W9-AWS-947

This book is on loan from the
Mid York Library System

When you are finished reading, please return the book so that others may enjoy it.

The Mid York Library System is pleased to partner with **CABVI** in assisting those with special vision needs. If you found the size of print in this book helpful, there may be other ways **CABVI** can help. Please call today toll free at **1-877-719-9996** or **(315) 797-2233.**

MID-YORK Library System
1600 Lincoln Avenue Utica, New York 13502

DARK BEFORE DAWN

DARK BEFORE DAWN

Kay Stephens

G.K. Hall & Co. • Chivers Press
Thorndike, Maine USA Bath, England

This Large Print edition is published by G.K. Hall & Co., USA
and by Chivers Press, England.

Published in 1997 in the U.S. by arrangement with Chivers Press Ltd.

Published in 1997 in the U.K. by arrangement
with Severn House Publishers Ltd.

U.S. Hardcover 0-7838-8104-5 (Romance Collection Edition)
U.K. Hardcover 0-7540-1047-3 (Windsor Large Print)
U.K. Softcover 0-7540-2026-6 (Paragon Large Print)

Copyright © 1997 by Kay Stephens

The moral right of the author has been asserted.

All rights reserved.

All situations in this publication are fictitious and any resemblance to living persons is purely coincidental.

The text of this Large Print edition is unabridged.
Other aspects of the book may vary from the original edition.

Set in 16 pt. Plantin by Minnie B. Raven.

Printed in the United States on permanent paper.

British Library Cataloguing in Publication Data available

Library of Congress Cataloging in Publication Data

Stephens, Kay.
Dark before dawn / Kay Stephens.
p. cm.
ISBN 0-7838-8104-5 (lg. print : hc : alk. paper)
1. Large type books. I. Title.
[PR6069.T4293D37 1997]
823′.914—dc21 97-18510

DARK BEFORE DAWN

Chapter One

Sheila was holding her breath, waiting for the verdict.

"I'm afraid Johnnie'll never get any better. Not as long as he stays in Yorkshire," said Dr Morrison.

He was sighing as he finished sounding the boy's chest where Sheila could see every rib outlined in the sunlight, which was now so rare she suspected it was rationed along with everything else.

Clouds tore across the sky, darkening the window, and she had to check the urge to rush to the lad and hug him. He looked so dismal, more forlorn than ever. But Johnnie had been distressing her for months by always shrinking from any affection. She could only contain the tears now surging up to choke her by glancing away.

She met Dr Morrison's concerned grey eyes. "Whatever's wrong with him, Doctor? I can't understand it, none of us can. I mean — on a *farm*. Where could he have meals that were as good? In wartime."

"I know all that, Mrs Calvert. It's nothing to do with the food he's been given."

"Then what? My mother's marvellous with kids, all the other evacuees have doted on her. Every one of them that's ever stopped with us since the war began. Louise and Billy don't want to go home."

"I'm sure that's true. I've known Enid Hardaker and the farm since the day I took over this practice, haven't I?" He lowered his voice, but Johnnie had turned his back on them anyway, when he'd hurried across to stare out of the window at the troubled sky. "It's this little lad himself, nothing at all to do with the care he's been receiving. And nor is it basically a health problem. There's no sign of infection of any kind."

"But —"

"The lad's pining — pining for his mother. For his own home."

"Are you sure?" Johnnie had been with them for over a year. And before that had stayed somewhere up in the Dales. Sheila couldn't believe that after all this time a five-year-old would remember enough about his real home to experience this degree of yearning.

"You say you've not had a reply from his mother?" said Dr Morrison.

"I've written three times now. When he stopped eating the other week I thought she'd better be told. As I've explained, I'd sent her letters before, an' all. Mainly, to ask if there were some reason she knew of why he never wanted to play with the other kids."

"What sort of a person is she? How did she strike you, Mrs Calvert?"

"She seemed nice enough when she first brought Johnnie to us — bright, quite chatty. That makes it worse, somehow — him being so quiet. She was smartly dressed an' all. Blonde . . ."

She noticed the doctor's gaze travelling to Johnnie's dark curls, and smiled. "Bottle-blonde, I dare say. Fairer than me, certainly. And her eyes were brown. I remember what a contrast they were to her hair."

"Is there someone who could take him back to his home? There are hardly any air raids down south again, now that the bombing a few months ago seems to have ceased. And that wasn't as severe as a couple of years back in 1942. In any case, I believe we've got to take that risk. What Johnnie needs is surroundings where he no longer feels out of place."

"You're serious about this, aren't you, Doctor?"

"There's no real alternative. The lad's retreating into his own little world — and from what you say, near enough starving himself."

"I'll see what I can do." Sheila was supposing already that it would be up to her to take Johnnie back to Kent. Her mother had her hands full enough with Billy and Louise, the two evacuees reluctant to leave the farm. Enid Hardaker's work didn't end there — she kept an eye on the Land Army girls, and did the cooking for everyone.

"Come here, Johnnie love," Sheila called, holding out his clothes.

He came obediently, dispiritedly, and raised his arms for the Chilprufe vest which had been preserved since before the war, darned, and handed down to him. He took his shirt from Sheila, thrust in stick-like arms, and fastened the buttons carefully.

"He can manage anything, you know," she told the doctor.

He nodded. Johnnie Richards seemed more intelligent than most children of his age, which made his decline all the more sad.

"And how's your own tiny lass?" Dr Morrison enquired.

"Barbara's fine, thank you, Doctor. And not so tiny either now."

"How old is she — four?"

"Five, same as this one here." Barbara, though, couldn't be more different. Vivacious and outgoing, without a single inhibition, she charmed anybody she met, was just as popular at school as with everyone on the farm.

"And your husband? Is he still based over here?"

"Aye. The Army hasn't sent Edward abroad yet. I'm afraid he rather regrets that. He feels he ought to be on active service. Especially now that there's so much going on all over Europe."

"Well, maybe it won't be all that long now. There's a lot more hope since the D-Day landings."

While they were talking Johnnie had tucked his shirt neatly into his short trousers and had put on his pullover. Sheila handed him his school cap as she stood up and thanked Dr Morrison.

The wind met them as they opened the outer door. Tearing down from Midgley Moor and from Oxenhope Moor beyond that, it would often assail them here, even on a June day like this. And in winter the bleak gusts made the local folk believe they were nearer to the Arctic than to Halifax, only about five miles away.

Johnnie's hand was unresisting when Sheila took it in hers. It also seemed unresponsive, just as he failed to react when she tried to jolly him along by suggesting that they should run down the lane.

Running wasn't a good idea. Despite the doctor's assertion that nothing ailed the lad, she was obliged to slow to a walk as soon as Johnnie began panting.

"Your chest doesn't hurt, does it?" she asked anxiously, not entirely convinced that he wasn't suffering from TB or something.

Johnnie shook his head.

Sheila hadn't expected a verbal reply. These days, he seemed to prefer silence. Cutting himself off from folk. They wondered if somehow he was punishing everyone; for what, none of them could imagine.

Even her dad had become concerned about young Johnnie Richards, and Nat Hardaker worked such long hours and was always so tired that he rarely had time to pay much attention to their evacuees. But he had seen Johnnie, as Sheila had, mooching around their hillside fields on his own, and detaching himself from the other youngsters on the walk to and from school.

"Is it the school that's upsetting him?" her father had asked her. "Does his teacher say how he's getting on?"

Sheila had told him how her own alarm had deepened when the school confirmed that Johnnie had the makings of a clever little boy, if only he would communicate. The story there was all too familiar, judging from his behaviour around the farm. The lad just didn't participate.

Approaching Hardaker Farm now, Sheila wondered how anybody could fail to be content beneath its slate roof. A sandstone house, with her cottage across the yard, and barn and byre on the third side. It all looked reassuringly solid and, even with vegetables now replacing her mother's garden flowers, bright and welcoming.

"Something's happened to young Johnnie somewhere along the line," her mother said later that evening. Sheila was relating the doctor's opinion as they tidied the old-fashioned kitchen, which smelled of rhubarb tart. "Summat that bad that it's turned the poor kid in on himself. It isn't only since he's started school either. He's had very little to say for himself ever since he got here. And as for the way he eats — well, I've never known a lad like him. He ought to be ravenous, all the fresh air and that, out there."

"Happen he is just missing his mother," Sheila suggested as she washed one of the many pans stacked beside the stone sink. "That's what the doctor seems to think. But what I can't understand is why he doesn't *say*. Other youngsters have, afore they settled, haven't they? Most of 'em have had a good cry for the first day or two."

"Is that what you're going to do then — take him back to his mother?" asked Enid, her hazel eyes serious as she pushed a lock of greying hair behind her ear.

"Looks like it. I'll give her till the end of the week to write back. If I haven't heard owt by then, I'll have to be making plans."

"Well, you know we'll manage here while you're away. Them Land girls are very good, they'll see to everything out in the fields. They usually do the milking now, any road. And I can cope with the youngsters on my own."

"Even our Barbara?" Sheila enquired. "With her being on the go all the time like she is . . ."

Her mother looked up from the plate she was drying and grinned. "Me and Barbara get on all right, we have an understanding."

Sheila laughed. "Oh, aye? That she can wind you round her proverbial little finger! I might ask our Pauline to have her to stay over yonder. She must find it a bit quiet since Ken were killed."

"Well, quiet it won't be, if she has your young madam there!" Enid exclaimed, but then she nodded to herself. "That mightn't be a bad idea, you know. In any case, if you're not at home,

Barbara will have to move out of her own room, won't she? Couldn't leave her by herself in your cottage, even if it is only t'other side of the farmyard."

"Pauline's only working part time still, isn't she?"

"That's right, love. With her being under the doctor ever since losing her husband. They've been very understanding at the factory, considering."

"Does that mean she'll be able to adjust her hours to the times when Barbara's at school?"

"I dare say. And if she can't, the little lass could come here with the others. Just sleep at Barbara's, like."

"It'd be less work for you, Mum. I don't know how long I'll be away, remember."

"Nay, I'm not bothered about a bit extra —"

"All the same," Sheila interrupted. "You've more than enough on, as it is. With the jobs you do around the place, looking after folk, and keeping an eye on Billy and Louise."

"Bless 'em! I shall miss them two when they go," her mother admitted. She'd been pleased that Billy and Louise loved Hardaker Farm so much. And if they were still reluctant to go back to their homes near Portsmouth — even though the bombing there had decreased some long while ago — the arrangement suited their families. Both kids had mothers who were on war-work and fathers abroad in the forces.

"You won't know what to do with your time

when this war's over!" Sheila exclaimed, wondering what she herself would do. She had worked on the farm throughout the war, a fact which meant she wasn't obliged to be drafted into a factory or to the forces. In 1939 she had been a new mother, relishing domesticity. Edward had courted her while she was still a student at art college, and she had never experienced working anywhere but on the farm. These days, she felt as though taking up art again might be a luxury, even an irrelevance.

"I'll see you have some sandwiches with you," her mother announced suddenly, jolting her back to 1944.

"Sandwiches?"

"When you set off for Kent with young Johnnie."

Sheila grinned. "Trust you to have it all worked out! It won't be for a day or two yet, you know."

She would first have to explain to Barbara, and she had no means of telling how her daughter would react to such an absence. Ever since Edward joined up, she and Barbara had been very close. The girl might be upset by thoughts of their being separated. Sheila herself wasn't at all sure how *she* would feel away from her.

"Do you mean that, Mummy? Can I really stay with Auntie Pauline?" Hopping from one foot to the other, blue eyes gleaming, Barbara was leaving her in no doubt that the plan was approved.

"I don't know how long it will be for," Sheila continued. Still rather apprehensive about having her daughter realise that they could be apart for more than a couple of days, she had waited until the Friday in the hope that a reply from Johnnie's mother might remove the need for making that journey.

"But I will be able to sleep there, you said . . . ?" Barbara's eyes were round with wonder.

"That's right, love. We're going to take your nightdress over to Auntie's. Teddy and Bunty as well — and some books."

"She'll tell me stories out of her head, she's good at that. I won't need books."

Sheila ought to have been delighted that both her daughter and her sister were pleased with the arrangement. Pauline had been enthusiastic when she called to ask her if she would be able to cope with Barbara.

Those lovely green eyes of hers had lit up with the genuine smile missing since Ken had died serving with the Eighth Army at El Alamein. "It'll be fair grand to have somebody to cook for again. And Barbara's getting to be right good company."

Somehow though, Sheila still felt uneasy about going off and leaving them.

A few hours later, when Barbara had had tea with the other children and she was getting her ready for bed, Sheila believed that she knew the reason for her earlier reluctance to go anywhere, which had seemed so groundless at the time.

Barbara was excitedly telling her about some game they had played around the sandpit at school, when the outer door of the cottage opened.

"Are you up there?" Edward called from the tiny hall below.

Sheila ran out onto the landing and leaned over the bannister. "Hello, love! I didn't know you were due another leave," she exclaimed.

"Only a forty-eight," Edward told her, dropping his kitbag in one corner. He came running upstairs, kissed Sheila hastily, and strode past her to find his daughter.

"Daddy, Daddy!" Barbara cried ecstatically, and flung herself at him. She was warm and flushed from her bath, her light brown hair gleamed after Sheila's careful brushing.

Edward hugged her to him, then flung her around, holding beneath her arms while sturdy legs flailed behind her. Sheila felt like telling him that it was Barbara's bedtime, and she certainly didn't need encouraging to be overexcited. Instead, she reminded herself silently that Edward's visits home were always too short and too infrequent. He must be given the freedom to play with his daughter without anyone's intervention.

"I'm going to stay with Auntie Pauline," Barbara told him. "You will come and see me there, won't you, Daddy?"

"Of course, my sweet." He looked over his shoulder towards his wife. "What's all this?"

"I've got to take Johnnie home to Kent. Dr

Morrison's sure he's pining for his mother, that's why he's losing weight and so on. But it needn't be for another few days yet. Not now you're home, love."

"When were you planning on leaving?" Edward asked.

"We'd thought tomorrow, but it really doesn't matter."

"It does to Johnnie, from the sound of it. Why don't you go? Barbara and I can spend a Saturday having fun together, for once."

"Oh, yes, Daddy, yes!"

Hurt by the alacrity with which Edward had dismissed her departure, Sheila left them in Barbara's bedroom and went out onto the landing. She caught sight of herself in the mirror, and frowned. She'd washed her face and hands since coming in from the fields, but her fair hair was untidy, like a heap of tangled corn. Her eyelashes, bleached by the sun until they'd grown invisible, did nothing to enhance the eyes that she'd always disliked for being neither blue nor truly grey. And which tonight looked reproachful. Feeling ridiculously emotional, she stared out of the window, determined to pull herself together.

Just outside the door of the farmhouse, Johnnie was leaning against the sandstone wall. She saw her father crossing from the milking parlour to the house, and the way he bent down towards the lad, speaking to him. A couple of times Johnnie shook his head, but he seemed not to say one word. And then he turned sharply away and began running in the direction of the field gate.

"I've just got to pop out for a minute," Sheila called to the other two. They didn't respond. As she dashed down the stairs, she heard them singing 'Wee Willie Winkie', in unison.

She caught up with Johnnie in the field. He was sitting in one of its corners, his back pressed into the angle of the drystone wall.

"All right, love?" Sheila asked.

He nodded, but she saw that his cheeks were tear-streaked. The urge to cuddle him was overwhelming, but as she came nearer, the lad visibly withdrew until Sheila cringed, certain the rough stones of the wall must be digging quite fiercely into his bony body.

"Why won't you tell us what's wrong, love?"

Again, he did not speak.

"You don't like it here at all, do you? Never mind, I'm going to take you home. To your mummy."

This time Johnnie looked her in the eyes, for once. His own were the brown of plain chocolate, wide with appeal.

There was no way that she could make him wait even one day longer. "Shall we go there tomorrow?" she asked.

Once more, Johnnie nodded.

It was all she could do. And at least she and Edward would have tonight. The long evening as well, as soon as she had taken Johnnie into the farm, and checked that her mother would pack his belongings.

"Time for bed then, love," she insisted, and held out a hand. "If we're going all that way tomorrow we'll have to be up early."

Enid was waiting for them at the farm door.

"Do you want me to put him to bed, Mum?" Sheila enquired.

"Eh, bless you, no. I'll see to that, lass. I saw Edward crossing the yard. Now he's home you'll want to be together."

"Well — I shan't have much time for talking to him in the morning."

"You're not still thinking of taking Johnnie home tomorrow?"

"I'm afraid I'd better. He's not going to pick up until he's back where he belongs. And Edward says it's for the best."

"Well, I've got his clean stuff ready for packing. He hasn't got so much that hasn't worn out by now, has he, poor lamb?"

They arranged that Enid would have the boy ready by eight o'clock the following morning. Nat Hardaker had to go into Halifax and would drop them off at the station.

I wonder if he can spare the petrol to call round at our Pauline's and leave Barbara with her later tomorrow, thought Sheila. She ought to have asked him, but she wouldn't turn back to the farm and enquire now. Very conscious that she and Edward only had tonight, she didn't want to waste any more of it.

He was still upstairs with Barbara. Sheila could hear his voice reading from the *Chick's Own Annual.* Their daughter should have been asleep by now, she reflected. And then felt guilty. She suspected she herself rather resented Edward's concentrating on the child.

"Do you want something to eat?" she asked him from the bedroom doorway. "I haven't a lot in, but the hens have been laying well — I could rustle up an omelette."

Edward turned and smiled. "It's all right, lass. Don't bother. I — I had a meal earlier on."

"Before you left camp? Bet you could do with another by now —"

"No. Like I said, I'm all right."

"I'll just do myself an egg then."

While the egg was boiling, Sheila wondered why she wasn't happier simply to have her husband home. From the moment his unexpected arrival had sent her heart racing, she'd been determined to make the most of these few hours, and that she wouldn't spoil them by regrets about having to make that journey tomorrow. Somehow, though, everything felt wrong. And if he didn't finally tuck their Barbara in for the night, the child would be tired to death in the morning.

Edward came down to the kitchen when she was washing the dishes. The egg seemed to have given her indigestion, or was that due to her eating hurriedly while thinking all the time that he might have wanted to keep her company, even if he wasn't hungry?

"How are things?" she enquired, turning her back on the sink, and failing to quell the knowledge that normally Edward would have her in his arms long before this. Perhaps he was as tired as she felt. Now into this fifth year of war, everybody was worn down by its effect.

"Not bad, I suppose. If you don't count feeling that you're not doing your bit."

"You are training other chaps for the front, that's important. Happen it'll all be over soon, anyhow. Then we'll be back to normal."

Edward didn't respond; he seemed anything but reassured. She knew he felt trapped over here by his peacetime skill as a cartographer, conveying an understanding of maps to troops preparing to depart.

"So long as we all survive, that's the main thing, isn't it?" Sheila persisted. "That's what we've said all along, haven't we?"

"Aye, love, aye."

Still he made no move to hold her. She took a few paces towards him instead, put her arms around him, raised her face for his kisses.

Edward stiffened. For one dreadful moment Sheila was reminded of little Johnnie and the way he avoided physical contact. But then she felt his hands on her back and the familiar longing surged right through her.

It was ten o'clock though before they went up to bed. They had listened to the news on the wireless at nine, and still Edward had seemed content just to sit there.

By the time they were between the covers disappointment had taken the edge off her own desire. Nothing was the same any longer. During the early days of the war, each leave had been exciting when Edward had come rushing in, hardly able to wait for her until Barbara had been placed in her cot. There had even been occasions when he had suggested that her mother should have Barbara for the night, to allow them more time on their own.

Rather than eager, Edward seemed slow to respond, and then less enthusiastic than she might have hoped following an absence of several weeks. Sheila could have wept, but reminded herself that he probably was exhausted. Perhaps in the morning they would make love again.

She awakened to find she was alone in bed, the sheets cold beside her. She grew perturbed. Where was Edward?

Even when Sheila heard his voice and Barbara's from the next room she experienced no surge of relief. Sighing, she got out of bed and hurried towards the bathroom. She had a job to do, hadn't she, one that would not allow for preoccupation with her own frustration.

As Sheila emerged from the bathroom to go and dress, Barbara came running out of her bedroom with Edward on her heels. With his light brown hair still tousled from sleep, he looked younger and very appealing.

“Daddy’s going to take me to Auntie Pauline’s today,” the child exclaimed. “We might be going for a picnic.”

“Before you go to Auntie’s, you mean?”

“No. After breakfast. Then Auntie Pauline can come out with us.”

“She might not want to,” Sheila began. She didn’t wish her daughter to become enthusiastic about an outing that might not materialise.

“I’m sure she will,” Edward asserted, blue eyes glinting. “It’s just what she needs after all this time stuck there on her own.”

“Well, you’ll soon see, won’t you?” She was not going to enquire into the details of their plans. She had enough of her own to finalise. Although she had packed her small case on Thursday, she needed to gather together various last-minute items, and there was only half an hour before she must pick Johnnie up from the farm.

Sheila felt subdued during breakfast, but the other two did not notice. If Edward had been overtired last night, he had recovered swiftly. He was teasing Barbara, who was giggling so much that the toast soldiers and her boiled egg were cooling in front of her.

“I’m afraid you two will have to wash up,” Sheila told them.

“I’m good at drying plates, Daddy. I’ll help a lot,” Barbara assured him.

“That’ll be fun,” Edward responded. “Another thing we can do together, love.”

Upstairs a few minutes later, Sheila made the bed, then looked slowly around the room. She didn't want to go. Despite being well aware that young Johnnie Richards needed to be taken home, she could hardly bring herself to leave this place.

She struggled to control the emotions rushing to the surface with a force that wasn't like her at all. Swallowing, she strode across to stare out through the window. The view to the west didn't help. Lush with summer greenery, the woods and fields stretched out to either side of the valley surrounding the Calder. Up to her right the steep-sided hill soared towards open moorland.

"Get a grip on yourself, lass," she murmured aloud. "You're taking a homesick boy to his mother, that doesn't mean *you've* any excuse for becoming homesick for Hardaker Farm."

"Are you coming across the yard to say goodbye to Johnnie?" she asked Barbara. Dashing downstairs to pick up her case, Sheila was checking that she had a key in her handbag.

"No," her daughter said firmly. "Johnnie doesn't talk to me."

"Only because he's upset while he's a long way from his mummy. That's why . . ."

"I should leave it," Edward suggested. "It's not worth making an issue —"

"All right," Sheila interrupted. They seemed suddenly to be totally out of step with each other. He wouldn't normally give in to Barbara when she might be taught a bit of consideration for others.

Whether or not it was through her own irritation with him, Sheila couldn't be sure, but Edward's hug felt cool and there could be no mistaking the token kiss that merely brushed her lips. But Barbara did stretch up her arms to be lifted into a warm embrace that heartened Sheila. And the pair of them remained at the open door, watching as she hastened across the yard to the farm kitchen.

Johnnie was waiting already, his cardboard suitcase fastened with string to contain the bulges, and his gasmask in its scuffed case suspended from his shoulder.

"What do you think?" her mother said, turning from the sink. "Billy and Louise have given him some of their toys, bless 'em. That's why his little case is fair swelling now." Enid was beaming with satisfaction, seeming as proud of her evacuees as she might have been of her own grandchildren.

"That's nice, isn't it?" Sheila smiled down at Johnnie. "Are you going to say bye-bye to your Auntie Enid then?"

She was delighted when the lad rushed to her mother and hugged her around her faded cotton skirts before raising his face to be kissed.

"Thank you," he said in a barely-audible voice. "I do like you," he insisted, as though aware that Enid needed to be reassured.

Sheila looked up as her father's boots were heard approaching around the side of the house.

At the door he gazed towards them.

"Ready, are we?"

"Thanks, Dad, yes." Sheila had sensed her mother was about to begin admonishing her to take care of herself, and to come home safely. Today, she needed simply to set out. She couldn't bear to entertain the possibility that anything might occur to prevent her from returning. But the kiss she gave Enid was warm and sincere; a silent assertion that she knew what she was feeling.

Taking Johnnie's hand and walking round to the front where her father's Morris Eight was parked, Sheila was pleased to see Edward and their daughter still at the cottage door. She waved to them and called, "See you soon." They waved back, but silently. She ached for a few words to send her on her way cheerfully.

Before passing around the corner of the farmhouse and out of sight, Sheila glanced back again. Edward had his hand on Barbara's shoulder and they were looking at each other and laughing.

How could they *laugh* while somewhere in the region of her heart she herself was weeping? While she was setting off for the south of England where nothing was the same — where folk had suffered so much bombing.

It had been so much better round here: all through the war there'd been nothing like that quantity of air raids. The only really serious damage had been that bomb in 1940 which fell on Halifax, near Hanson Lane, where eleven people had been killed and ten severely injured. Over five hundred houses were destroyed then, but since that night most of the bombs locally had caused relatively little damage. And although there'd been plenty of incendiaries dropping, again, they hadn't created much havoc.

Her father was puffing on his pipe, watching the road with the deep concentration that he always applied when driving. Sheila felt torn, longing for him to insist that she must take care while she was away, yet also being aware that it wouldn't take much to make her give in to this irrational foreboding. As she had with her mother, she sensed that too many reminders of the nature of this journey could just be her undoing.

She couldn't understand herself. She wasn't seriously scared that she might be injured or worse, it was more this feeling that travelling to places she did not know was only a small part of the unfamiliar turn her whole life was taking. And she felt so ill-prepared. Years ago she'd have gone to church before tackling anything out of the ordinary, but working a seven-day week had eroded her church-going until she wondered if she warranted such assistance.

Beside her, Johnnie was looking out over the valley, staring at the mills of Luddenden Foot now coming into sight below them. To her, even these grey stone factories looked good; she would miss them as greatly as she would miss the West Riding countryside which earlier had seemed to urge her to remain where she belonged.

"Happen it won't be so long before I'm back," she heard her own voice saying. And was sorry that her thoughts had somehow tumbled out ungoverned.

"You'll get a real welcome from us, whenever," her father asserted gently. "You know that, don't you?"

"I know, Dad, I know."

She only wished that she felt half as certain about her own husband's reaction on her return. Never in all the years she had known him, had she felt this insecure in her relationship with Edward. Never had she sensed like this that something was gravely wrong.

"Are we really going on a train?" Johnnie asked in a whisper so hushed that she could barely distinguish the words.

"We certainly are," she confirmed, and resolved to begin looking forward. If this little lad could enthuse about trains, the journey ahead might prove to be less of an ordeal than she had imagined. And Johnnie was what counted now, not her own uneasiness, not her own private misgivings about what she was attempting.

Chapter Two

Darling, at last!" His kiss interrupted his own words, and he drew Pauline against him. The attraction was so intense between them, he stirred and felt her responding before his lips left her mouth.

"I couldn't believe it when she went off while you were still on leave, Teddy."

"Didn't take much persuading either, thank goodness. I might have felt bad about it if our Barbara hadn't been so glad to come and stay with you."

"We *are* lucky, aren't we? This is so much better than snatched evenings when you've dashed over from camp."

"And this time we really can be certain she won't call on you while I'm dropping in here on my way back off leave."

"You do understand it isn't only sex, don't you, Teddy? I have said, haven't I — your friendship's kept me alive since I lost Ken."

"You've said, Pauline, countless times. And you've shown me as well, just by being here for me, for wanting me."

"Like now . . ."

"Like always. Whenever we can be together."

"Until —"

"Until this lot's over," he stated firmly. "And we can sort ourselves out. Like we agreed."

"I think Barbara's fast asleep now. Shall we go up? Or did you want the news at nine o'clock?"

"Don't even consider it. Have you locked up?"

He waited in Pauline's bedroom, listening while she went around downstairs, shutting windows, dropping the latch on the front door. He could pretend, just for the one night, that this was where he lived, where he belonged. The room was more elegant than the one in the cottage, its walls had been papered before the war in delicate peachy tones, and Pauline had taken good care of this place. The walls at home were distempered, but had faded from cream and looked more like whitewash.

The bed here was more modern altogether, with a sprung mattress, not flock that formed itself into humps. The cover was a shade deeper than the walls, satiny, and matched the curtains that still hung at the large window with the blackouts beyond them.

She came to him already undressed, wearing a nightgown so diaphanous that his breath caught in his throat. He felt ill-prepared suddenly in the thick sweater and serge trousers which had been worn for their picnic on the moors.

Pauline seemed not to consider him unready, coming to press herself against him, while she began attacking his buttons. Still firmly adjoined below the waist, she leaned back slightly to pull the sweater up and over his head.

Her fingers were light and swift, unfastening his shirt, and then her hands were on his chest, caressing, until they slid to his back and slowly traced the length of his spine.

Discarding trousers, he reached the bed ahead of her to lie between the satiny cover and the insubstantial silk of her garment, savouring the sensation. Only then did he feel regret, that this experience was outlawed — by convention, and by his own inherent sense of right. But senses more powerful were flooding his entire being, forbidding thought, denying the existence of anything beyond himself and this woman.

Her touch was on him again, inflaming, exploring, *loving* her musky scent lingered in his nostrils, increasing his longing. Passion could not wait, or only for now-familiar nuances of its expression. Anticipation was its own reward when each moment's bliss enhanced desire, and drove him onward to its ultimate conclusion.

Unable to withhold any longer, he covered her mouth with his own again, turned her to lie beneath him, and thrust home into the haven prepared by his searching fingers.

"No one but you," he sighed into her tangle of hair. "No one but you was ever this gorgeous!"

He'd said those words before — or others of similar content — so many times since that first occasion, when she reproached him for making comparisons. Pauline had accepted now that he needed this release, and needed perhaps to justify his turning from her sister. He drifted into sleep, reassured, knowing love imbued passion with tranquillity.

Towards summer's early dawn, he awakened to the pressure at his back, to fingers tracing over his hip, and further. The answering surge swam through his veins, a massive delight that brought him fully awake, brought the laughter of sheer pleasure to the mouth which tingled with latent kisses. Relishing her touch, he lay there, obedient to her hands, until he felt her weight moving over and across him and they lay face to face, kissing.

"One day," she promised, "every morning will be like this. Every night will be spent together."

"No more partings, my love. No days when you're alone, none when I have to be — elsewhere." He hated to leave her. Each time that he went off to camp, the parting became harder. And as for those other times . . .

"How long will she be away?"

"I don't know, Pauline, how can I? She does not know herself."

"But it's miles away, and even when they get to Kent she has to find the boy's mother."

"I'll be here again before she's back. One evening this week, if I can't manage more than a few hours."

"Meanwhile, your daughter will be here. She so reminds me of you."

"You'll have to insist she has an early night,

have her asleep before I get here or she'll refuse to go to bed."

"And if we don't use the opportunity now, she'll be awake before we're ready. Don't forget Barbara's used to a farm routine."

He smiled. "You shouldn't worry. I suspect I shan't hold out much longer . . ."

If only he were free, he would be happier than ever before, more alive, alive to the perfection of the ecstasy now compelling him towards the bliss that sent all his senses rocketing.

"I wish that it was coming dark now instead," Pauline murmured beside him as their breathing evened once more, their bodies relaxed. "I need to keep you here, to feel you at my side, to know you're safe. Oh, why can't we just stay here in the dark?"

"Why isn't there any light?"

The tiny voice from around her elbow made Sheila smile. Johnnie was speaking.

The train journey had become horrible, nightmarish in this dim blue lighting which made seeing clearly across the compartment difficult. They had halted several times; once while a siren's wail reached them through the sound of the chugging engine, curdling her blood and making her fearful. Blacked-out windows sealed them in, away from the rest of the world, as though they might remain isolated for ever. But Johnnie had begun talking to her.

Whether or not in dread, Sheila could not

know, but his turning to her was strangely beneficial. The only person here who was familiar, she relished the warmth of his head pressing into her sleeve, but most of all his sudden willingness to communicate.

Even the hardly-discernible voice, little more than a breath, seemed more acceptable in this place. It barely stirred the air that smelled so badly of sweat, and of one wound at least that was turning gangrenous. Around them other folk slept: soldiers, airmen, several nationalities — men and women injured and wearied by years of onslaught. Even the few civilians like herself bore hardship on their faces, behind eyes shadowed by deprivation, anxiety, bereavement.

Johnnie's hushed little words disturbed no one, while they aroused in her immense satisfaction. They had been right to get him away; starting this journey had been enough. Reassured, he seemed different now, content to have her beside him, to let his hand stray to her fingers, if only to attract her attention.

"Will we be in London soon?"

"I don't know yet, love. We can't see where we are, can we? But we'll be there sometime. Happen it will be soon now."

The train from Halifax, running late, had failed to connect with the intended mainline train; they'd waited on a platform while rain soaked their clothes and they dried out again. They had stopped and started so many times afterwards: shunted aside to allow troop trains through, some of the men had said before they relapsed into sleep. The long summer evening had turned to night during further delays.

Sheila had accepted hours ago that all her ideas had gone by the board; they would be arriving in London far beyond the time that she had anticipated. What they would do, how she would care for the boy if they got there in the middle of the night, she could not imagine.

Her watch had broken. It wasn't Johnnie's fault. He had begun talking last night, telling her how at school he was learning to read the time. Here in the darkened carriage he'd been unable to see the tiny hands and the dial while the watch was still on her wrist. It had slipped from his fingers onto the dusty floor. The soldier sitting opposite had nodded approvingly when Johnnie retrieved the watch and said how sorry he was for dropping it. His being contrite hadn't altered the non-existent ticking, but Sheila had concealed the damage from him. Moving its hands around, she had made time go by whilst helping him to perfect his understanding of minutes and hours.

Hours, though, were often interminable. Unmarked by any kind of diversion, while diversions of another sort took this train of theirs off at some tangent somewhere, on to lines that had not yet suffered under enemy bombardment.

Sheila couldn't shrug off the unease that had dogged her for a very long time. She thought about home, and longed for her own child, but reminded herself firmly that Barbara was perfectly happy to go to Pauline. That thought produced no comfort at all.

Perhaps I'm being extremely selfish, she reflected. I wouldn't be nearly so perturbed if Edward hadn't turned up out of the blue like that, making me decide between sharing his leave and bringing Johnnie away. But, in fact, Edward has not made me decide — *he insisted that this was what I must do.* Only that knowledge does not help at all. Because this isn't all right, is it? Nothing feels right . . .

It was still dark when they finally pulled into London, and according to the station clock, only three-twenty A.M.

"I want to wee," Johnnie confided urgently while Sheila struggled along the platform with his luggage and her own.

"All right," she assured him. "We'll find somewhere in a minute."

At least here, although a surprising number of people were around, she wasn't faced with the congestion they'd had to negotiate in the corridor of the train every time he had needed the lavatory.

The difficulty now, Sheila discovered, was deciding which one to choose. Weighing the alternatives, she rejected sending Johnnie alone into the correct one for him. She preferred the possible disapproval she'd face for taking a boy into the Ladies to the potential problems in retrieving him if he failed to reappear from the other one.

She did receive a few funny looks from several women, but she ushered Johnnie ahead of her into a cubicle and leaned against the door, urging him to get on with it.

Johnnie refused. "I can't," he whispered, furiously. "It's not nice with you here."

"It'll be even less nice if you have wet pants while I take you through London and home to your mother. Now, come on, Johnnie — I've seen you in the bath often enough, haven't I?"

"That's not —"

"— The same? Happen not, love, but it really doesn't matter."

Johnnie still felt differently. In the end, Sheila was obliged to wait outside the cubicle, where she found herself explaining to the queue of women that she was waiting for her little boy.

One lady smiled sympathetically. "Taking him to the country, are you?" she enquired. "Thought the evacuation was over and done with, didn't we? Till this lot began . . ."

"This lot?"

"These here pilotless planes that's coming over. That is why you're getting the boy away from London, isn't it?"

Sheila closed her mouth firmly, she couldn't admit that she was returning Johnnie to the south. She'd heard rumours about this new German weapon but she hadn't realised how serious it was becoming down here. God, what was she doing bringing the lad away from Yorkshire?

By the time Johnnie had washed his hands and

she had checked once again that they were complete with gas-masks, suitcases and her handbag, tiredness had overtaken her to the degree where the alarming prospect of these pilotless planes seemed unreal. A problem to be shelved while she contemplated more urgent matters.

Will we ever get to Kent? she wondered. She had planned every mile of the journey before leaving home, but the re-routing of that second train they'd taken had perplexed her. They had been diverted into another station. For the moment she couldn't for the life of her think how to get across London. There was the Underground, of course, but did that run during the night? Or they could try and hire a taxi, but they seemed rationed like everything else — the queue was daunting.

Crowds were surging towards the entrance of the Underground, one or two people were emerging. Perhaps they were in luck and the trains were running. If they could only reach Charing Cross and the lines into Kent, she would feel a lot better. All they need do would be to wait there until that day's services began operating.

Johnnie was clinging on to her coat, clearly apprehensive of the throng, as they began descending the steps.

"That's right," Sheila assured him. "You hang on to me, stick by my side and you'll be okay. And when we get on the tube, make sure you still hold on." With both of her own hands occupied, she couldn't make a grab for the lad if that should become necessary.

Even before they descended the final flight of stairs to reach the platform, Sheila realised how mistaken she had been to suppose that any trains might be coming along these lines before daylight. The scene before them was just like those she'd seen in the papers during the blitz. The entire platform was taken up by people using the Underground as a shelter.

A middle-aged man shifted along the step where he was sitting. "Here you are, missus — room for you and the lad. Don't want to risk being caught by none of Hitler's secret weapons . . ."

Sheila thanked him and sat, pulling Johnnie down beside her, urging him to leave enough room for people to pass up and down the steps alongside them.

"Getting him out of London, are you, dear?" the man asked, nodding towards their luggage. "Best way, I'm sure. Looks like he could do with a bit of feeding up in the country, doesn't he? My grandchildren will be evacuated again. Up north somewhere, Yorkshire, I think."

Sheila suppressed the hysterical impulse to laugh. I hope to goodness Johnnie doesn't feel like confiding. If he tells this chap where we've just come from, they'll all think I'm barmy!

Johnnie, however, had grown silent again. His dark eyes were round with amazement as he stared out over the mass of people — many of them recumbent — adapting to surroundings which had, no doubt, been all too familiar a couple of years ago while escaping repeated bombings.

Sheila wanted to ask how much damage these pilotless aircraft were causing, but she was too exhausted to form the right questions. All her energy was concentrated on assuming her new role — that of a mother whisking her boy away from the renewed danger here.

Whatever would Johnnie's real mother think of her for bringing him back to this? How would she make Jane Richards understand her reasons for getting him away from Yorkshire? Even to herself, the state Johnnie was in seemed no longer to excuse exposing him to danger. She prayed she would find some means of convincing Jane that she was doing her best for the lad.

For about an hour they rested on the cold steps, until Sheila couldn't endure inactivity for another minute. The only good thing about the time they were spending together in these strange circumstances was that Johnnie had leaned against her and left a hand in hers in a way that seemed touchingly reliant. She wished with all her heart that the lad's confidence in her might be justified, but at the moment she felt too worn out and bewildered to be much use to him.

When they stretched their cramped limbs and slowly picked their way between people and up the steps, Johnnie began talking again. Sheila sensed that he was bemused by the crowds he had seen down below, and needed to chatter to restore some kind of a link with the life that he remembered.

"Is this even earlier than your daddy gets up at the farm?" he asked, sounding quite pleased to be thinking of Nat Hardaker.

Sheila smiled down at him. "Aye, love, I dare say it could be. And Barbara'll still be tucked up in bed at her Auntie Pauline's."

"Louise and Billy might be awake," Johnnie suggested. "They used to get out of bed and come and tell me stories."

"That was nice —" Sheila began.

The boy interrupted, shaking his head vehemently. "They weren't nice stories."

Oh? thought Sheila and wondered if this was one clue to Johnnie's inability to settle as readily in Midgley as those other evacuees. Had they persistently tormented him with frightening tales? One day she would try to find out more but, at the moment, with London dark and unfamiliar all about them, she wasn't going to risk anything that might introduce an even unhappier element.

"Does Barbara like living at her auntie's?" he asked suddenly.

"She's only stopping there for a day or two," said Sheila hastily. "Just till . . ." her voice trailed off. If she mentioned that she hoped to be on her way back to Yorkshire before long, that might give the poor lad the impression that she was going to abandon him here. He couldn't know that even talking about Barbara made her feel as though she hadn't seen her daughter for weeks, never mind a few hours. If this brief separation induced such a fierce yearning, she mustn't forget that she was here because Johnnie had *got* to be reunited with his mother. Realising how much pain being apart generated should make her really sure she was doing the only thing possible.

Forty-five minutes later Sheila again questioned the wisdom of what they were doing. Still too early for them to find any form of transport, they were trudging slowly through the West End streets.

Johnnie was stumbling along now, so exhausted that she could well understand that his legs must be giving out on him. She herself felt as if her arms were being dragged from her shoulders after carrying their suitcases for so long that they now seemed to be welded to hands that were becoming numb.

"Shall we rest for a bit in this shop doorway?" she suggested.

Before Johnnie replied they both stared upwards. The roar of an aircraft engine had turned into an appalling rattle. And then they saw the plane appearing over rooftops to the south east. It looked to be on fire as it sped overhead across the sky that was beginning to grow lighter. The sound died just as abruptly as Johnnie screamed, and the thing fell from the sky in the distance, seconds before an explosion that hurt their ears — and terrified them both.

"Grab hold of my sleeve, love, we're getting

away from here as fast as we can," Sheila exclaimed. Even encumbered with luggage like this, and tired out, she would have to run now until she got Johnnie to somewhere that was safer.

They reached Charing Cross without seeing another of the objects which she now realised must be those pilotless planes that only last week had started attacking England.

They didn't have long to wait for a train, but their journey into Kent was slow, with such frequent stops in between stations that Sheila wondered uneasily whatever was going on around them. Above the sound of the steam engine they often heard aircraft; she hoped they were our own, and not those appalling German vengeance weapons.

Most of the people cramming the carriage and filling corridors were service personnel. As in the other trains, many were wounded and all looked tired out. Sheila felt inhibited by their more serious troubles — couldn't bother them by asking about the best way of reaching Johnnie's village of Benenden. In any case, these folk in uniform most likely would be as much strangers here as she herself. But then she noticed a woman of roughly her own age, making her way back from the toilet with a little girl hanging onto her hand.

"Excuse me," Sheila began. "I wonder if you can help. I'm in a bit of a predicament. We've got to get to Benenden, and I'm not sure which would be the easiest way."

The woman smiled reassuringly. "New to Kent, are you, dear? Your best bet's to change at the next stop, Paddock Wood. You want the hoppers' line then."

" 'The hoppers', you say?"

The woman nodded. "Hop-pickers — they use it a lot, all the way to Hawkhurst the line goes, but you want to get off at Cranbrook. That's the third stop after Horsmonden and Goudhurst. We're only going as far as Horsmonden, but I can show you the right train. So long as it is running . . ."

The woman helped with their luggage when they changed at Paddock Wood, and told Sheila how long this branch line journey to Cranbrook should take. While they sat in the train waiting for it to move off, she nodded towards the main-line platforms.

"You should have seen Paddock Wood in 1940, it was one of the feeding stations for troops on the way back from Dunkirk. And at Tonbridge — the one we passed through a few minutes since — the stationmaster collected for the wounded men sent to Pembury hospital."

"We're getting a lot of wounded chaps up north where I come from," Sheila told her. "Especially airmen, some have been terribly burned."

"Have you had it bad up your way?"

Shaking her head, Sheila smiled. "Nothing like down here."

As the train pulled out they grew silent, Sheila

gazed over the rolling countryside, and thought that it appeared so serene that the war might have been miles away. Only the sky, its blue criss-crossed with white lace ribbons of vapour trails, witnessed to air battles.

"You'll have to watch out — don't forget it's the stop after the next one," the woman advised before leaving the train. "They took the names off the stations when the war started. Some have been put back again, but I don't know what's happened further down the track."

"We've got to try and get a bus now," Sheila explained to Johnnie when they finally alighted at Cranbrook. She prayed there would be a service running on a Sunday to somewhere near Benenden.

With no bus stop in sight on the main road, and no signposts even to point them in the right direction, Sheila wondered what to do. Never before in her life had she felt so *lost*. But she mustn't let that show. She was here with Johnnie because he was disturbed. She'd got to appear calm and in control. She listened to the steam engine drawing the train out of hearing, then shuddered at the aircraft droning constantly overhead — reminding her of that pilotless plane crashing on London. They couldn't just stand here forlornly. There was just one chance of help, an old man walking an elderly spaniel.

After explaining about trying to get a bus to Benenden, she was disappointed as soon as he began solemnly shaking his head.

"I don't think you'll find one along here, especially on Sunday. Don't use them myself, so I can't be certain. Never go far, you see."

"Can you tell me which direction to take, though?"

"I'll show you the road. It's this way . . . Uphill, round that bend, then you want the first lane off on your right. It's quite a walk, though. I hope somebody'll give you a lift before you've gone far."

Not knowing what to expect out here, Sheila didn't have much hope of that happening. With petrol in short supply, few cars were around.

Johnnie had been silent for ages, he'd shown no interest in chatting to that little girl on the train. And now, trudging gamely beside her though he was, she could tell he'd had more than enough.

"You'll be all right when I get you to your mummy," she promised.

The words appeared to have little effect, Sheila thought back to his reaction a few days ago when she'd first said she would bring him here, and she swallowed down a sigh. The poor kid probably remembered hardly anything about his real home and the mother he'd left there.

They had been walking for about ten minutes when she heard a horse and cart approaching from behind them. As it drew near a man's voice hailed her.

"Are you going far, missus? Your little boy looks as if he can hardly put one foot in front of the other!"

"I know. He's not been so well, bless him, and we've come ever such a long way."

"Where are you going?"

"Benenden. How much further is it?"

"A mile or so yet. I can give you a lift, if you don't mind sitting among a load of turnips. I've just fetched them out of my brother's store at Glassenbury — for fodder, you know."

"I know. My dad's a farmer," said Sheila, smiling up at the elderly man who reminded her of Mr Pickwick.

"Not round here though," he observed with a grin as he lifted Johnnie up onto the cart and began taking their luggage from her.

"No, in Yorkshire. How could you tell?"

"You certainly haven't a Kentish accent, have you?"

"I suppose not, no."

"And what's your boy's name?" the round-faced farmer enquired, as he resumed his seat and encouraged the horse to walk on again.

"Johnnie. He's only been staying with us, though. I'm taking him home now, to his mother. Jane Richards, do you happen to know her?"

"Can't say I do. Strange, that. Out here we know most people. But I farm just outside Benenden. Not in the village itself."

A few minutes later he was pointing out his farm to them. "Where exactly did you say the woman lived?"

"New House Farm."

He nodded. "I'm sure that's between the village and Goddard's Green. I'll drop you off somewhere along here. Are you certain you've got it right, though? I should know her name if —"

He paused, they both gasped, staring ahead into the distance where the road was blocked by vehicles standing alongside heaps of debris that stretched back from the roadside to what remained of a building.

"Bloody hell!" the farmer exclaimed. "I've been staying at my brother's to give a hand. I heard something come down yesterday, but I thought it was further away than this, over towards Tenterden. Looks bad, that. I hope to goodness it's not part of the sanatorium."

"So do I. Do you think it was one of those pilotless planes then?"

"Afraid so. And my missus will have seen that happen from our side windows! Oh dear — her heart's not so good, as it is . . ."

"You'll be wanting to get home to see she's all right. Why don't you drop us off here?"

"If you're sure you can manage now. Doubt if I'd get through there anyway . . ."

He helped them down with their baggage, and Sheila thanked him warmly for giving them a lift.

As they walked on, Johnnie's brown eyes grew wide with horror when he gazed towards the ruined house. Men were sifting through some of the rubble, placing furniture, a cooker, and a wringing machine, lopsided now on its iron stand, to one side of the wreckage. Further into the mass of dust and debris, others were digging.

Trying to hustle the child past the devastation, Sheila began talking, and recognised in her own voice an alarm no less than his.

"Do you remember anything at all here, Johnnie love?" She had to pause to cough. That dust seemed to be everywhere, she could even taste it, and she could smell burning. "Do any of the houses further up the road there look familiar?"

Johnnie shook his head. Sheila wasn't surprised. She had questioned him to no avail about his home in the past, and increasingly since deciding to bring him here. "Don't worry, I'll find somebody to ask. They'll tell us where New House Farm is."

A lady in a WVS uniform had been passing hot drinks to the men wielding picks and spades. When she turned away Sheila beckoned to her.

"I wonder if you can help me, please," she began, as soon as the woman noticed her. "I've brought this little lad home to his mother. He's not been so well, and the doctor said he was pining for her. Any road, she was living somewhere round here called New House Farm."

The woman was pale already, her face immediately turned to almost the shade of her white hair.

"Oh, my God!" she cried. "What a terrible thing to happen. Why did it have to be just now?"

"What do you mean, love? Are you all right? Had you better sit down or summat?"

The woman swallowed hard, and shook her head, then went on shaking it. "Oh, dear," she moaned, "oh, dear."

Sheila began to guess at the appalling truth. "You don't mean? Please tell me it isn't . . ."

"This house that they got yesterday with that damned pilotless plane! You can see how bad it is. It wasn't until the afternoon that they extinguished the blaze that had broken out in the rubble."

Sheila glanced towards Johnnie, who appeared too tired to comprehend the gist of their conversation, even if he heard it all.

"Where've they taken them? Are they in hospital, the folk that lived there?"

"I don't know for sure. But if he's related to them I wouldn't take him anywhere near. They're dead, you see. All three of them."

"Three?" She had expected to find Jane Richards living alone. Jane had never mentioned her husband being at home, or anyone else.

"A married woman and her parents," the WVS lady confirmed.

"I see." So that was it. She should have thought that Jane would be with her parents while her husband was wherever the war had taken him. "Thank you," Sheila said dully and turned to hurry Johnnie away.

"Just a minute," the woman called, mustering her shaken composure. "I say —"

But Sheila had gathered up both cases and urged Johnnie ahead of her down the road, so desperate to get the boy away that they only just avoided colliding with a pair of middle-aged men with spades, who were intent on joining the others to help clear up.

"I think we'll go and see that farmer," she told Johnnie. "He was ever so nice. And he only lives a little way down the road here."

That elderly man was the only person in the whole of Kent she knew how to contact, and otherwise she certainly couldn't think where on earth to turn for advice on what to do now.

"Don't let it upset you, love," she urged Johnnie, who was glancing back towards the wreckage of the house. "Don't keep looking back. We'll soon see that kind farmer again."

"They're dead, aren't they?" said Johnnie, and his tiny voice quivered. "The people that lived in that house."

"I think so, yes. But they might not be." She hoped to God that the woman she'd spoken to could have been mistaken.

Dismally, she wondered how she was ever going to break the news to him. How could she manage to explain to the child that she'd brought him all this way, only to arrive on the day after his home and his mother — and with them his future — had been blasted off this earth?

I'm not up to this, thought Sheila. But if Jane had been killed there was no one else. She couldn't let Johnnie down. Whatever happened now, she'd have to see that the boy was all right.

Chapter Three

The farmer frowned as he opened the door to them. "What is it?" he asked. "What's wrong?"

"I'm sorry to trouble you," Sheila gabbled, distress making her heart race. "I just wondered if you can advise me what to do. About Johnnie, here. It's that house, you see. The one that's been bombed. That's where his mother was living."

"Are you sure?"

"I asked a lady from the WVS who was handing out tea to the men there. She said it was New House Farm."

"You'd better come in. But I'm all at sixes and sevens. The wife was taken bad yesterday with the shock of watching that thing crash down; she's in bed. The woman next door had to send for the doctor."

"I'm sorry to hear that," said Sheila, about to turn away. "And I can see you've enough on as it is. I mustn't bother you . . ."

"No, no. I can't let you go off like that. Not when you say you've come a long way. Now just give me a minute, let me think . . . What was I doing? Oh, yes. Starting to make a pot of tea."

Sheila couldn't avoid noticing how helpless he looked. "Could I do that for you perhaps, if you show me where things are?"

His blue eyes in the round, weathered face brightened. "Well, now — don't mind admitting I'm not much of a hand about the house. May always manages to cook, and all that. Or she has done up to now."

He led the way through to a kitchen which, with its fire oven and black-leaded range, reminded Sheila of her mother's. He pointed to the kettle sitting on a gas ring. "We've got water laid on in the house now," he confided proudly. "You only have to fill that at the sink."

"I'll soon have it boiling up, Mr . . ." Sheila hesitated, realising she didn't know his name.

"Fred. Call me Fred. Everybody knows me as Fred, we don't go in for ceremony out here. And what are your names?"

"Sheila, Sheila Calvert. And this is Johnnie."

"You say you're not his mother then? That you're looking for her?"

"That's right. Oh, this is a blow, I don't seem able to think straight," Sheila sighed, watching the kettle while it began to murmur as it heated up on the gas.

"Me neither. Although May's been bad before, she's hardly ever taken to her bed."

Sheila nodded sympathetically, realising that even the fatalities in the village were failing to distract him from his wife's illness. "What does the doctor say about her, has he been again today?"

Fred nodded. "According to May, he's pleased with her, says she's improved a lot. She might only need to rest."

"That's good. Well, if there's anything more I can do to help before we leave, just say the word. I'm still ever so grateful —"

"Leave?" Fred interrupted. "But I thought . . . Have you somewhere else to go then?" He seemed worried about having to cope. She saw the table was so covered in provisions you couldn't put a pin down.

"Well no, not really. I was wondering if they'd have accommodation in a pub in the village or something."

"You don't want to go there. Not with the little boy, 'specially these days when there's so many servicemen making a night of it there. Yanks as well now. Not that I blame any of them, mind you. Not with what they go off out to face. They deserve any chance they get to let their hair down. Their lads as much as our own."

"But if you don't think the pub's suitable, is there anywhere you can suggest? Do any of your neighbours take in lodgers?"

"Neighbours?" Fred shook his head at her. "What do you want to go there for? Isn't this nice enough for you?"

"You mean . . . ? You don't mean you'd want us to stay here?"

Fred grinned, smoothed the snowy hair round

his tanned pate. "Only if you're as willing as you say to lend a hand while May's in bed!"

When the tea was brewed he took a cup upstairs to his wife, while Sheila tried to encourage Johnnie to talk. He had been staring silently around the big farm kitchen, which had a flagged floor with a rag rug in front of the range, white plastered walls and lots of dark wooden beams that looked very old. Even older than the farm at home.

"This is nice, isn't it, love?" she said. "Won't we be lucky if we are able to stop here tonight?"

Johnnie did not speak.

She tried again, wondering aloud if Fred and May had any children, but still the boy remained silent. I suppose he's still suffering from shock, thought Sheila. And prayed that Johnnie couldn't really have sensed that his mother had died in the ruins of that house.

"May says I've got to talk you into staying the night with us," Fred told her as soon as he reappeared. "And she says you make a grand pot of tea. She always tells me you could stand the spoon up in the cup when I make it."

"Some men aren't domesticated, are they?" Sheila observed, smiling. "Especially farmers who've always got another job they ought to be doing outside."

"You will stay here then?"

"We'll be glad to, thank you. Certainly until tomorrow, I might have some idea by then what to do for the best."

"You can have our Harry's room. There's a sofa in there as well as a bed. He liked to play his gramophone and that up there, before he went off into the army. Used to ask some of his pals in. They could have a bit of a laugh and so on, without disturbing us."

"That'll be lovely, won't it, Johnnie?"

The boy nodded, this time his lips moved as he murmured the 'yes' that remained inaudible.

Sheila noticed that Fred was looking curiously at the lad, and read in his eyes concern that Johnnie might have some disability.

"He's tired out, poor little love," she explained.

"And not the only one either," Fred observed, scrutinising her face so sympathetically that Sheila felt quite weepy.

"Well, what can I do to make myself useful?" she enquired. "If you want me to get a meal going or something, it'd be no trouble."

Fred's neighbour evidently kept pigs, and four chops were waiting in a meat safe in the larder. "I've plenty of peas and potatoes, and I dare say you'll find something you can make a bit of gravy out of."

Sheila encouraged Johnnie to help by shelling peas, a job he'd often done to please her mother, and one which now ensured that she could keep an eye on him whilst preparing the rest of the food.

It wasn't until later that evening, after they had eaten and she had put Johnnie to bed, that she was able to begin enquiring more closely into the family who had died when New House Farm was damaged.

"Do you remember the young woman's married name?" she asked Fred. "Did they call her Richards — Jane Richards?"

Feeling puzzled, she watched Fred shaking his head dubiously. "Don't think that was it, doesn't sound right to me. May might know for sure, only she did say she was going to go straight to sleep when I brought the tray down."

"Then you mustn't disturb her. We'll just hope that she's a lot better in the morning."

He nodded. "And I suppose if that young woman who was killed is the one you're seeking, another few hours isn't going to make a lot of difference."

"Aye, that's true, right enough. Do you know her parents' name?"

Fred nodded. "I knew them, but only slightly. They weren't farming people, you understand. Her father had worked at the sanatorium for years. Abreheart — Charles Abreheart. But are you sure his daughter's name was Jane? I thought May called her Joan."

"Oh, Johnnie's mother told me Jane all right. In fact, had it written down, had to have in case of needing to contact her. Only recently she hasn't been replying to my letters. That's the whole trouble, that's why we had to come down here."

Sheila suggested that Fred should forget about it until there was something they could do. She herself had no desire to dwell on the wreckage of that house. She had hardly dozed in the train last night, she needed to make up for that tonight or she'd be no use to anyone by morning.

Although aching for a bed, Sheila could sense that the elderly farmer wanted company, and she hadn't the heart to go upstairs immediately. When Fred spoke it was of Johnnie, and his blue eyes echoed the concern in his question.

"The boy's very quiet, isn't he? Is — is there something that prevents him from talking, like?"

Sheila sighed ruefully. "There is, and I wish I could tell you what it is. He's never had much to say for himself, not since he came to us. Did I tell you my mother took him in as an evacuee? It's because he's like he is — withdrawn, and eating so little that he's losing weight, that I set out to bring him to his mother."

"But his talking — or *not* talking — isn't he ever any different?"

"Not so often. Although he did have a bit more to say on our way down to Kent, happen because it were such a difficult journey. Even when he does talk, though, you can scarcely hear what he says. Sort of whispers, he does. It's as if he doesn't really believe folk want to listen to him."

And how is he going to be now? thought Sheila as she finally went up the narrow stairs to the room they were sharing. If his mother is dead, who on earth *is* there who'll get Johnnie to respond to them?

He was asleep when she went in, the light from

the landing illuminating his dark head as it contrasted with the white of sheet and pillow. He looked utterly contented in the bed she had made up for him on the sofa.

She undressed without lighting the gas mantle in case that disturbed him, found a nightdress in her suitcase, and slipped it on.

Before going to the bed, she paused again beside Johnnie, gazing down while her eyes misted. Whatever was she to do with him now that the urge to bring him to his mother had ended so abortively?

"There'll be some way done," she murmured aloud.

"I know," said the boy, awake suddenly, his huge brown eyes meeting her own. "You'll look after me," he told her. "It wasn't all frightening in the train, was it? And I like this house you found. Can we stay here with Fred?"

"Well, for a little while, yes. You're not a bit of trouble, are you, bless you?"

"Not stay here *always?* Not for ever? Doesn't he want us to stop here?"

"It isn't where we belong, is it, love? Not really. Only for a day or two . . ."

Johnnie nodded, smiled. "But you'll take me somewhere else that's nice. I know you will. Somewhere to live for always."

His sudden confidence in her warmed her heart, but Sheila could not let it lull her into any false feeling of well-being. This lad was going to be forced into facing the worst trauma of his already troubled life. And she still didn't know how the hell she was going to cope with telling him, or with the aftermath.

Despite her exhaustion, Sheila lay sleepless for hours wondering over and over again what on earth she was going to do for Johnnie. If he had lost his mother, there was nothing to keep them down here in Kent. Unless she was able to trace his father, she would be obliged to take him home to Yorkshire. However would she get the lad to accept going back there? She could only be thankful that at last he was showing signs of becoming attached to her, but she was going to need a lot of luck if she hoped to overcome all the unease that had inhibited Johnnie for such a very long time.

Even through the blackout material at the window, Sheila could see that the sky was bright with restless flashes that might have been lightning, but could equally have been a blaze somewhere. Alarmed, she hurried to the window and drew aside the black cloth. She recognised the flaring of anti-aircraft fire, its sound had been disguised by the moaning of the wind battering the house, reminding her of her own home and the gales that often beset Hardaker Farm.

She wished she was there; that Johnnie's problems had been sorted out. And the wind here wasn't the only disturbing noise. The drone of aircraft went on and on, seeming worse than she'd first noticed when arriving in Kent. Most terrible of all though, was the clattering, like the engine of some massive, badly-tuned motor bike, a sound which she now knew was one of those dreadful planes that needed no pilot. She returned to bed, perturbed, praying that they hadn't come all this way to become the victims of these diabolical weapons.

Sheila slept far later than she'd intended the following morning, and wakened to hear Fred's boots clattering across the farmyard. They were not the only sound: the wind had actually strengthened during the night and was wailing in nearby telephone wires, soughing through trees and rattling a door somewhere. For these few short moments she was prevented from noticing any aircraft, piloted or otherwise.

Johnnie was awake and dressed, sitting on the sofa and gazing anxiously towards her. He smiled when he realised she was awake.

"I knew you hadn't died," he announced. "I watched your chest, it was going up and down."

"Eh, love — you weren't frightened summat had happened to me, were you?" she said, wondering what other potential insecurities the lad had been contemplating.

He shook his head. "Not when I could see you were breathing. Can we have some breakfast now?"

"When we've both had a wash and I've got dressed. We can't go downstairs like this, can we?"

"I washed my hands and face," said Johnnie.

"Did you, love? You found the bathroom again all right?"

He nodded. "But I got washed in the kitchen. Fred said I could. While we talked."

He would be surprised that you did talk! thought Sheila. But then she realised that Fred might have been responsible for getting Johnnie to chat. The boy's reaction to attempts at conversation always seemed unpredictable. She wished she knew what the key to it was.

When she eventually went downstairs, their host's jovial smile convinced her that his encouragement had loosened Johnnie's tongue.

"You're looking a lot better that you were," he greeted her. "And the boy's quite chirpy. I've got good news as well. The doctor called on his way to his surgery — May can get up this afternoon."

"Oh, I am pleased. You must be very relieved, Fred."

"I am indeed! I'd rather be ill myself than have the wife laid low. And she wants to see you, soon as you've had a bite to eat."

"I'll certainly be pleased to meet her."

"We don't get to see many new people, these days. I'm afraid the chaps in the services billeted round here look on us as a bit old and past it. Not that they're stand-offish, or not according to what I hear, but if they mix with local folk it's generally so's they can make a beeline for them with attractive daughters!"

"And you — am I right thinking you've only the one son?"

"Now — now we have. Our Alice was a nurse, we lost her during that last bad raid on Canterbury."

"I'm sorry. War's diabolical, isn't it?"

Fred nodded. "But you can't go on being miserable for ever. Them that have gone wouldn't have wanted that. Her mother and me just pray that our Harry comes home after this lot's over. We'll try and be thankful then that we still have part of our family." He swallowed. "Listen to me going on like this. And today I was just going to be content. Because of May getting better . . ."

"And so you should. When did you say she wants me to go up and introduce myself?"

May was a large lady and, sitting up in the old-fashioned bed, reminded Sheila of illustrations of Jack Spratt's wife. She had a ready smile which belied her recent poor health, and was soon inviting Sheila to sit in the wheel-backed chair to chat in comfort.

"I hear you've brought one of your evacuees home to Kent. Fred tells me you're afraid his mother's been killed by that Jerry missile that's crashed just along the road there."

"It certainly sounds like it. I had the address, and a woman making tea for the men clearing the site said it was that house."

"And what was her name, dear? When Fred was telling me about it he'd forgotten what you'd said."

"Jane. Jane Richards."

May sighed, slowly shook her head. "Richards

doesn't sound right to me, you know — not that I can remember what their lass was called after she got married. But she definitely was Joan, not Jane."

"Oh, I do hope you're right! I'd give anything to find out that Johnnie's mother isn't dead after all. He's not at all well, you see. That's why I had to bring him down here. He's not been eating properly for ages, and he's that withdrawn. Hardly talks at all."

"Poor little beggar! Tell you what — I'll have a word with the doctor when he calls in again. He has to pass the door on his way back home and he's promised to bring me a bottle. He knows everybody. He'll be able to tell us if that young woman were called Richards."

Although determined to make herself useful by preparing food and doing what jobs she could manage round the farm, Sheila found time dragging until she saw the man she took to be the local doctor arrive.

She was out in the yard, with Johnnie following her around as she finished mucking out the stable. The wind had not abated and was howling round the farm buildings, rustling the trees and surging between the stable and the barn with such force that whenever Johnnie crossed the gap he was almost lifted off his feet.

The boy appeared happy here, grinning up at her whenever he was buffeted by the gale. Even though he still didn't have a lot to say for himself, Johnnie did seem to no longer be resisting her.

It might be, as she had thought previously, that the traumatic journey from Yorkshire really had drawn them closer together.

Earlier in the day they'd had torrential rain, driving across the fields and obliterating the horizon. Now the sky was darkening yet again, presaging a further downpour, and endorsing May's insistence that Sheila and Johnnie must remain here until the gales lessened.

"Whether you plan on taking him back home to Yorkshire or intend stopping for a while in Kent, you can't go dragging a bit of a boy like him around in this weather."

As soon as the doctor left, May came to the kitchen door and called Sheila to come in.

"Doctor thinks I am right, and Johnnie's mother isn't the young woman that was killed," May began. "Their daughter was definitely called Joan and her married name was Blakey."

"Oh, thank goodness!" Sheila exclaimed. "But I wonder how it was that Jane Richards came to give me that address?"

May smiled. "Ah — well, that was another thing the doctor mentioned. I'd forgotten, but a long while ago they had a lodger staying with them. A friend of their daughter's."

"And that could have been Jane. Nobody knows what happened to her, I suppose?"

May shook her head. "Not for sure. Although Doctor says she worked at the sanatorium for a while, with Joan. You could try there."

"I certainly will."

May looked through the window where the wind was lashing rain against the glass. "I should wait till tomorrow, though, dear."

Sheila grinned. "I've got an umbrella, I shan't melt. I can't wait to find out as much as possible about what happened to Jane Richards. I wonder, though — would you mind if I leave Johnnie with you? I don't want him upset by seeing the ruins of that house again. And besides, I'd rather he wasn't with me if I have to ask a lot of questions about his mother. If it's bad news, I'll break it to him."

The hospital wasn't more than half a mile or so from the farm, but Sheila had been unable to hold up her umbrella against the force of the gale. By the time she arrived at the entrance she was drenched and her bare legs were smothered in splashes of mud from the lanes.

She was compelled to smile to herself when the first woman she approached gave her a look which conveyed that Sheila gave the impression of having been hauled from the nearest hedge. But the disapproving glance was replaced quickly by a professional smile.

"Yes? What can I do for you?"

Sheila swiftly explained about her efforts to trace Jane Richards. "I don't suppose you happen to know if she is still employed here?"

"Was she on our nursing staff?" the woman asked, but distractedly. When Sheila looked around she could see why anyone working here was preoccupied. Several windows had succumbed to the blast, even some of the interior walls were damaged and plaster had fallen from ceilings. Her face was prickling as if she could feel the dust that still hung in the air settling on her skin.

"I'm sorry, I don't know. And I'm sorry to be troubling you, after what's happened. You all must have a lot of extra work."

"You'd better come to my office. This may take some time, but I must warn you I can't spend long on it, you've seen what it's like. We're just very thankful that it wasn't more catastrophic here — we only had three minor injuries. However, to business. We've been employing lots of extra staff — on the domestic side as well as nursing. I'll see what our records show."

After going through a doorway damaged by the blast, the woman went to a large filing cabinet, and began sorting through.

"I have a Jane Richards here," she said eventually, reading from a document. "But this was a long time ago, before the war. She was an assistant in the kitchens. She left in early 1939."

Sheila frowned. This information didn't seem to tie in with what she had learned today. "I was looking for somebody who'd been here more recently than that. I think she was living at New House Farm for a time, with the people that were killed."

The woman sighed and then was interrupted to answer the telephone. After a brief, evidently urgent, conversation, she turned to Sheila.

"It's possible she has worked here since that first occasion, I suppose. She certainly isn't currently on our payroll, or I'd have remembered her name. I've been at the sanatorium for two months now."

Delving further into her files the woman finally smiled. "Ah — this is more like it! Someone had mis-filed it. Jane Richards was employed here again for just over twelve months, terminating in March last year."

"And do you have an address for her?" asked Sheila eagerly.

"Afraid not, sorry. Says here she was seeking temporary accommodation, she must have failed to give us her address when she did find a room."

Sheila sighed. "I thought for a minute that we were onto something then. Oh, dear. I don't know what to try next."

"*Why* did you say you're trying to trace this woman?"

"I'm from up north. We've had her five-year-old son evacuated with us for over a year and he's not very well. Our doctor's sure it's that he's pining for her. So I brought Johnnie down here. I'd written to his mother, you see, and she hadn't answered. This was the only thing I could do."

The woman's smile became sympathetic. "Tell you what — if you'd care to take a seat, I'll ring through and see if any of the women she worked with remember her."

Despite the invitation to sit, Sheila felt so wet and bedraggled that she remained standing rather than spoil the upholstered chair.

The woman explained down the telephone that she picked up, and asked if anyone working in the kitchens had been particularly friendly with Jane Richards. There was an extended pause whilst even from a distance Sheila could hear the clattering of pots and pans. At last, the woman replaced the receiver and turned back to her.

"You're in luck. Jane Richards left to go and work on one of the local airfields — Woodchurch."

"That's terrific — thank you ever so much for finding out for me. Would that be in the NAAFI, do you think?"

"Or the equivalent, I should imagine. You may discover that it's rather less organised than the NAAFI; some of these Advance Landing Grounds are very small bases, with few facilities."

Sheila thanked her again. Almost running in her eagerness to follow up the lead, she hurried out into the rain. The strong wind had abated slightly but she hardly noticed, she was desperate to carry on with her search. Johnnie would be so delighted. Although it was late afternoon now, the summer evenings were long and she ought to be able to make her way to Woodchurch today.

As soon as she arrived back at the house she was obliged to revise her plans. Johnnie, who had seemed happy here, had in fact only been content whilst Sheila was somewhere around the farm.

"We've had quite a time with him," Fred explained. "He's gone up to your room now. If it were any other lad I'd say he was sulking, but I don't think that's it. May got herself quite upset because she couldn't do anything to please him."

"That's right," his wife confirmed. "You'd only just set out when he ran through the rain to the far field — Fred had a job finding him."

"Tucked away into a corner between the angle of the hedge and an oak tree, he was," Fred continued. "I couldn't get a word out of him."

"I'm so sorry," said Sheila. "He used to do that a lot at home, only our fields have dry-stone walls round 'em. I often thought the stones must be digging into his thin little body like knives." She sighed. "You mustn't let Johnnie upset you, either of you. It's just the way he is. Any road, I'll take him with me another time. That's if we haven't found anywhere else to stop . . ."

"You needn't do that, you know," said May. "It's nice having young company again."

Young? thought Sheila, she felt at least fifty. "Well, we'll see what else I can find out tomorrow. I've got a lead now to where Jane Richards might be. I'll tell you all about it later on." First, though, she must go upstairs and see what she could do for Jane's son.

She saw from the doorway that Johnnie was curled up on her bed. She could have been cross with him because he hadn't taken off his shoes, and she didn't like to think he'd been so careless of the bedspread. But she hadn't the heart to reproach the lad. He was lying with his face pressed into her nightdress, and murmuring away under his breath while he tugged anxiously at one of his dark curls. Before he became aware of her, she caught a few of his words.

"Please God, make Sheila come back. Make Sheila come back."

She was forced to swallow before speaking, and even then her voice sounded hoarse to herself. "What are you doing up here, love? I thought you liked being at the farm with Fred and May."

He shrugged his bony shoulders. "Yes, but not all the time," he whispered. "I only like it when you're here."

"All right then. Never mind. I'm back now, aren't I? And I've got some news, about your mummy."

She sat on the bed beside him and was surprised when Johnnie submitted to a cuddle, nestling his head against her. It's only a bit of loving that you're short of, she reflected, running a hand over his head, then raising it so that his brown eyes met her gaze.

"I've been talking to a lady who thinks your mummy is working at one of the airfields not so far from here. We'll be able to go there tomorrow, start looking for her."

She had hoped that Johnnie would enthuse, or at least show some interest. This whole excursion to Kent was in order to reunite him with the mother for whom he was yearning, wasn't it?

"What's the matter, love?" she enquired. "Is it that you can't remember her very clearly now?

I'm sure you will as soon as you see her again."

"But she might not like me . . ." the lad murmured.

"She loves you, Johnnie. That's even better than liking you. You're her little boy, that means you'll always be special to her."

On the following morning Sheila was awake before Johnnie and went downstairs to ask if she might give him a bath. She was determined to have him looking as good as possible when Jane Richards saw him again.

Before they set out from Midgley, Enid Hardaker had washed two pairs of his short trousers which were lying all neatly pressed at the top of his suitcase. And he still had one clean shirt to wear with them. In a fresh pair of socks and his good school shoes, he looked really smart by the time they were ready for leaving the farm.

Fred had lent her a train timetable and another for the buses, but they knew that both services might be disrupted by one of those terrible flying bombs. The number of missiles falling daily on Kent and London seemed to be increasing. Only last Sunday the Guards' Chapel at Wellington Barracks in London had been destroyed during morning service. Rescue parties were working for hours afterwards to bring out the dead and wounded, and the total number killed was feared to be well over a hundred. Locally (according to Fred) these pilotless planes were coming down in all the villages. Frittenden, Goudhurst and

Lamberhurst had been hit.

"I don't like you going anywhere while it's as bad as this," said May. "Can't you leave it for a while, dear? See if things get better. You can stay with us."

"It's ever so kind of you, but I want to get this sorted out as soon as I can."

"Couldn't you let Sheila have the car then?" May suggested to her husband. "It might be quicker."

He checked that she knew how to drive.

Sheila nodded. "My dad taught me at the beginning of the war, but I've not driven so much with there being such a shortage of petrol."

"Well, you're welcome to have a go, if you want. I tend to use the cart and horse, these days, if I need to go anywhere."

When he took Sheila to one of the barns where the car was kept, she was relieved to see it was an Austin Seven. She wouldn't be too daunted by handling a vehicle of that size. And although they might be just as vulnerable to air attack as they would be on the train, she ought to feel more in control than if the track were damaged. Ever since that journey down to Kent she had dreaded the possibility of being marooned miles from anywhere because rails were destroyed.

Johnnie thought setting out in the little car was exciting and began singing nursery rhymes to himself as they headed east. The roads were fairly quiet, allowing Sheila to adapt to driving a different car without too much trouble. She had studied the map Fred had lent her, memorising the route to Woodchurch, and was surprised how soon the airfield came into sight.

The place was nothing like pictures of airfields that she had seen on newsreels or in the papers. Much smaller than she'd imagined, Woodchurch resembled a base thrown together hastily, where even the hangars looked insubstantial. From this distance, the end of one of them appeared to be just massive sheets of tarpaulin.

Explaining her purpose as she opened the car window at the barrier, Sheila was shaken when the American airman on duty laughed as soon as she asked for directions to the NAAFI.

"There's the mess hut, that'll be what you're wanting. But we don't have any *young* women here. Only wish we had!"

"But I was told this was where Jane Richards was working . . ."

"*Was* perhaps — but there sure is no one of that name on the base now."

"Do you think somebody might know where she's gone to, though? Is there someone I can ask?"

"Just one moment, if you please." He nodded towards the huge tanker and trailer about to turn in behind her. "This guy's bringing fuel for our Mustangs, kindly park over to the side there, lady, and let him through."

When Sheila had moved the car out of the way she saw Johnnie was craning his neck to look up at the tanker driver. The lad was smiling and another glance at the man told her why Johnnie was so interested.

Once the tanker and its trailer were inside the airfield, Sheila stared towards the planes and the men loading several of them with bombs. The entire place smelled strongly of what she took to be aviation fuel, and was noisy. Shouts from the men accompanied the clattering of metal on metal, doors slammed, and vehicles tore purposefully across the field. An aircraft engine started up, and Johnnie flinched, but grinned when Sheila covered her ears. The car quivered as the ground vibrated.

Another man in USAAF uniform came striding in their direction. He paused to instruct the tanker driver, pointing out where he should go, and continued on towards the man on duty at the barrier.

She heard him ask what business she had on site, and then he walked on again, to address her through the car's open window.

"Sorry, lady, but civilians are only admitted on official business, after producing a pass. I assume you don't have one."

"I'm afraid not."

"Then I must ask you to leave. You're seeking someone, I believe?"

"Jane Richards. I was told she was working here."

"Could be she was once upon a time, I sure know that name. But she ain't here now."

"And would no one here remember her, know

where she moved on to?"

"Sorry, we don't have the time to go searching out answers to those sorts of questions, not concerning civilian personnel."

Sheila noticed that his tone suddenly chilled. He had seemed firm originally, but his statement that they were unable to assist had sounded quite reasonable to her until those few seconds ago. Now she sensed his open antagonism. Perturbed, she looked in the direction that he was gazing, beyond her into the car.

"How old's your son?" he asked sharply. "Was he born in England?"

"Johnnie's not my son," Sheila responded, but softly, she didn't wish to upset the boy. "Actually, it's his mother we're trying to . . ."

"Oh, yeah?" The man shrugged, shook his head. "If you say so, lady . . ." He gave Johnnie another assessing stare, then turned from them and strode away from the car.

Sheila smiled at the boy. I hope to goodness he doesn't realise what that was all about, she thought, aching to give him a hug. She hadn't understood these Yanks would take this attitude.

"Never mind, Johnnie, we'll go somewhere else and look," she told him. She was longing to hold the child until the alarm was driven from his wide brown eyes. But the fellow on duty here was watching them intently, she felt obliged to start up the car and drive away.

"It's all right, love," she said to reassure him. "We don't have to come here again."

But what of all the other airfields they must visit? she wondered anxiously. Would every American airman act in a similar way as soon as he saw Johnnie Richards?

Chapter Four

Don't want to go to any more airfields, not ever!"

Sheila wasn't surprised when Johnnie objected to visiting other air bases, but she had *got* to locate his mother. She couldn't give up looking, even just for that one day. "But this is why I've brought you to Kent, love. When we find Mummy you'll start feeling better."

He did not respond, just sat there beside her so dejectedly that her heart felt weighed down by his distress. As soon as she found a place where she was able to park the car, Sheila switched off the engine and turned to him. His dark eyes looked haunted, staring out from his thin brown face.

"It isn't that they don't like you, Johnnie," she began earnestly, and stroked the curly black hair that always felt springy beneath her fingers. "It's more that they don't understand. Where they come from, you see, they think that people like you are different somehow. They're wrong to think that, but they don't really mean to be unkind."

"But it's everybody, everywhere. The other

kids keep asking why I'm brown. Billy and Louise always laughed at me as well . . ."

I should have known, thought Sheila. That's why you've hated everything about being away from your own family. She hadn't realised, none of them had, he was just *Johnnie* and so appealing with huge brown eyes and skin only a few shades lighter. "It'll soon be all right," she assured him. "When you're back with your mum and dad."

Johnnie sighed. "Who is my dad, please?" he whispered.

Sheila swallowed. God, but she needed help with this, it was worse than they'd thought! Although Jane Richards had never told them anything about the boy's father, no one at Hardaker Farm had suspected that the child might remember nothing at all about him.

"Oh, we'll find that out when we get to your mother," she asserted, and hoped that there might prove to be some grain of truth in her words. For the present, she could only persist in searching. "Let's look at the map, shall we? We've got to find her, haven't we, Johnnie? We'll see where else she could be."

The word Newchurch seemed to spring off the page. She'd heard Fred talking about squadrons there of Tempest fighter planes which could reach speeds of over four hundred miles an hour.

As she started up the car and headed towards Romney Marsh, she began telling Johnnie what little she could remember from Fred's account of those planes. Anything to get the boy interested. To make him forget those cruel reactions to his colour. "They go that fast that they can intercept these horrible pilotless aircraft."

"What's intercept?"

Sheila smiled to herself, realising that if she wasn't careful Johnnie wouldn't be the only one out of his depth! "Well — stop them, I suppose, before they can do too much damage." But she suspected that already some of these wretched Vls had done just as much damage when coming down short of their target of London.

"Is that why all these aeroplanes are up in the sky now?"

"Yes, love, that's right. They're up there to protect us." She had hoped that by trying to ignore the constant zooming of aircraft and the sight of them overhead she would contain her own alarm and, more importantly, would avoid passing it on to Johnnie. Twice so far while they were driving along had she seen what had only this past day or so been christened a 'doodlebug'. Each time, the missile's fiery tail had been visible against the still stormy sky — a reassurance (if she believed what she'd been told) that the engine was not about to cut out and send it plummeting straight towards them.

I wonder if we are in even more danger than necessary while continuing to look for Jane, she thought, her concern deepening. The area surrounding air bases could well be at infinitely greater risk than elsewhere. Dare she hope that their purpose in coming to Kent might eventually justify endangering this boy beside her?

They had travelled only another mile or so when they saw a small wooden hut and beside it the notice: POLICE BARRIER STOP. As she slowed to a halt and leaned across Johnnie to enquire what this was about, a uniformed policeman touched his helmet to her.

"Sorry, madam, but I've got to ask all the usual questions . . ."

"Usual?" Sheila didn't understand.

"You're not local then?"

"No, I'm staying just outside Benenden. Does that matter?"

"Indeed it does, I'm afraid. Since before D-Day there's been restrictions on movement within ten miles of this coast. Along here, we're still pretty strict. Gun batteries all around, and landing strips. In the main, it's only residents who're allowed through, except for servicemen, of course."

"Oh, dear."

"Visiting somebody, were you? Best thing is to get them to vouch for you, then we'd have to see —"

"That's just the trouble," Sheila interrupted with a sigh, and went on to explain their reasons for trying to reach the airfield at Newchurch. "I've got to find out for sure where she is, there's no way I can contact her otherwise."

"You could write to her, care of the base. If that is where she's working you'd get confirmation, and maybe then we could find a way to grant permission for you to go through to Newchurch."

Sheila thanked him and turned the car round. She was terribly discouraged. Everything seemed so complicated.

Despite feeling that she had been compelled to bring Johnnie to Kent, Sheila was beginning to wish with all her heart that she had never left Yorkshire. Before coming here she hadn't realised how wearing this constant noise of planes would be, nor had she fully understood what it would mean to be surrounded by evidence of the earlier bombing that had taken place — some towns had a lot of damage. And now there were these terrible doodlebugs. Even the local people who had seen so much destruction appeared unnerved by them.

As she abandoned their search for a few hours and headed back to the farm, Sheila ached to be going home to someone close. To someone with whom she could talk out her unease. Here in Kent, she was very conscious that, compared with everyone who'd lived through the rest of the war, she'd experienced nothing. She couldn't go on to them about her feelings of dread. If only she could have had Edward waiting for her, she'd have been able to share all this apprehension.

"There's no reason to feel so anxious, I'm sure. Sheila'll be as right as rain, you've no cause to worry about her like this, love."

"But every news bulletin says there's been

more of them flying bombs," Pauline persisted.

"Happen so, love, but Jerry's aiming them at London. She'll be miles away in the country. You know that's where they were going."

Edward had managed a few hours away from camp, and had wangled enough petrol for driving over to see Pauline. Barbara had been in bed when he arrived, but he had been reassured by seeing how peacefully she was sleeping. Not having her mother at home seemed hardly to have affected her, and that was giving him hope. His daughter might not be too distressed if he was eventually able to do what he wanted with his life. And as for tonight — he'd no intention of letting Pauline spoil everything by fretting about Sheila.

They had just finished their meal. She'd insisted on going to the fish shop and, yet again, there hadn't been anything better than the battered 'sandwiches', with more potato than fish in them. But the chips accompanying them had been good and hot. Sitting across the table from Pauline, he'd been acutely aware of her: of her smile which always made him feel like a twenty-year-old again, and of her eyes. Those beautiful green eyes of hers roused passion right through every vein until he could have cried out for her.

He was going to risk staying the night, or until just before dawn. He had good pals at camp who were covering for him, and it wasn't that far to drive back before first light. It would feel as if they really belonged together already. And what a relief that would be after years of wondering if he really belonged anywhere.

Edward suspected these days, that it was on account of their cottage being adjacent to Hardaker Farm that he'd never felt that it was *his*. Sheila had always been so at home there, while he — well, it wasn't his fault, was it, that he'd felt more like a lodger?

"Shall we go up, Teddy? Barbara was asleep ages ago, wasn't she? And the only time she's ever woken here was when the siren went. That false alarm, the other night."

It was bliss knowing that they'd have hours together again this time; despite the force of his need, he could woo her with caresses, undressing her slowly, while all his senses yammered.

At his first touch, Pauline stilled the moan rising in her throat, even as she fought down the guilt threatening to mar their pleasure. It isn't only for me, she reminded herself, it's for Teddy, because I can't help loving him. And if she didn't quite surrender completely to him, mightn't that become a sort of — well, an *offering* for her sister's safety?

Teddy had said it all during these past months, had assured her time and again that if Sheila had kept him happy there'd have been no one else. There would have been no need.

By the time they reached the bedroom his urgency seemed even fiercer, but its expression was being restrained. And that sent Pauline's emotions surging. Her will to deny herself the total abandonment that she craved began eroding. The now-familiar conflict of concern for her own sister and yearning for this man joined the tumult deep inside her, creating tremendous agitation.

Beneath expert fingers her skin grew sensitised, aware, until every outer inch of her echoed the inner screaming. God, don't punish us through Sheila, she thought, and gave in to her own impulses that were compelling her to reach for him.

Edward smiled against her mouth before they kissed. "That's right," he murmured when she started on his buttons. Only with Pauline was it ever like this. No one else ever had snatched at his clothing with such insistence. How could it be wrong, how forbidden, when they came together so well-attuned?

Their bodies, instruments tautly-strung, they touched, clutched, strained at each other. Hazed by longing, almost stumbling with eagerness, he drew her with him towards the bed. She was as ready as he himself, her breathing no less urgent than his own while his final caress gave way to taking possession.

Before they eventually slept he had quieted every last vestige of their unease along with their passion.

Edward's only regret was leaving while Pauline was sleeping. But she smiled beneath his kiss, and again at his whispered vow to return. He would make her relinquish all that destructive guilt, he knew that now. Pauline hadn't resisted him in any way last night. No part of her was withheld, any more than he was capable of reserving anything of himself for the woman he had married.

Sheila had never cared enough, not for him, not to have them become one person. There was always somebody else. Parents, Barbara, the farm evacuees. Sometimes, he'd wakened in the night and found her side of the bed empty while she tended a calf, helped with the lambing, nursed a sick sheepdog. No one wanted to feel they came second to everything else. He had got the message.

The word from Newchurch airfield was tantalising. If Jane Richards had worked there, they weren't willing to confirm that. Reading between the lines of their reply, Sheila sensed that they knew more than they were saying, perhaps there had been a dispute? She didn't know where to begin looking next. And nor did she know how to raise the subject with Fred and his wife. Amid their distress, her problems and Johnnie's suddenly appeared less imperative.

There had been a terrible incident further north in Kent on the Saturday morning. Shot down by a fighter, a doodlebug had hit the Newlands Military camp at Charing. Dozens of men had been killed and many seriously injured. Fred and May had lost a nephew and had gone dashing out to try and comfort the lad's widowed mother who lived in Tenterden.

Sheila had spent the day looking after the farm, after assuring them that she would cope willingly. During the early evening they had come home, grief for their relative written across lined faces, while speaking of his death resurrected the pain of their daughter's.

Johnnie had watched them from his seat in the farm kitchen, his dark eyes hauntingly saddened in the little brown face that looked somehow thinner than ever.

"Will we all die?" he asked Sheila that night in their room. "Will there be nobody left?"

Reassuring him meant reminding herself that there must be no let-up. If she couldn't trouble these new friends of theirs, she must rely on her own resources to continue seeking the boy's mother.

At Sunday breakfast May was more herself, and remembered the letter that had arrived for Sheila yesterday. "Did it bring the news you wanted?"

Sheila shook her head. Glad that Johnnie was across the yard with Fred, she admitted her own confusion and how daunted she was by the difficulties of locating Jane Richards.

May nodded sympathetically. "I wish I knew where to tell you to look for her," she exclaimed. "But all I can think is that you'd better check out every airfield near here. And there's a lot of them — if you count the small landing strips that have been constructed."

"Are there really so many?" asked Sheila. She felt torn. In one way she was glad to learn that so many opportunities for locating the woman existed; but she was also overwhelmed by the prospect of having to investigate so many possible places. They were only names to her.

"Maybe if you start with the ones nearest to Benenden you'll be lucky," May suggested. "She knew this area, didn't she? She might have wanted to work somewhere familiar."

"So where do you think I ought to try next?"

"High Halden's not so far away. Then there's Headcorn Airfield that's between Smarden and Egerton Forstal. If you've still got the map that Fred gave you, I can show you whereabouts they are. I'll just find my glasses."

As soon as Sheila approached the landing strip near High Halden she became afraid that their journey would prove fruitless. There wasn't a single aircraft in sight, and the whole place appeared strangely quiet.

"There's nobody here," said Johnnie from the seat beside her, sounding so relieved that she realised afresh how greatly he'd been dreading another confrontation with an unsympathetic US airman.

When she halted the car however, she discovered that the base wasn't totally deserted; a man in a blue RAF uniform came striding towards her. As soon as she began explaining who she was seeking, even a faint hope of seeing Jane there evaporated.

"Sorry, love," the man said, his warm voice identifying him as from her native Yorkshire. "We've no one of that name here now. I dare say she left when the Yanks went off to France after D-Day. There's only a handful of us based here at present, although 616 squadron are due in any day now."

Trying not to let Johnnie see she was despondent, Sheila glanced towards him after thanking the airman and driving off. "We'll try Headcorn now, shall we?" she said briskly.

"Where's that? Is it a long way?"

"I don't suppose so, love." Sheila certainly hoped that it wasn't. They had been out for less than an hour, but already she was longing for the comfortable farmhouse. The weather was still miserable for June, quite wet and with a wind blowing up to make it feel colder. The constant droning of aeroplanes continued of course, even though the sound was growing so familiar that she noticed them less frequently. What she did notice, and each time felt her entire being cringe, was the appalling roar of doodlebugs passing overhead in greater numbers. She could only be thankful that Johnnie rarely seemed perturbed by them. But then the lad often appeared so uninterested in everything that his very lack of fear was alarming.

Heading north along the winding lanes, Sheila soon found they were in the village which she took to be Smarden. After pausing long enough for another glance at the map, she drove on again through a maze of narrow roads until Headcorn airfield finally came into sight.

Three planes took off one after the other, their roar deafening her. She saw their American markings, and thought they were Mustang P.51s reported in the papers for long-range flights as far as Germany.

When Sheila explained her purpose to the man on guard duty he waved her through, but with instructions to park just inside the perimeter.

As soon as Sheila got out of the car she was approached by a second airman who had been standing to one side when she drove up. She had to listen carefully when he spoke, his accent made his words so difficult to understand. But the glance he gave Johnnie unfortunately needed no interpretation.

"If you're after tracing some guy, I think you've come to the wrong place. The only black troops that ever visit this base bring in aviation fuel, and they're stationed at Wye."

"I beg your pardon?" Sheila began, outraged by his tone as well as the look he was directing at Johnnie.

"Didn't I hear you're seeking somebody? It has to be the boy's father."

"Actually, it doesn't," Sheila retorted. She resented his evident assumption that she'd had such a casual relationship with someone that he now needed to be traced. "It's his mother I'm trying to find."

"Oh, yeh? Dumped him on you, has she?"

"Johnnie was evacuated to my home in Yorkshire, because she wanted him to be safe. Not because she didn't care."

"Sure, sure . . ." he said, but cold eyes revealed total disbelief.

"Her name's Jane Richards," Sheila persisted. "She's working in the mess at one of —" The slamming of her car door interrupted her. When she swung round she saw Johnnie running away. He ducked under the barrier and darted through churned up mud beyond the entrance.

Sheila shouted his name and sped after him as the barrier was hastily raised for her. "Johnnie!" she shrieked again, appalled as he ran into the road. A jeep was roaring towards them from the south, so close to the boy that there seemed no hope of its stopping.

The jeep swerved, missed Johnnie by no more than the thickness of his little school coat. And the lad had stopped abruptly, in the middle of the road, shaking so much that Sheila could see the tremors.

She ran to his side, scooped him up into her arms, and pressed his cold little face against hers.

"You're all right, Johnnie love, you're safe, you're safe."

She felt tears sliding down his cheeks. They were matched by those spilling from her own eyes. The child could have been killed and his alarm showed he realised that, which made it even more dreadful.

"Say, I sure am sorry. Are you two OK?" The

man who'd been at the wheel of the jeep was crossing to them. Concern darkening his grey eyes, he swept off his peaked cap and grasped her shoulder. "Is the boy all right? Are *you?* I really could not see him, you know."

Sheila mustered a smile. "I know. It was Johnnie's fault, he simply ran off."

"And why was that?" he enquired gently. "Were they turning you away from the base?"

"Not quite, but . . ." Sheila didn't know how to explain, didn't want to, not while the boy whose colour had evoked that cruel reaction back there was clutching her so fiercely, was sure to hear every word.

"Look — why don't I take you back in there. Could be I'll be able to explain for you. I gotta do something, for heaven's sake. I feel so responsible."

"Not there, not there!" Johnnie gasped between sobs.

"I really think we'd better just be on our way," said Sheila, looking up at the man, noticing how smart he was in his belted uniform jacket which was a dark greenish brown more than khaki. He wore a tie with his neat fawn shirt, and she wondered how she could tell if this USAAF uniform meant he was an officer. "You must be extremely busy." And important, she thought; he certainly looked important.

"Is that your car through there?" he asked. When Sheila nodded, he grinned suddenly. "Then I don't think you're able to argue, ma'am.

You've had quite some shaking just now, I'm gonna insist you take a few moments to recover before you drive on."

He took Johnnie from her arms and led the way to his jeep where he smoothly lifted him aboard. Smiling, he placed a hand beneath her elbow as he assisted her up into the vehicle.

Sheila had expected him to return to his seat behind the wheel; instead, he leaned against the side of the jeep, one foot resting on its step.

"Should have introduced myself," he said. "Lieutenant Todd Albany, and mighty ashamed that I so nearly hit the boy. I didn't strike him at all, did I, with this thing?"

"I'm sure you didn't. And it wasn't your fault, not in any way. Johnnie should never have —"

"— Been distressed by the guy back there?" Todd suggested, a frown creasing his deep forehead and tensing a strong jawline. "You don't have to tell me, lady. I guess some of these guys from the south of the US have a lot to learn. And I sure believe you English aren't accustomed to this kind of prejudice. Your boy here . . ."

"Actually, he's not my boy," Sheila corrected him softly. "Johnnie's been staying with our family, he was evacuated to us. But nobody wants to know that. If they'd only listened. It's his mother we're looking for, I was told she was working at an airfield, in the NAAFI or — or whatever you call the equivalent."

"PX, it's PX to the USAAF. But on these ALGs, sorry — Advanced Landing Grounds there aren't many refinements. There are few civilian personnel here at Headcorn airfield. What's his mother's name?"

"Richards, Jane Richards."

Todd shook his head. "No, ma'am. Sorry, but we don't have anyone of that name here. Which other bases have you tried?"

Sheila told him. "Oh, and there was Newchurch, down on Romney Marsh. Couldn't even get near, there was a police roadblock."

"Still? Thought that only applied up to the Normandy landings. But I guess there's still a need for security in some areas."

Just listening to the airman and telling him about all that she was attempting was calming her. She no longer felt so distressed. And Johnnie was distracted from his fright — listening, looking from one to the other of them, taking in their conversation.

"Look, I feel real bad about the way you were treated back there," Todd said eventually. "The way they assumed —"

"That I was searching for some chap who was Johnnie's father?"

"Well — yes. That, and more. You can have no comprehension what it is like in the States, especially where too many folks hang on to old ideas. It's mighty different over here, when you get away from US bases, mighty different. And that sure is good."

Sheila smiled. "Well, you've certainly made up for the attitude of some of the others. You've been more than kind."

"Not at all. Only wish I could help . . ." Smiling back at her, Todd grew pensive. "Say — why don't I give you a hand, some other day? If I took you around . . ."

"Oh, no — I couldn't let you," she protested. But she was longing to have this American assist her. He was so *genuine,* a quality Yorkshire folk appreciated, made her feel she could depend on him.

"You'll offend me if you don't," said Todd. "Now why don't you tell me where you're staying? And you haven't yet revealed your name," he finished with a grin.

Sheila told him, and gave him directions to Fred's farm. Todd insisted that he would call for her and Johnnie on the following day.

"I've a forty-eight due me, hadn't taken it because I wasn't sure how I'd use the time. Now I've found me some real good motivation."

When Sheila eventually drove off Johnnie was smiling beside her, and she herself felt altogether different. Todd Albany had impressed her with the concern so evident in those lovely grey eyes. Tall and fit, and strong as well, he made her feel more confident. With his assistance, they could well be able to locate Johnnie's mother.

She sensed already that in his company none of his fellow-countrymen would risk insinuating that the lad was any less worthy than they themselves were. Some Americans might see nothing wrong in demeaning their black personnel. It seemed they were only employed in menial jobs, for tasks like driving the tanker that they had seen, and were segregated. But with Todd around she might be able to prevent people from making Johnnie more inhibited than he already was.

When she awakened next morning Sheila heard the rain pounding down yet again. Somehow, though, she could not let the weather depress her. Todd was picking them up in just over an hour's time, even in a deluge he would keep them cheerful. Johnnie liked him unreservedly.

She had been surprised yesterday when the boy had chatted on and on to Fred and May, describing Todd, recalling what he had said, telling them all about the jeep. She had thought that he was yearning to remain in touch with the American airman simply by remembering everything he could about him.

They were almost ready for setting out when the local postmistress brought the letter. Sheila had written to her parents soon after arriving in Kent and had been looking each day for the reply that would provide the much needed link with her home. It seemed a very long time now since she'd left Yorkshire, and her life here felt rather unreal. She wanted a reminder of where she belonged.

Enid Hardaker's letter was short, but full of everyday events on the farm, and assurances that they all were well. Sheila had carefully avoided mentioning the pilotless planes which had become a part of daily life here in Kent and was relieved that her mother didn't refer to them either. She had been hoping that no one at home was becoming preoccupied with fears for her safety.

Enclosed with her mother's letter was a note from Barbara. Sheila turned to it eagerly. Headed by a drawing which was supposed to represent her Auntie Pauline, it must have been written with her help for Barbara couldn't yet manage more than her own name unassisted. The text was simple enough. *I am having a lovely, lovely time here.*

I am glad that she's settled all right without me, thought Sheila, I wouldn't want her to be miserable. But she would have appreciated just a hint that her daughter was missing her.

Reminding herself that she could go home just as soon she had located Johnnie's mother and reunited him with her, Sheila quelled a sigh. She must continue to set her own feelings aside and give all her attention to putting things right for the boy.

Everything seemed better when Todd Albany knocked on the door. He paused, smiling, just long enough to be introduced to May and her husband. And then he was scooping up Johnnie under one arm and running with him through the rain to the vehicle. It was a car today, instead of the jeep, he laughed as he held the passenger door for Sheila after he'd placed the boy on the back seat.

"I borrowed this from one of the guys on the base. I couldn't have you in that jeep with the wind forcing in rain every which way!"

"You're very thoughtful," she said. "I only hope we're not being too much of a nuisance."

As he drove out of the farmyard, Todd assured her that they were being nothing of the kind. "Didn't I say? I'm simply thankful to have some purpose today. There's nothing worse than having time off due to you, and not wishing to take it."

"But I thought you all went dashing off, seeking the high life?"

"Not me, ma'am. Not since — since some weeks ago."

He sounded suddenly serious, Sheila gave him a sideways glance and was surprised by the hurt look in his eyes. She longed to ask what was wrong, but she hardly knew him, did she? He might resent personal questions. And something told her that the problem was very personal.

She was still wondering whatever had gone wrong when Todd began telling her anyway.

"Most of the guys on site would insist this is just the reason why I *should* be living it up. I guess I must be odd or something, it's just not me to be drinking or dancing the night away while I'm feeling this cut up. It was my girl back home, see. She wrote me the classic 'Dear John' letter. You know? Like she'd been going around with this other fellow, a marine. And like she is having a kiddie."

"I'm sorry," said Sheila, and thought how dreadful war could be, creating so many means of destroying lives.

"I took it kinda badly, you know. I'd set my heart on buying a home for her, raising a family. Been counting the weeks, I guess, since news of the Anzio beachhead broke, and I began hoping that I would be home in the States one day."

"Maybe when you do go home you'll find you feel better about everything . . ."

"Or maybe I won't go back."

Sheila felt her eyebrows raising. Could he really care that little about his homeland? "What's your job in peacetime?" she asked.

Todd grinned. "Same as now, Sheila, same as now. Or I intend that it should be. Always wanted to fly, the one good thing about the war is it gave me the opportunity, completed my training. I reckon being an airline pilot will do me just fine."

"So, at least you've a good career to look forward to."

"Sure have. And what about you — are you married?"

"Yes, my husband's in the Army."

"And overseas?"

'No, actually, to his perpetual dismay, he's never been posted abroad. Always been involved on the training side."

"So you get to see him often?"

"Quite often. He's not been out of Yorkshire — our home county."

"And kids, do you have any?"

"One — Barbara. Same age as Johnnie here, five."

"I'll soon be six," the boy declared from the back seat.

"Not quite yet," Sheila confided to Todd, who was laughing. "He was only five in March." She was delighted though, that the lad was speaking up for himself.

"You haven't said where you're taking us first, where are we heading?" she asked.

"Newchurch was the place you mentioned as inaccessible to you the other day. I figured we oughta take a look down there. I believe I can wangle our way through any roadblocks. The uniform, you know . . ."

Sheila knew. She also was gathering already that Todd Albany had quite a way with him, and the sort of determination that finds a route around most obstacles.

Sure enough when they encountered the same police officer at the same point on the road, Todd had them through after offering his ID along with a smiling explanation.

Sheila grinned. "I can see we ought to have had you on our side from the outset."

"Yes, yes!" Johnnie chanted. "We like you, don't we, Sheila? Ever such a lot."

"Well now, that's real kind, young fella!" Todd responded over his shoulder. "It's mighty nice to be appreciated."

Sheila certainly appreciated his skill in handling everything when they reached the Newchurch airstrip. Winning a salute from the guard on duty, Todd drove them straight on to the site and headed over towards a makeshift building with MESS painted on its door.

He took Johnnie by the hand as they left the car and Sheila felt Todd's other hand on her elbow as he urged them through the rain to the hut's entrance.

Once inside, while they were hesitating, Todd detached himself from them, but only to stride towards the counter where an elderly woman was pouring what appeared to be coffee from a cheap looking pot.

When they entered Sheila had been aware that the men grouped about tables were talking loudly, calling to each other and laughing. Uncannily, they became silent and stared at the three of them.

She was beginning to feel uncomfortable when Todd completed his hasty conversation with the woman and strode back towards them, shaking his head.

"Sorry — no go. The good lady back there has worked this place on her own but for an old guy who does the dishes, since Lord knows when. No young lady here, I'm afraid."

"Well — thanks for trying," said Sheila.

"Yes, thank you very much," Johnnie echoed.

Todd smiled down and ruffled his tight curls. "That's the spirit, son. We make up our minds that we gotta keep on looking, right?"

"Right!" Johnnie asserted loudly.

Behind them as they left the hut Sheila heard the men sitting around there laughing again, but their tone was indulgent. I certainly could have used Todd's influence earlier, she thought, if he always evokes a sympathetic response for the boy. Despite the rain coming down in torrents, searching with Todd might not be such an agonising struggle.

Chapter Five

May was standing at the farmhouse door when they drew up there in the early evening. She asked Todd to join them for a meal and although he declined he smiled as he thanked her, and Sheila could see that he was pleased to be invited.

Sheila herself was strangely relieved that he wasn't spending the evening with them. Todd Albany had a powerful presence, overwhelming her with his courtesy and consideration until she felt . . . Well, that was the whole trouble really, she couldn't tell what her exact feelings were.

Although they had found no trace of Jane Richards — even after visiting airfields at a place called Brenzett as well as New Romney — she was quite elated in Todd's company. Without saying much about it or making obvious efforts to cheer them, he was generating optimism that Johnnie's mother would be located. And his effect on the boy was astounding. Several times in the car Sheila had listened while the pair engaged in earnest conversation. She hadn't known that Johnnie was so interested in the countryside. During all the months on their Yorkshire farm she'd been too busy to discover that he relished the green of trees and field, the gold of ripening grain, that he loved darting rabbits, that he could identify various birds. Todd prompted the lad to express his affection for them all. Most importantly, he continually encouraged him to communicate. He was succeeding in unlocking some reserve that she herself had failed to release.

I could like that man a lot, Sheila acknowledged when she was alone, and admitted privately that she needed a bit of a break from Todd Albany if she was not to be harmed by his personality.

His grey eyes seemed just as genial when morning again brought him to their door, this time with the jeep which Johnnie immediately declared 'terrific'. The day was fine, at last, and Todd came with the suggestion that they should venture rather further afield.

"I have an idea that your friend might be working on a large base," he said as Sheila got into the jeep with Johnnie sitting between them. "I reckon we should make for Biggin Hill, learn what goes on there."

"And how far's that?" asked Sheila. "Will it use a lot of fuel?"

Todd laughed. "I sure don't believe the USAAF will expect me to account for every gallon! Just let me worry about that aspect, eh? You're making me feel useful, don't forget. That's pretty important."

He *is* a nice man, thought Sheila, and felt the

previous day's response to him widening to include more personal emotions. If she were younger, and free, she'd be losing her head over this one.

"If we find my mummy at one of your airforce camps," Johnnie began seriously. "Will my daddy be like you?"

"Wow, that is a question and a half!" Todd exclaimed, and Sheila watched his mouth forming a smile of sheer delight. "We can't know that, can we, son? But I tell you what — I reckon he must be pretty good to have a boy like you."

Todd couldn't be doing more to restore young Johnnie's self-esteem. Looking back, Sheila recalled the main reason why yesterday had been so agreeable. On those busy airfields he had succeeded in deflecting any antagonism displayed by those of his fellow Americans who had assumed that she had given birth to this brown-skinned boy.

As they headed north-west she noticed again that Kent was far less flat than she'd believed originally. They were climbing most of the time, passing through towns and villages that she'd love to identify, but they were made tantalisingly anonymous by the absence of signposts.

"I hope you're more sure where you're going than I am," she remarked to Todd with a smile. "I didn't realise just how confusing it is without place names when you're on unfamiliar ground."

He grinned at her. "You haven't ventured away

from your home territory very often, I guess. Right?"

"You certainly are! My parents farm, you know. That means there's never time for anything. Since the war began I've felt obliged to remain there and help. It beats going on munitions, any road."

"Sure thing! I'd never survive being cooped up in some factory."

"And you love flying."

"Too true, I do. Can't imagine any other life, especially now."

"Now?" Sheila prompted. Todd had suddenly sounded wistful. She remembered then all that he had told her earlier, about the girl he had lost. She longed to make him feel better. "I'm sure you'll find a lot of satisfaction in civilian flying when peace finally comes."

"I shall put all I've got into making a success of it."

As they were driving on, the skies over the fields, woods and scattered towns changed quite radically. Barrage balloons hung suspended above, hundreds of them, silver-white, against the blue. Even though she had seen plenty of these previously they had never been congregated in this quantity.

Before they had travelled much further Sheila recognised how necessary such a barrage had become: above the noise of the jeep's engine they heard the menacing rattle and roar of flying bombs.

"Maybe I shouldn't have brought you this way," Todd began, awkwardly. "I should have given it more thought."

"But I've got to try every airfield I can, haven't I, if that's the only way to find Johnnie's mother?"

"I'd never forgive myself if we became a target, though. Croydon's only just the other side of Biggin Hill and the town's beginning to be the worst hit of anywhere by these darned things."

The rest of the journey on towards Westerham and beyond seemed to Sheila strangely incongruous, surrounded as they were by exquisite countryside, picturesque villages, the drone of planes, and the all-too-frequent menace of doodlebugs overhead.

More than once they saw the flame of a missile extinguish, heard its engine cut out, then watched as it sped earthwards. They agreed that the only consolation they experienced was because the ones they saw rushing to the ground seemed to land away from any buildings.

I just hope we get there and back today without witnessing any carnage, thought Sheila. And then she had a strange feeling. *If* the worst happened and they came across some kind of devastation, she sensed that being with Todd would make everything more bearable.

They reached Biggin Hill during a lull between flights of V1s. She became aware then of the din created by aircraft taking off, as they were constantly when Todd halted at the gate. The noise, a hundred times worse than at smaller bases, shook the ground. The smell of aviation fuel was overwhelming, more obtrusive than anywhere else.

Todd showed his papers to the man on duty and began asking about Jane Richards.

The man reacted immediately. "She's not here now!"

"You do know the lady then?" said Todd.

The response was a snort. "Lady? You evidently don't, or not well enough! There's scarcely a man left on this base who'd make the mistake of calling her that."

Appalled by what they were hearing, Sheila glanced towards Johnnie, wondering how much of that tirade had reached his ears. He seemed oblivious to their conversation while he stared wide-eyed as a Hurricane fighter taxied quite near to them, preparing for take-off.

"Is it long since Jane left here?" she asked.

The man shook his head. "Just the other day, otherwise I mightn't have recalled the name. Sacked, she was for — well, being over-friendly with too many chaps here is the polite way of putting it."

"I suppose you've no idea where she's living?" Todd enquired.

"Are you relatives or something?"

"No, but I do need to contact her urgently," said Sheila.

"I can tell you where she moved on to from

here, she telephoned with some query about her pay. I got lumbered with taking down details, no one else had time then to sort it. Just hang on a tick . . ." He turned and went inside the hut behind him.

When he emerged, the man was grinning. "Thought so — another air base. That's where she is now. Lashenden. Let me see, that's —"

"It's OK, thanks," Todd interrupted, smiling. "I know Lashenden."

"So where is it?" Sheila enquired when he'd started up the jeep once more and was turning it around. "Is it far?"

"From here, quite a way. But not from where you're staying. It's just outside Headcorn village."

"But I thought we'd tried there. Wasn't that where we met you?"

Todd shook his head. "It's confusing, I know. Headcorn airstrip is where I'm based, but Lashenden's even nearer to the village, I guess. Only a mile or so to the south."

He understood when Sheila couldn't wait to visit the airfield. "We'll call there on the way back to Benenden," he assured her as soon they were on the road again.

Sheila was wondering anxiously how to prepare Johnnie for the imminent reunion with his mother, but the lad still seemed more interested in the aircraft they had seen at such close quarters.

"Are the planes you fly like those?" he asked

Todd, craning his neck to watch from the jeep until the airfield was out of sight.

"Almost," Todd replied. "But ours are called Mustangs. And they're capable of travelling all the way to Germany."

Sheila suddenly felt cold. She didn't want to contemplate the dangers Todd faced during every day of his working life. His love of flying could not be denied though; it was evident in his tone of voice as much as the actual words while he began explaining the power of his favourite aircraft.

I'm going to concentrate on what's likely to happen when we finally meet up with Jane, Sheila resolved, determined not to allow concern for Todd to outweigh the purpose of her coming to Kent. She would need to handle the encounter between mother and son very carefully. She'd been afraid for a long time that it wouldn't be easy, that Johnnie now had only vague memories of what his mother was like.

As for Jane, the meeting was bound to be a shock. Having received no response to those letters, Sheila could only assume that they'd never reached their destination. Jane Richards couldn't have the slightest notion that her boy was on his way home to her.

"You all right?" Todd enquired eventually, making her realise that she had been preoccupied for quite some time, and silent.

Sheila grinned. "I think so, really. Just a bit nervous, about — well, you know . . ." She was very conscious of Johnnie sitting between them; she'd no wish to infect him with this anxious anticipation of the encounter which finally seemed about to happen.

"Just leave everything to me when we arrive there," said Todd. "I'll make all the enquiries, then we'll take it from there."

"I'm ever so thankful you're with us today," she exclaimed. Yet again, he had got Johnnie to chat enthusiastically during the journey. The lad had improved greatly during these two days. Surely that would help him to be better equipped for meeting up with Jane?

They had driven for miles since leaving Biggin Hill and now were well away from the area where the sky was clustered with such a mass of barrage balloons. And for the past half hour or so there'd been no sign of approaching flying bombs. I just hope to goodness there isn't an air raid or anything now, thought Sheila. She'd not be able to bear the tension if anything should happen to delay that reunion.

"Not much further," Todd told her as they passed between the houses and inns of a hilltop village.

Before them a long, straight road dropped steeply downhill to the south, with fields to either side where Land girls worked, their tin hats reminding Sheila how much more hazardous this was than Yorkshire. There was a difference also in the landscape, a panorama of farms with oast houses and hop-gardens stretching towards the distant line of low, blue-hazed hills.

"Headcorn is only just out of sight after the terrain levels out over there," Todd continued. "Then we press on south in the direction of Tenterden. You know that town perhaps?"

Sheila shook her head. "Afraid not — I've been too busy trying to locate airfields to spend time exploring the local towns."

"You must make time to take a look, some of these places are mighty fine. That's if you love old buildings."

Headcorn when they reached it had plenty of those. Timbered shops and houses, some of the latter quite large. One or two, on their right as they drove through, were showing their age in walls that leaned out of true and windows not quite vertical.

Glad of a diversion for him, Sheila pointed these out to Johnnie.

The boy chuckled. "They look like they're out of one of the nursery rhymes that your mummy taught me!"

Mention of her own mother at that moment, just when they were expecting to reunite Johnnie with *his*, affected Sheila rather strangely. She felt torn — eager to take the boy to his real home, but moved by his recognising the lasting influence Enid Hardaker had on him, despite his distress while staying at the farm.

"We used to see army tanks along this high street, Johnnie," Todd was explaining. "During the lead-up to the Normandy landing this part of Kent saw a lot of military equipment, and personnel."

"Were you here then?" asked Johnnie, sounding awed.

"Sure was, young fella. That was the reason we were assembling around here. Did you know, though, that not all those tanks and army vehicles were the real thing? They had dummies made up to fool the enemy reconnaissance aircraft."

"Really?" Sheila was intrigued.

"Straight up! And some airfields round here were fakes as well, to mislead the Luftwaffe."

"What — into thinking that we had more strength than we had?"

"That sort of thing, I guess. And to confuse them as to where allied troops were either gathering or actually operational."

Absorbed in considering an aspect of warfare which hadn't been known to her previously, Sheila hadn't noticed that he had left behind the last few houses of Headcorn village. She felt ill-prepared when Todd turned in at the entrance to Lashenden airfield.

"You wait in the jeep," he suggested. "I know some of these guys here, I'll soon learn what gives."

"It's not very good, is it?" Johnnie remarked, looking around them. "I mean, it's kind of little."

Sheila laughed. Certainly, after Biggin Hill, this base seemed small indeed, anything but impressive. There appeared to be few permanent buildings, and there could be no mistaking the tents which looked as though they were all that provided accommodation for the airmen she could see hurrying purposefully about the site.

"Do you know why we've come here, Johnnie?" she began, conscious that she must somehow prepare the boy for meeting his mother again.

"So's Todd can see his friends?"

Before she could answer Todd was striding back towards them.

"No go today, sorry," he told her. "The good news is we have found the right place. It's just that she's not on duty. Try again tomorrow. I'll explain later."

When Todd stopped the jeep in the farmyard Johnnie jumped out and ran towards Fred who was urging the cattle out to their field after milking.

"We've seen ever such a lot of planes!" the boy exclaimed, and they smiled, hearing him begin to describe their visit to Biggin Hill.

"So, when will I be able to see Jane Richards?" Sheila asked Todd.

"In the morning, they say. She's only on duty during that part of the day. There's something else, though —" He paused, glanced towards Johnnie. "Do you think we might talk somewhere where he won't interrupt?"

"We could go inside. Or take a walk maybe . . ."

"A walk. What d'you say if I drive us to the

centre of Benenden?"

He was surprised by how small the village was. After a quick glance to either side where there were a few shops and houses, they began walking towards Benenden church which was set back some distance from the high street. Passing an old school on their right, they strode in silence until they reached the church.

In the shadow cast by the building the day felt quite cool suddenly, a factor which seemed to emphasise Sheila's unease. She watched Todd as he mustered the right words to impart the news he'd gleaned at Lashenden airfield.

"You're going to have to be careful how you handle this, or young Johnnie's about to develop one almighty chip on his shoulder. They told me back there that his mother has another child, a baby girl."

"Oh, Lord," Sheila sighed. "That's not going to help the poor little lad at all, is it?"

"My sentiments exactly. And I'm afraid my furlough's up, I'm on duty tomorrow. I can't be with you."

Sheila smiled. "I didn't expect that you could. And I'm just very grateful for the time you have given us."

"It's been a real pleasure, Sheila. I mean that."

"I'm sure I'd never have located Jane without you, certainly not for weeks. I'll have to try and prepare Johnnie a bit, perhaps suggest that he might have a tiny brother or sister waiting to meet him."

"Good idea. You may find there's no real problem with there being a baby. But I thought if you knew —"

"It's vital that I do! It should help me anticipate Jane's attitude to the situation, as well as her son's. I don't want her making it obvious that coping with Johnnie in addition to the baby is going to be difficult."

Todd agreed, and continued to look pensive. "You'll have the first hurdle also — getting Johnnie to his mother without encountering any more nastiness on account of — well, of his colour."

"I just wish people would get to know him first, before they —"

"— Judge him by his skin?" Todd sighed. "One day, maybe things will be different in certain states back home. Despite what you've noticed here, there is hope that attitudes could change. If only we can overcome years of believing segregation is acceptable."

She asked where Jane was living, but Todd hadn't been told. I wonder who's looking after the baby while she's at work, Sheila thought. She couldn't recall whether Jane's mother lived in the area.

"I suppose you'll be hurrying back to Yorkshire once you've delivered the boy to his mother," said Todd, sounding regretful.

"Of course. There's more than enough work for all of us at Hardaker Farm. I felt quite guilty leaving them to cope, and I've already been away longer than intended."

Todd nodded, his strong features looking taut with concern. "It's just — well, I guess I need to know what happens when you do meet Jane Richards. How Johnnie settles, and so on . . ." He sighed. "Trouble is, we never know from one minute to the next when we'll take off on another mission."

"I don't suppose I'll be dashing back to Yorkshire tomorrow. You could ring me here at the farm, I'm sure neither May nor Fred would object."

"I'll do that, I surely will."

"You've been so good, Todd, I wouldn't just go off like that." And all at once she didn't want to even contemplate not seeing him again. This earnest young American had made up for any prejudice she'd been confronted with on account of Johnnie's colour.

"I'll be in touch then, sometime tomorrow," he confirmed.

Reluctant to let Todd go, Sheila was happy to stroll at his side, listening while he began telling her about his parents' home in Virginia. Describing the Blue Ridge Mountains, he made her long to see their splendour. Suddenly, though, the tranquillity was shattered. Drawn by the noise, they looked towards the south-east and saw not one flying bomb, but two.

Todd clutched her arm and drew her against his side. "I'm going to see you home to the farm. There's no way I'm gonna keep you out here with that lot passing overhead."

Sheila sensed that he was equally perturbed by this reminder that they were never quite safe from these V1s. Away from the hum of the jeep's engine, there was no disguising the menacing roar of impending destruction. Even though they had seen those tin hats worn by workers in the fields, there was nothing like the sight and sound of these weapons to make them realise how vulnerable they were in the open.

There seemed no adequate way of thanking Todd for all his assistance, but thank him Sheila did on the steps of the farm before he got into his jeep again.

All at once Johnnie appeared, running from the stable where he left Fred to lean into the jeep and hug the tall airman. "Thank you for today," the lad said, beaming shyly. "For — well, everything."

"That's all right, son. My pleasure."

Sheila was remembering Todd's reassuring presence next morning when she set out with Johnnie to return to Lashenden. Fred had loaned her the Austin Seven again, and she had felt better about accepting this time, feeling sure that before the end of the day she would need the car no longer.

Johnnie was sitting beside her, cheerfully anticipating seeing more American airmen who must, he claimed, be lovely. Because Todd was lovely. About his forthcoming reunion with his own mother, the boy was less specific. "All right, I guess," had been his comment when Sheila enquired how he was feeling.

That was first thing today and, because she had decided last evening to tell him something about his young sister, Sheila was daring to hope that Johnnie would not react too badly.

When she had explained the situation he had seemed unperturbed. "So, I'll be the eldest now," he'd said in a voice that suggested he might be glad to be regarded as someone older and more responsible. Sheila could have hugged him because he sounded so ready to adapt. He hadn't mentioned either his sister or his mother afterwards.

The drive to the airfield took less time than Sheila expected. They were approaching the entrance long before she was prepared with what her first words should be on seeing Jane Richards. But she did know enough to smile confidently as she wound down the car window and looked towards the man at the barrier.

"We called here yesterday," she began. "With Lieutenant Albany. We were told that Jane Richards is working here. Her boy and I need to see her."

"*Her* boy? You sure you're not gonna give her one almighty surprise, lady?"

So irritated that she forgot to be diplomatic, Sheila glared hard at him. "If you stopped to think, you'd realise that his mother must have been there when Johnnie was born! Would you please tell me where I may find Mrs Richards?"

Once again, Johnnie was more interested in the numerous aircraft, some just visible inside a hangar where mechanics were servicing them. Although thankful that he did not seem agitated about being reunited with his mother, Sheila began to fear that the next few minutes might provide something of a shock for him.

She need not have worried on the boy's behalf. They saw Jane as soon as they entered the building, little more than a hut, which housed the mess.

Johnnie recognised her at once. "That's my mummy," he said, pointing towards her while, still clutching Sheila's hand, he began skipping along.

Jane Richards was the person who was shaken. She stared from her son to Sheila, then back again to the boy. "Oh, crikey!" she exclaimed. "Oh, my God . . ."

Hypnotised by the woman's shattered expression, Sheila quelled a sigh and continued walking towards her. Jane had paled, then flushed to the dark roots of her yellow hair. But then she reacted in a way that instantly generated Sheila's admiration. Scurrying around the end of the counter where she'd been serving, she was down on one knee with her arms outstretched before Johnnie reached her.

"Oh, my little darling!" she cried. "You hadn't forgotten me at all, had you? My, but you're thin, dear . . ." she added, and gazed questioningly at Sheila.

"That's the main reason I've brought him home," she told her. "He's not been getting on particularly well with us. The doctor thinks he's been pining for you."

"Ah — the poor little chap." Jane released her son and straightened her back. "Don't quite know what to say, you bringing him here without warning, and that. You could have let me know."

"I did try, Jane." Sheila was conscious of attempting to keep her voice low and even. Johnnie would not be helped by any disagreement. "I wrote two or three times."

"Oh, yes — well . . ." Jane avoided eye contact with her, and refused to meet her son's adoring look. "That place where I was staying had a direct hit, you know. I lost my friend, and both her parents were killed."

"I know, just the other week. But I wrote long before that. Were you staying with them until quite recently then?"

"Well, no — not exactly. They said — said there wasn't enough room. You see, Johnnie's got a little sister now. It's made everything — different. I had to move . . ."

"Who's looking after your daughter today?" asked Sheila, long before she'd intended, but she was so anxious to learn the truth.

"She's well cared for, make no mistake. I've got a room, not far from here actually, in Frittenden. The woman the house belongs to is ever so good. She keeps an eye on Gloria while I'm at work. That's why I work the early shift, makes it easier for Mrs — Mrs Foster."

Everything in Jane's manner was screaming to Sheila that the move and the arrangement with her landlady were quite new. She tried not to give space to her own growing suspicion that Jane had been asked to leave her friends near Benenden, that since then she had moved her accommodation quite regularly.

It was none of her business. She had brought Johnnie home to his mother and, on the face of it, Jane was welcoming him cheerfully.

"How did you find me?"

Sheila was starting to tell her about Todd's assistance, but Johnnie was explaining already. "A man helped us, an American man. He's got a jeep, and he knows how to drive aeroplanes . . ."

"That's nice, dear. Is he stationed here?" Looking at Sheila now, Jane seemed more animated, eager to be acquainted with Todd.

"No. Not far away though. Like Johnnie says, he helped a great deal. I wasn't getting very far at all till he stepped in."

"I'd like to thank him," Jane announced. "Can you arrange that?"

"I'll try, but now Johnnie's safe with you I shall have to be off back to Yorkshire."

"Already? But — I mean well, I haven't got a bed for him or anything, have I?"

"And nor have I." Sheila sensed that she needed to be firm. "Johnnie's been sleeping on a sofa in my room. And we've been lodging with a farmer and his wife. I can't expect them to put up with the inconvenience any longer."

She was recognising increasingly that this young woman (despite her initial outward show of affection) was reluctant to cope with Johnnie. She herself would have to continue to insist that Jane should at last take responsibility for her own son.

"Can you hang on to him until later today then?" asked Jane. "When the others come on duty I'll go and see my landlady. She'll have to find us a bed or another cot or something."

"I don't sleep in a cot, they're for babies," Johnnie protested. "I haven't slept in a cot for years."

If the situation hadn't been so pitiful, Sheila might have found his assertion amusing. Instead, she felt like hitting Jane for being so unthinking in her treatment of the boy.

"You'd better tell me where you're living, and how to get there," Sheila said. "I'll bring Johnnie to you this afternoon."

Returning to the car, she asked the boy what he wanted to do until it would be time to go to his mother.

"Go with Todd in the jeep," he answered swiftly.

"I'm afraid you can't do that, love. He's busy today. Is there something else you'd like?"

"Help Fred on the farm. I won't be there soon, will I?"

"Not when you're living with your mummy,

no. But you will be able to have fun with your little sister. It'll all be very exciting, won't it?"

Johnnie's expression told her he was not impressed. Sheila decided not to labour that particular point. Since meeting Jane Richards again her own emotions had been in turmoil. I hope I'm never so grudging in my treatment of our Barbara, she thought. I know I get harassed trying to do right by her as well as pulling my weight around the farm, but I trust I haven't ever made her feel that she was in the way. There had been occasions, she was compelled to admit, when giving her mother a hand with the evacuees had exasperated her own little girl. She could hear Barbara's voice now: 'But you're *my* mummy, not theirs. You should be playing with me.'

Oh, God, she thought now; I'm coming home, Barbara love. I'll be with you just as soon as humanly possible. Tomorrow, so long as I can travel all that way in one day in wartime.

She would be especially good to her own daughter, compensate her with all the attention she deserved, until she herself was certain that Barbara hadn't suffered because of these days of being apart.

Sitting after lunch in the farm kitchen with May, Sheila remembered suddenly that Barbara hadn't been exactly miserable. That she'd declared she was having a lovely time with her Aunt Pauline. Perhaps that meant there was all the more reason to hurry back to Yorkshire.

Johnnie's things had been ready in the car since

that morning, but Sheila made sure that he had a thorough wash and looked neat and tidy before they set out to leave him with his mother.

She was moved almost to tears when he solemnly thanked both Fred and May for letting him live in their house. Whatever the shortcomings of the boy's stay at Hardaker Farm, he'd evidently acquired good manners. Now that he'd begun to unfreeze, he was showing considerable charm.

So long as your mum treats you right, Sheila thought, you'll make out nicely. Away from folk who disparaged his colour, he would grow and progress, learn to face life head-on, yet without any arrogance.

The telephone interrupted just as May was saying quietly that Sheila must tell them afterwards about Johnnie's reunion with Jane.

When Fred called Sheila in she was delighted to hear Todd's voice. "I've just resurfaced after a few hours' sleep. We were out most of the night, headed back at dawn. I just — well, was kinda anxious about how things went. With Johnnie, you know."

Sheila related brief details of the visit to the airfield. "As a matter of fact, I was just setting off to take him to Jane now. She's renting a room in Frittenden."

"I'll take you there. So long as that's right with you?"

"I'd love you to. And Jane did say she wanted to thank you."

When Todd arrived, transferring Johnnie's few belongings into the jeep took no more than two or three minutes. The boy then decided he must reiterate his thanks to the elderly couple.

Todd exchanged a smile with Sheila. "We sure do have one different kiddie there. Where's the Johnnie who wouldn't talk at all a couple of days back?"

"I think the change is your doing — it can hardly be mine, when he's been in my company for ages! Until very recently he was only retreating further into himself."

"Whatever the cause, the result is great."

Bouncing along in the jeep, the journey to Jane's lodgings was altogether brighter than Sheila had feared. By the time they were parking outside the address she'd been given, both she and Johnnie were laughing.

A woman of about sixty with fading hair that once had been an attractive sandy shade opened the door. She pushed a pair of spectacles up onto the bridge of her nose, and looked first at Todd's uniform, then towards Sheila. Last of all, she gazed to where Johnnie was wriggling uncomfortably beside them.

"You can't be —" she began.

"We are bringing Jane's son Johnnie home," Sheila confirmed briskly. So, Jane hasn't told this Mrs Foster about him, she thought despairingly. Hadn't she the sense to prepare her?

Jane appeared in the tiny hall, and her gaze also went immediately to Todd. "Well, hello!

Come right in . . . All of you," she added, very much the afterthought. She was holding a girl who looked to be a year or so old, a beautiful child with hair as pale as hairdressing skill rendered her own.

"Isn't my Gloria lovely?" she demanded of Sheila. "I keep saying she's such a picture! I am so lucky." For all the notice she was taking of Johnnie, he might have been from another planet.

It was disastrous. I have to get away from here, thought Sheila wildly. I can't stand this. I shall have to say something. I've brought the lad here, for heaven's sake, because he was pining for *you!* Or so we thought. Pining for something, certainly. But however would he find that here? With this woman?

Chapter Six

Sheila honey, you had to do it. You had to leave him with his mother. Johnnie's not your responsibility. You knew that all along. Didn't you? *Didn't you . . . ?*"

They were in the jeep. She was making an utter fool of herself. They had only got away from Jane's lodgings a few seconds ago. Todd had offered to help move a small bed from another room into the one Jane was renting. Her landlady Mrs Foster had insisted then that she must make them all a cup of tea.

Sheila had almost choked on hers, she was developing such an enormous lump in her throat. Jane had told Johnnie to take off his coat, but had instantly reproached him for putting it on a chair. Why doesn't she take it from the lad, hang it up, show him where his things belong, where he belongs? she had thought. But Jane had been fussing with the baby.

Bottling up her thoughts for so long had been the wrong thing for Sheila. As soon as they emerged and crossed to the jeep she was weeping. Great sobs that nothing on this earth might suppress.

"Hang on, just for a minute or two," said Todd, determined to get her right away from the place.

He stopped the vehicle a mile or so out of Frittenden and switched off the engine. They were somewhere along the hillside they'd visited the other day where the Weald of Kent stretched out below them. A handful of US fighters scoured the sky to the east, reminding Sheila of Todd's work, that he'd be up there soon. She felt totally bereft. Lost without young Johnnie, and suddenly, painfully aware of how lost she would feel without this man whose warmth was penetrating right through to her skin on this unseasonably chilly summer day.

"I thought you'd accepted that you were doing the best thing in bringing the boy back to his mother," he said reasonably.

Her sigh was rueful. "I'd accepted that, yes. But it doesn't feel right somehow. Does she strike you as a good mother, Todd?"

"I'm no expert, am I? The baby seemed well cared for. Jane herself is quite smart."

"She was always that." It wasn't a compliment.

"When are you going back to Yorkshire?"

"Tomorrow. It's high time I did. Happen I'll be more use looking after my own daughter."

"She'll sure be glad to have you home."

I wonder? thought Sheila miserably. "It's only that I wish I was happier about Johnnie . . ." What did that woman, with her bright hair and tight, slinky frocks, know about the needs of little boys?

When her voice trailed off dismally, Todd drew her against him. She felt his lips on her forehead.

"If it'll make you feel better, I'll keep an eye on things this end. I could call on Jane Richards once or twice, it's no distance from the base. And I am kinda fond of Johnnie."

"Would you, Todd? If you could just let me know how he's settling."

"You only have to give me your address." And that was something he needed, some way of maintaining contact between them. It wasn't by any means only the boy he'd grown fond of during this incredibly short while. And now Sheila was about to travel miles away to the north, while he himself would be drafted very shortly. And who could prophesy where his destination might be?

"I *will* keep in touch," he reminded her later when they parted at the farm.

Those words seemed to be the only comfort as a succession of trains carried her back towards the West Riding next day. She had spent a restless night trying to rationalise her unease, telling herself repeatedly that Johnnie would be all right now that he was with his mother.

Today, Sheila was trying to resist additional emotions which were threatening her peace of mind. Alarming though those wretched flying bombs were, and disturbing to think about the people risking their lives to combat them, she had felt somehow more alive in Kent — part of this war still being fought above its fields and orchards.

Even the yearning to see her own little girl again did not quite erase the urge to remain in this area. She had come to feel more strongly than ever that she *belonged.* Gazing out of the carriage towards the changing landscape she wondered if she would ever stop picturing those airfields, if she would ever be able to cease this overwhelming concern for the men stationed on them. And for one man in particular . . . ?

She must learn to forget Todd Albany. He had played a role in her quest, had transformed the struggle to find Jane Richards, for her and for young Johnnie. She could be thankful that the boy had learned from him the ability to begin to enjoy his life. For herself, the interest that Todd had brought must be relinquished.

After passing through Doncaster Sheila began looking forward to arriving home. Excited now, she couldn't wait a moment longer than necessary to see Barbara. She would go straight to Pauline's house.

It was late afternoon, school would have finished for the day, Barbara would be there. She would take her home to the cottage. It would be marvellous to have her under the same roof again.

Familiar soot-darkened mills, public buildings, and masses of houses interspersed the woods and fields of her Yorkshire hills. She felt she was home already, began to resent the rest of the journey, and then they finally were pulling into Halifax station.

So eagerly that she scarcely noticed the weight of her suitcase, Sheila hastened up Horton Street and found the bus that would set her down near her sister's house in Luddenden Foot. The weather here was dull, and felt still cooler than the days in Kent, but even this inclement temperature had ceased to worry her. She was over her reluctance to return — all she wanted now was to be with her family.

Pauline paused for a moment as she opened the door when Sheila knocked, seemed just for that second to be uncertain what to say. But then she was urging Sheila to come in, exclaiming that they hadn't known when to expect her.

And there Barbara was, looking quite enchanting with a pink ribbon in gleaming brown hair, her sturdy little body suddenly noticeable in a floral print frock that Sheila didn't recognise. But Barbara only gave her a smiling glance and a brief "Hello, Mummy"; she was receiving help with her jigsaw puzzle.

Sheila could have told no one why she was astonished to find her own husband with their daughter. Why then should this dreadful unease have returned, causing her heart to thunder and something close to panic to surge into her throat?

"Didn't know I'd find you here, Edward," she said.

"One of us had to be around for Barbara," he snapped.

She smarted from his rebuke, but contained her own retort. "Well — I'm sure it's nice that you're able to be with her. But I was confident anyway that our Pauline would cope very nicely."

"I'm the last person to deny that," Edward told her sharply. "I just happened to feel that this was for the best."

Pauline, still looking uncomfortable, began fussing that she must make tea. Sheila was trying not to resent the settled way that both her husband and her daughter continued to sit at the table. Suddenly, she knew that she had to get away, that she had got to take Barbara with her. She'd been longing for them to be together.

"Thanks, Pauline, but I'd rather we got off home. By the time we've unpacked and everything it'll be long past Barbara's bedtime."

"But, Mummy . . . I want to stay here. Don't want to go home."

Her daughter's protest couldn't have hurt her more.

"She could stop another night," Pauline suggested. "It'd give me time to pack up all her stuff."

"We can pick up her things some other time. She's got everything else at home, hasn't she?"

Sheila noticed that Edward and her sister exchanged a glance. They might have been resigning themselves to letting the child go home. But why on earth should it matter to Pauline that her niece's visit was curtailed? And as for Edward —

he'd be going back to camp, why should he care so long as Barbara was being looked after?

"We'd better do as you say, I suppose," he said. "It'll only upset Barbara's routine all the more if we're late home."

"You're not due back at camp then?" Sheila asked. She seemed to have lost track of his comings and goings.

"Didn't I say? I'm on leave."

He didn't seem inclined to discuss plans for his leave, any more than to enlighten her about how long it would be. After years of conditioning herself to *not* asking the despised question "When do you go back?" Sheila resolved to wait and see how long Edward would be with them. But she could have done without his coolness. Her homecoming was turning into a disappointment.

All the way in the bus up to Midgley, Barbara alternated complaining about being whisked away from her aunt's home with enthusiastic descriptions of the fun that she had had there. And wasn't her frock lovely? Her auntie had made it out of one of her own skirts.

By the time the three of them reached Hardaker Farm, Sheila was wondering how her daughter's stay there could possibly have been so marvellous. Pauline did make a fuss of the girl, she'd always known that, but what else had been so exceptional during the visit?

Sheila's own mother welcomed her so warmly that it ought to have compensated for Barbara's lack of enthusiasm. Enid came dashing out of the farm kitchen when she noticed them through the window.

"Eh, I am glad to see you, Sheila love. And you two an' all, of course," she added swiftly, and hugged each of them in turn.

Sheila was thankful that, for once, her mother had put her first; and immediately reproved herself for such foolishness. Of course they were all equally welcome here. And, *of course,* she was always glad the three of them were included together. They were a family.

Happier now, Barbara dashed into the farm to tell Billy and Louise the latest episode in the adventure of sleeping away from home. She had seen them daily at school, but needed to remind them that she had become somehow different.

"And my Daddy came to see me a lot," she added loudly.

That must be childish exaggeration surely, thought Sheila, well aware of how infrequently her husband managed to get home from camp.

She turned to ask him if the situation had improved, but Edward was calling "See you later" to her mother and crossing to the cottage.

"I'd better go, or we'll never get her ladyship settled down in time for bed," said Sheila.

She was glad when Enid seemed not to mind, hurrying indoors instead to shoo Barbara out towards her own home.

"We'll have a nice tea, then you can tell me what you've been doing while I was away," Sheila promised, reassured because her daughter had bounded out of the farmhouse and seized her hand.

"We've had our tea," said Barbara chirpily. "Auntie Pauline made it as soon as Daddy came."

She would, naturally, thought Sheila. Who would not, when the child's father arrived to help look after her? She herself would have done likewise in a similar situation. It was only logical.

"I had to keep an eye on Barbara, couldn't let your Pauline think we didn't care," said Edward later that evening.

"I know, you said," Sheila agreed. And wondered why he was going on about the matter. Unless it was to rub in the fact that she had been absent for those few days?

An hour or so ago while unpacking, she had told them about the long search for Johnnie's mother. Beginning with that protracted journey down to London, she had explained how different things were away from the West Riding, and about the flying bombs causing such devastation.

"We'll just have to be glad you've got back all right," said Edward.

She wished he *sounded* more glad — about anything. For a man on leave he was showing remarkably little enthusiasm. She had looked for some evidence that he was thankful to be in his home, and had found nothing substantial.

He would be tired, naturally, she reflected, silently rebuking herself for lacking understanding. And there was his continual disappointment. He'd never accepted not being posted overseas. She must make allowance for that. Tomorrow would be better.

Sheila went into her daughter's bedroom after a while, not only to check that Barbara was asleep. She needed something to reassure her that everything was all right now that they were at home again. Draped over the back of the bedside chair was the dress Pauline had made. Barbara had refused to have it put away, insisting that she wanted it to be the first thing she saw in the morning.

Sheila hated the dratted thing, could have snatched up her scissors and cut it into pieces. But what a sin that would be. All material was in short supply, and everybody was desperate for clothing coupons.

In bed that night, while Edward slept, Sheila thought about the family who had been killed by that V1. Jane's friends. And she hadn't even really commiserated with her concerning their loss. She felt awful now for neglecting to say how sorry she was. A whole family wiped out. People with whom Jane had once lived.

That Jane had seemed unaffected by her bereavement made Sheila feel no better. Jane had a frenetic life, caring for an infant and working at airbases to provide some sort of a home.

Happen Johnnie'll be company for her now, Sheila hoped. And sensed that the boy's need was to be the centre of someone's attention, to be reminded how greatly he mattered. How would he be affected by the presence of a baby sister? A demanding baby. A white baby.

Together with the boy day and night in Kent, she herself had hardly had an opportunity to think through all the implications of those varied reactions to Johnnie's colour. It had been a shock to her when first confronted with such overt disapproval of the lad. Almost from the day of his arrival here on the farm, she and her parents had accepted him as he was — Johnnie. She had supposed — blindly perhaps — that the attitude *they* found so natural would come just as easily to everyone else. She had never suspected that some people, even other evacuees like Billy and Louise, were making him feel different, disadvantaged.

I hope Todd does keep in touch with them and let me know how Johnnie is, she thought, still unable to accept that accomplishing her mission to return the boy to Jane had put things right.

Todd did, in fact, write to Sheila very swiftly. She was glad to hear that he had called on Jane and the children one evening, and had been pressed to spend a few hours there. Johnnie had appeared relaxed, and had talked about his 'Auntie Sheila' a great deal. And whilst Jane did seem harassed as she tackled a pile of ironing, she had proved talkative, quite entertaining.

She would be, reflected Sheila, with an attractive man like Todd around; and wondered what was inducing such sour thoughts.

Glad of a reason to write back to Todd, she settled with pad and pen one night as soon as Barbara was in bed. Writing the farm address at the head of the paper, she smiled to herself, pleased about something else. While she was away her father had had a telephone put in. By letting Todd have her number she was able to feel that he could contact her if that were necessary.

Today, she needed reassurance that she wasn't quite as alone as she had begun to feel. The sensation of facing problems in isolation was all the more ironic with her parents only a few yards distant in the farmhouse, and Land girls and other workers always around. It was nevertheless a feeling that was growing unbearable.

Edward's strangeness throughout his leave had been the first thing to generate the emotion. He had talked far less than usual, and sexual relations between them had been reduced to one swift occasion, which had felt to her devoid of all affection, never mind love.

She had sensed that he was blaming her for the shortcomings now developing in their marriage. Worrying and worrying for hours while she was busy working out in the fields, she had concluded that her short absence from home could be responsible for creating awkwardness between all three of them. Barbara was too young to be made to understand, but Sheila had tried to explain to her husband that she had been compelled to do her best for Johnnie.

'I know, you said,' had been Edward's only comment.

He was not the only person causing her anxiety. As soon as he had gone back to camp, their daughter had started being difficult.

Before Sheila had gone to Kent, Barbara had understood that everybody at the farm had to work hard, and that this was to help the war effort. Only rarely had she grumbled about having tea with Billy and Louise after school, and spending time with them instead of always with her mother. Now suddenly she was wandering about the place, protesting that she was bored, and demanding that Sheila devote more time to amusing her. With depressing regularity her complaints were linked to assertions that she always had fun with Auntie Pauline.

Whilst realising that her daughter was missing being the centre of attention, Sheila was trying to make up for the time that she'd been away from the farm, and could not neglect the tasks there.

The school holiday began, and Sheila got up early to put in a few hours' work while Barbara was having breakfast in the farm kitchen and playing with the other children. She had arranged that she would take time off later on around midday; that would ensure that Barbara was given some of her attention. She then intended to tackle the evening milking and get her daughter to help, something which normally went down well with her.

Sheila enjoyed being back in her own kitchen which, although not elaborate, was compact and lit by the big window above the sink. But her attempt to please failed as soon as Barbara smelled the corned beef hash simmering in the Baby Belling oven.

"Auntie Pauline never has corned beef," she said, the look on her normally pleasant face so arrogant that Sheila itched to slap her. "She knows I don't like it."

Sheila had brought Barbara up to eat most of the food that was put in front of her, drilling her into accepting that in wartime nothing should be wasted. But on this occasion no amount of persuading would encourage her to eat more than a couple of mouthfuls. Being told that she wouldn't be given a helping of the rhubarb and custard that was to follow proved to be a disaster. The news that Auntie Pauline did not eat rhubarb was not something which Sheila wanted to hear.

Sorry that her efforts to please her own daughter had ended so dismally, she spent the afternoon trying to interest her in first one and then another of the many toys and books acquired over the years.

Barbara refused to take any notice of them. Worst of all, she went on and on about wanting to go and see her Auntie Pauline. Thwarted and in despair, Sheila finally turned on her.

"All right, I'll take you to see her, but it'll only be for an hour or so. Happen you'll find out then that she's not really doing anything very special."

"Ooh, thank you, Mummy, thank you, thank you. Can we go now?"

"You'll have to wait a few minutes. I can't drop everything just like that to take you over there. I'll have to have a word with your Grandad. I was going to help with the milking, you know."

Barbara was angelic in the bus. Not surprising, thought Sheila, she's getting her own way. *Once*, like this, that might not do too much harm, but this child of hers would have to learn that today was an exception. It wasn't good for folk to grow up with the impression that making a fuss would ensure them whatever they most desired. Barbara must also be made to understand that people and places away from home usually seem more interesting than those seen every day.

In common with most West Riding wives, Pauline always left her door unlocked when she was in the house. When no one appeared to hear her knocking, Sheila turned the handle and called "Hi, there — Pauline, are you in?" as they entered.

She saw the living room was empty, and a quick glance confirmed that the kitchen beside it was also unoccupied. Sheila would have gone out again. She didn't believe in taking liberties. Barbara, however, had no such inhibitions. Darting towards the staircase, she put her finger to her lips and began to clamber quietly upwards.

"Hey — come back here," Sheila insisted, but was only answered by her daughter's giggle.

Oh, well, Pauline is my sister, after all, Sheila reflected; if she has popped next door or something this will be all right. She followed swiftly in Barbara's wake up the thickly-carpeted stairs.

The door of the bedroom facing them had been closed, but was closed no longer. Sheila arrived to see her daughter launching herself at the elegant bed with a shriek of "I'm playing too!"

But the people there were not indulging in any game. Pauline was struggling to wrap herself in one of the sheets, while the man had leapt away from the far side of the bed and was attempting to disguise his nakedness while he struggled to remove one foot from the left half of his underpants where both ankles seemed to be wedged together.

It's like some outrageous scene from a farce, thought Sheila wildly. But this was real, and the hurt was searing right through her.

"Did you really believe I'd never know?" she demanded, clutching at the oak handrail as she swayed backwards, dangerously close to the head of the staircase.

Barbara's little voice exclaimed "Daddy!" in a tone where delight mingled with curiosity as her wide blue eyes inspected the equipment that had made Edward her father.

Willing shock into control, if only for long enough to get them out of there, Sheila lunged forward, seized Barbara by the arm and hauled her from the room.

"We're going straight home."

"Oh, God, God!" she heard Pauline cry.

Anything further was drowned in Barbara's shrieks. "No, Mummy, no! Want to play with Daddy and Auntie Pauline."

"That's the last thing you'll ever do. You can put that idea right out of your head."

"But I *need* to stay," Barbara persisted.

"I don't care what you say, you're not going to." They were down the stairs now, across the classy living room, and at the front door.

As soon as Sheila had the door open, her daughter clutched its edge, screaming "I want my daddy, I won't leave him here, I won't!"

"Oh, but you will, young lady. Now *come on* —"

When Barbara risked trapping her fingers rather then removing them from the door, Sheila lifted her bodily, forcing her out onto the path so that she was obliged to relinquish her hold.

"Daddy, Daddy!" the child screeched. "Mummy's hurting me . . ."

Sheila sensed, rather than saw, curtains twitching across the road. Pauline's nearest neighbour appeared in her doorway.

"Your daddy's not going to help," Sheila snapped. "He's the one who's hurt us, both of us. You don't know what he was doing with your precious aunt."

Sheila's only satisfaction was seeing the woman dart hastily back inside her own home. Barbara was continuing to cry.

"You'd better stop that. The bus is coming."

No amount of admonishing would have any effect. Barbara was just as determined to stay with her father and aunt as Sheila was to get away from there to the refuge of their own home.

I can't sit in the bus with her yelling like this, she thought, I'll either lose my temper completely or give in to my own tears. They would have to walk. That way, so long as she kept a tight hold on her daughter, they would at least reach Hardaker Farm . . . Eventually.

She had never known Barbara to cry and scream for so long, or so loudly. All the way uphill to Midgley, Sheila had to control the urge to give her a spanking. Much as she hated resorting to physical correction, there were times when children were heedless of everything you might say.

To Sheila's relief, by the time they finally trudged into the farm-yard, her daughter's breath had run out. The only sound she was making was a painful gasping.

Sheila saw Enid at the farm window and waved to her, hoping her own expression was not giving away how distraught she felt. Her mother was adept at recognising troubles, even while they remained unspoken, and this was one matter that she would never bring herself to discuss.

"I'm sorry I had to get you away from there," she told Barbara as soon as they were inside their own cottage. "It wasn't my fault. I just had to. One day you'll understand. And I'm not cross with you, you know."

Still too short of breath to speak, Barbara glowered at her.

"I'll make you some tea in a minute. Would you like a nice boiled egg?"

The child shook her head vehemently.

"A spam sandwich then? You like spam, don't you?"

Again, the shaking head. Barbara flounced past her and stomped upstairs to her bedroom. Its door crashed to behind her.

Her own neat but homely living room no longer looked so familiar, but Sheila was thankful to be alone. She sank into the nearest armchair, closing her eyes as the sun filtered through the net curtains.

So — it had happened. Edward's unfaithfulness seemed now to have been something inevitable, unavoidable. She recognised suddenly that her own trip to Kent wasn't solely responsible for the recent awkwardness here. The thought was no comfort.

Why Pauline, though? And how long had it been going on — had they been *carrying on?* Right under her nose. Had it only begun while she was taking Johnnie home? She knew now why Edward had been so evasive about when he was due back at camp. But how many times in the past had he claimed his leave was up, when in reality he was simply making time for *her?* Her own sister.

They had been so close. Once they had, so close that some folk had asked if she and Pauline were twins. There'd been a time while they were kids when they'd pretended that they *were* — had tried to make something of the rare telepathic moments that occurred between them.

And when Pauline had been widowed, Sheila herself had felt the pain so keenly that she'd believed she knew what her sister was suffering. She had yearned to be with her all the time. Only the war making life on the farm so busy had prevented that. And she'd been glad, actually *glad* that Edward was willing to call on Pauline as well; ensure that she should not feel neglected.

Had he been more willing than she had ever suspected to call there? Had he, even then, had good reason to require family approval for visits which had perhaps begun much earlier?

What could she believe? Would she ever again believe anything Edward might say? Or what her sister might claim to be the truth? How could she live with the fact that her husband preferred their Pauline?

She would tell no one. Least of all her mum and dad. This would break their hearts. They were just an ordinary Yorkshire couple, but they'd treated Edward so well from the first day that she'd brought him to meet them. She could see them now: Enid at the table, always serving him the best portions; Nat Hardaker overcoming his natural reticence to learn what Edward's interests were, to discuss them.

Only by keeping the truth to herself would she maintain her one remaining scrap of dignity.

"I'm not going to cry," she told herself firmly. "Not for a long time yet. Because if I do give in, I could lose control." And that would not do. It would not do at all. Surviving depended on keeping control of her own life. And control over her feelings.

Chapter Seven

Sheila did not sleep in the bed made up with freshly laundered sheets and pillowcases. She had stripped everything off it. Too upset to know when she'd last changed the linen, she could not bear to get into the bed Edward had vacated. The suspicion that he'd regularly gone straight from her to Pauline was as painful as any part of the whole miserable business. Lying awake did provide one opportunity, though — for sorting out in her own mind how best to cope.

In the morning, while a still subdued, but calmer, Barbara devoured her favourite toast soldiers and egg, Sheila dashed across to the farm to have a word with her mother.

As she had feared, Enid's keen eye did not miss the haggard state she was in. "You look worn out, Sheila love, is it your poorly time?"

"I think that must be hanging over me, aye. And our Barbara's been playing up a bit."

"I thought you both looked fed up when you got back yesterday. It's not like her to cause trouble, though —"

"No, well — that's what I wanted to talk to you about. We called on our Pauline, and we caught her in a bit of an embarrassing situation. She had a chap there —"

"Oh, aye?" Enid interrupted, eyebrows rushing towards her hairline while her hazel eyes narrowed. And then she shook her head, as if condemning her own initial reaction. "Happen we should be thankful, eh? It's no good her grieving for ever. That won't fetch Ken back."

"No. Any road, what I wanted to warn you about was — our Barbara's all confused about it. Got it into her head that it was her daddy."

"Edward? But why on earth . . ."

"She didn't get a proper look at him, that was it," said Sheila hastily. She could feel herself going hotter. "Happen — happen he did look quite like her dad. I don't know. Daft really, I suppose. Anyhow — I had a job prising Barbara away after. She wanted to stop there, you see. Well, I could see we weren't wanted . . ."

Her mother was turning quite pale, "You don't mean — they weren't going to — you know — ?" She appeared appalled.

"Eh, Mum, don't ask me. Not my business. All I wanted to say was that you'd better ignore our Barbara when she comes out with her daft tales. About — about what I've told you," she ended lamely, unable to repeat even the supposition that Edward could have been involved.

"Right-o, love. Whatever you think best. Fancy her getting muddled up like that, though. Still, I dare say the little lass'll have forgotten in no time."

Barbara might, thought Sheila, as she turned to run back to the cottage. I hope to God she will. But there's one here who will never forget. Never for the rest of my life.

Work would have to be her solution. It had helped in the past, when — when Edward had gone into the forces. When she had been afraid that he would be sent abroad; that he might not come back alive.

And now he would not come back. She would have to think. He would need the clothes that he had left here, other possessions — things accumulated during the six years of their marriage. Was it six years, or seven? She was in no state to remember anything accurately. And from now on would resist remembering. But she did need to *think.*

She had to work out how to ensure that everything of his was removed from here, without her mother or father growing concerned or curious. More than that: it would have to be without any confrontation between Edward and herself. She couldn't bear to even see him again.

Barbara was playing with Billy and Louise, and Sheila was helping some of the Land girls with the haymaking, when her mother called her.

"You're wanted on the phone, Sheila."

I hope it's Todd, she thought immediately as she ran towards the farm. If I can hear his voice telling me that Johnnie is fine, that I've done one thing right, I'll be able to begin to endure this.

"It's Edward, isn't that nice?" Enid told her

when she was already holding the receiver. There was no chance of refusing to speak to him.

"You can't believe how sorry I am, Sheila. You can't begin to know how I feel," he said as her mother went out, closing the door behind her, as if to leave them to exchange loving words in private.

"That's right, I can't," Sheila heard herself saying. "And I don't want to try. I don't care, you see, not about how you feel. I just want you out of my life, for good. From today. You can collect your stuff sometime when I'm not in. And then you can leave your key in the cottage. You're not coming back, do you understand, not ever."

"But — there's Barbara, for her sake —" He sounded incredulous.

"For her sake, you'll keep your distance when I'm around. I'll not stop you seeing her. I can't. And anyway I know that wouldn't be right. But I don't want to set eyes on you again."

"But I can't move everything out, what'll your mum and dad think?"

"*You* should have thought — of that, and of what our daughter will think about you now. And since you mention them, I'd be obliged if you would clear your things out without Mum and Dad noticing."

"But that's impossible. You know they're always around, only a few yards away across at the farm."

"That's your hard lines. You'll have to use your

talent for scheming — you've grown adept at that. Just remember I won't have you causing them any agony."

"There's no need for any agony, for an upheaval. We can still make a go of it, Sheila. Start afresh . . ." He really did sound upset by having thrown so much away.

But she was upset too, more profoundly upset than anyone would ever know. She would never, never risk having that done to her again. By Edward or anyone else.

"No. Whatever you suggest, I'm not even going to try. You've sickened me, Edward Calvert. I've had enough." She hung up on him then, determined not to be influenced by anything he might say.

Avoiding her mother's perceptive eyes, Sheila left the farmhouse by a side door and stumbled her way over tussocks, out across the fields until she reached the one where the Land girls were haymaking.

I'm going to get on with this job, and I'm not going to think about another bloody thing! she resolved.

Not thinking was far easier said than done. Throughout the rest of that week and into the next, Sheila was repeatedly compelled to haul her mind away from Edward. She had loved him so much: from the day they first met she had felt that they were so right together. Until recently, of course, when the relationship between them had felt so strained. And now she knew the reason for that.

Harvesting certainly gave Sheila plenty of scope for throwing herself into hard manual work. There was a kind of satisfaction in labouring until she was exhausted, seeing the grain stacked at the end of a day, and joining the others afterwards in the big farm kitchen.

Enid had been glad when her daughter had suggested that she and Barbara would eat with everyone else during the school holidays. Only Sheila herself knew that meals in her own cottage seemed unendurable.

Barbara didn't help by demanding repeatedly to be taken to her Aunt Pauline's because her daddy might be there. Sheila had worried that the child might say something like that in front of Enid, but if she had no one was perturbed enough to mention it. She hoped her own explanation had been convincing. The only thing she could be thankful for was not being obliged to reveal what Edward had done to her.

The physical work she was taking on might be occupying her hands, but it was not keeping her brain from struggling with the situation. Emotionally, there was no let-up, the strain was too much. Shortly after that encounter in her sister's home, Sheila all but collapsed.

She was alone in the cottage living-room that evening, having put Barbara to bed quite late for a five-year-old. They tended to sit on in the farm after the meal, but this time her own mother had reproached her for letting the girl stay up so long.

"Them two evacuees were sent upstairs a full hour ago," Enid had pointed out, criticism hardening her hazel eyes. "This time of year everyone's up and about early of a morning," she'd added unnecessarily.

Being made to feel thoughtless as well as a neglectful mother was Sheila's undoing. She had managed to hold on to her composure whilst getting Barbara ready for bed. Now everything was different.

Downstairs once more and on her own, she visualised her future life as she believed it would be. There would be this daily ritual of getting up, seeing to whatever Barbara needed, washing, ironing, working somewhere — whether still on the farm, or wherever — and coming back to spend yet another evening on her own. She was aware already that she couldn't continue lingering on across at the farm every day without inviting her parents' concern about her home life. But solely responsible for Barbara, how could she take up any outside interest, something to get her away, even for an hour or two?

He's trapped me, the devil, she thought. He's the one who's done wrong, and he's trapped me here on this treadmill!

Too angry to sit still, she began pacing up and down the room, back and forth, back and forth, until her head throbbed. And then when she turned suddenly her eyes blurred and she almost fell. She staggered towards the nearest chair, wondered when she came round a bit if she was always going to resort to flopping down like this — to giving in.

Happen I'd better go and see Dr Morrison, she thought. And instantly dismissed that notion. He was the family doctor, wasn't he? Had known them all for ever. Even he himself would admit that guaranteeing not to reveal what caused her trouble would be difficult.

If he bumped into my mother somewhere he'd be bound to ask how I was, if nothing more, Sheila reflected. Then there'd be questions and more questions. They would all wonder what was so lacking in me that my husband has been compelled to turn to our Pauline.

Her father called Sheila to the telephone the following day when she was preparing food for the pigs. She was afraid that Edward would be on the line again and almost refused to come in. How could she though? If she began behaving oddly she'd invite those questions she was dreading, both parents would start asking what was going on.

Hearing Todd's voice was such a surprise that the tension emerged from her in a massive gasp of relief.

"Hey — are you OK, honey? What's wrong?" he asked anxiously.

Sheila made the excuse that she'd been running across to take the call. "But how are you?" she asked.

"Not bad at all. Better for hearing your voice."

"Same here," Sheila exclaimed. "You'll never know how much."

"Glad I rang then, although I have to admit I could be adding to your load. I'm not happy about those children, Sheila —"

"Johnnie, you mean? Whatever's happened?"

"Him, and his sister. Nothing's happened exactly, it's just that . . . Well — I thought you ought to know. That mother of theirs sure isn't treating them right."

"Are you certain, Todd? In what way?"

"Well, I've been helping her out. Sitting in with the kids when she wanted to go out. Jane seemed grateful and all that; mighty friendly towards me. Then there were a few times when I couldn't make it. When we'd take off at a moment's notice, you know what it's like."

"I know."

"One time we were on standby, waiting for take-off. Eventually it got cancelled. That happens, you know. Well, I figured I'd go round to Jane's, let her go out . . ."

"And . . . ?"

"What I found there really shook me up, Sheila. She'd only gone off out for the evening, left those kids on their own."

"Oh, but her landlady would be there, Mrs What-d'you-call-her . . . *Mrs Foster*'d be keeping an eye on them."

"That's what I thought at first, but she wasn't there either." Todd was reliving the awful experience. "I heard the baby screaming, and Johnnie shouting for their mother. I saw them then through the window; the little fellow seemed to have been looking all round the house for someone. He was carrying his sister down the stairs and into that front room of Jane's. I rapped on the glass, called to him to let me in, but he couldn't reach the lock on the door."

Sheila could picture it all. "Whatever did you do?"

"Hung around for a while. The baby stopped crying, but it fair shook me up to see a young boy like that left to cope on his own."

"It certainly shouldn't be allowed to happen. But what can we do? Have you spoken to Jane about it?"

"Oh, yes. Saw her as soon as I could, told her what I thought. She blamed the old lady, said Mrs Foster had promised to stay with the children. Somehow, I don't believe that."

"When was this?"

"Last week sometime, Friday, I think. It was Sunday I managed the word with Jane. But she took no notice. Promised it'd never happen again, all that sort of thing, and took no notice."

"Are you sure?" Sheila asked. She couldn't credit that any mother could be so careless of her children's wellbeing.

"Afraid so. I went by again last night. Same thing — kids crying, Johnnie and the girl both, this time. Nobody there, me unable to get to them. That hurt, I'll tell you. OK, they're nothing to do with me, I know. But that hurt."

"It's all my fault. I should never have taken him back to her."

"Don't say that, honey, don't even think it. Leaving him where he was when he wasn't thriving wouldn't have made a whole lot of sense, would it? You did your best."

"I can't just leave it at that though, can I? I've got to see Johnnie's all right — that they both are. I'll have to come down there again. It's the school holidays, I'll bring Barbara with me."

Sheila had reckoned without her daughter's reluctance to go with her to Kent. "No, Mummy, me stay with Auntie Pauline," Barbara insisted, suddenly sounding all babyish and whiney.

"You'll not stay with her, you needn't think that," Sheila stated. But could she ask her mother if she would have Barbara at the farm?

Enid agreed, of course, and agreed also that the child should not be allowed to visit Pauline.

She understood completely when Sheila said, "I won't have her there, Mum, not if that chap's still hanging round our Pauline."

Planning to get away was just what she needed. And because Enid was equally appalled by the probability that Jane wasn't looking after the children properly, returning to Kent so soon was all the easier.

"You mustn't worry about things this end, think on," her mother assured her. "Barbara can stop with us as long as she needs, you know that, love. One more doesn't make much difference, and you've both been having most of your meals with us any road."

"Bless you, Mum. I'll keep in touch, let you know how long I'm likely to be away. Now we've got the phone it'll be easy enough to keep you up to date on what's happening."

Todd had given her a number where she could ring him, and was delighted that she would be arriving in Kent the following evening. At her request, he had found her accommodation at one of the inns in Headcorn. She hoped to call on Fred and May, who'd been so kind, but didn't wish to be beholden to them for another stay on their farm.

Because he never knew for sure when they would have to take off, Todd couldn't promise to meet her; but just knowing that she would see him again was all that mattered to Sheila. He had been such a good friend to her already, she was yearning simply to talk.

Not that she would tell him about Edward. The days since witnessing his betrayal had only increased her determination never to speak of what had occurred. It was her business, no one else's — and nobody should be expected to sympathise or even to advise her. She'd made a mess of being married, how could she hope anybody would really understand?

There was also this matter of her rocky composure. Since nearly going to pieces in her own home, she was more on guard than ever outside it, determined she'd not embarrass anyone by breaking down. And besides, far away in Kent with Todd, she'd be able to behave so normally that he'd never suspect anything had gone wrong.

"Sheila honey, what on earth is it? You ill, or something? Have I got you to come all this way when you're not well?"

"I'm all right, Todd. It's just —"

"Now don't come that with me. We're buddies, remember?"

Todd took her by the shoulders, stood gazing into her eyes, his own so concerned that she felt dreadful about thinking of deceiving him.

"I am OK," she insisted. "Let's get on — we've got to check on those children . . ." They were standing outside the inn at Headcorn, and just being with him again was so *good* she could well go to pieces.

"We're going nowhere yet. Not before you tell me."

Telling him would be such a relief. Admitting to just one person, especially when that person was Todd, would make such a difference. It was the direct opposite of what she'd intended, but . . . He didn't know Edward at all, had never known them as a couple; he would not judge. She could let it all tumble out . . .

Sheila swallowed, sighed. "It's my husband — Edward." She closed her eyes, sighed again.

"He's been injured, worse . . . ?" His lovely grey eyes had clouded. Concern was tightening the strong contours of his face.

"No, Todd. It might be easier to bear if he

had. No — I don't mean that, I mustn't. Forget I said that. Please, forget it —"

"What's he done to you, honey?"

"He — he's sleeping with Pauline. And — oh, God, she's my sister."

"Christ!"

Todd released his hold on her shoulders, drew her to him. She felt his arms around her, strong, sympathetic, and safe.

"Are you certain about this?" he asked after a moment. "It sounds so incredible . . . Folks don't do that."

"I'm sure, all right. I caught them together. And Barbara as well."

"What? Your little girl? You mean they were having sex while she was there?"

"Not quite like that. Barbara was with me. Her dad had gone back off leave, or so I thought. And she was being an absolute trial — pestering to be at her Auntie Pauline's again. She'd been like that a lot since I got home."

"And you took her to visit?"

"Too right I did!"

"Honey, I am so sorry. I know just how you must be feeling."

"You never think it'll happen to you, do you?"

She felt Todd sigh, his breath stirring her hair while he seemed to hold her even more closely against him. "At least it wasn't my own brother did the dirt on me," he remarked at last. "Your entire family must be shaken."

"Oh, they don't know. No one does."

"But if your daughter says something . . . ?" Todd sounded bewildered.

"I thought of that." Sheila explained the version that she had told her mother, and her hope that they would believe Barbara had confused some other man with the daddy she was longing to see again. She surprised herself now with having thought up any means of explaining anything to anyone. "I suppose I'm hoping really that, given time, Barbara herself will begin to believe that it was some man other than her father."

"And in the meantime — are you having to pretend everything goes on as normal, when he's on leave and so on?"

"Oh, no. I couldn't. Not with him. I've told him he's got to get out. I just hope that when I arrive back his clothes and stuff will have been cleared out."

"And the house, do you own it jointly?"

The one fortunate thing about the entire wretched business made her smile slightly. "The house belongs to my dad really. A cottage on farm land, it was my gran's years ago. At least Barbara and I will always have a home."

"Even if there's no reconciliation . . . ?"

"There won't be one, ever. I'm not like that, I'm afraid. That's the one thing I am sure about. Especially because my own sister's involved. I don't want to set eyes on either of them again."

"Can't blame you for that, Sheila."

They seemed to have been standing locked together for ages. To her raw emotions Todd was the perfect balm, but she ought to bear in mind that it wasn't for this, wasn't for her own sake that she'd come back to Kent. Besides which, she would not rely on any man again.

"We'll have to get cracking," she said suddenly, stepping back from his embrace. "Are we going to see Johnnie tonight, did you say?"

"If you're up to that, honey."

"I'll be fine, don't worry. Tell me again what you have in mind."

Todd had arranged that they would babysit for Jane, allowing her to go out for the evening. The intention was that they would take things step by step, checking first of all that the children showed no signs of ill-treatment or neglect. Todd also proposed that some time later they should call unexpectedly at the house, to see if Mrs Foster was around now whenever Jane was not.

"And then we'll take it from there," he finished. "If there is continuing evidence of neglect we must take action."

"I'll have to find out what steps the authorities would take. If she's leaving kids of that age on their own it's very serious."

Today, however, Sheila was grateful simply for the opportunity to have a few hours away from mulling over her own problems.

Both children appeared to be well-fed and contented. Johnnie was still awake, although in bed, when they arrived and exclaimed gleefully as soon as he saw Sheila. He gave her a hug when she sat on the edge of his bed, and he began chatting brightly about going for a walk with Mrs Foster earlier that day.

"We saw lots of rabbits, and a squirrel. And a dog that weed on Gloria's pram wheel when we stopped outside the shop."

Sheila sought Todd's glance and smiled with him, glad to be able to enjoy simple amusement. Perhaps, after all, Jane would give them no further cause for anxiety about the children's welfare?

Her next visit to the house, on the following day while Todd was on duty at the airfield, made Sheila banish her brief feeling of relief.

Arriving just as Mrs Foster was putting on her hat and coat, she found her arm grasped even before she stepped over the threshold.

"Oh, am I glad to see you!" the woman exclaimed. "I don't like leaving them on their own, but she's not back on time again. And she knows I've got an appointment at the dentist's. You don't mind keeping an eye on the kids, do you? Just till Jane gets here?"

"Well, I was coming to see her, anyway," Sheila began. She was on the point of telling Mrs Foster what she thought of two young children being left on their own, but reminded herself that they were not the landlady's responsibility. "Yes, I'll hang on here."

Half an hour went by. Both children were good, although Gloria had a wet nappy and kept crying until Sheila searched for a fresh one. Several were soaking in a pail in the kitchen sink, but she located one that was clean among tea towels on a rail.

"This isn't aired," she murmured, picking it up.

"You can hold it in front of the electric fire. It plugs in here — shall I show you?" offered Johnnie, eager to help.

"I'll do it, thank you," said Sheila swiftly. She couldn't bear to think of a five-year-old boy playing around with an electric fire. She only hoped he was never encouraged to help dry things off in front of it.

That's something else I'll have to talk to their mother about, thought Sheila grimly, and began to dread Jane's arrival.

She had quite enough opportunity to work out what she ought to say: a full hour passed before a jeep drew up outside and Jane paused to give the driver a lingering kiss before dashing indoors.

"Oh, *you're* here," she said as soon as she saw Sheila.

"Just as well too! Mrs Foster had a dental appointment, hadn't she?"

"Was that today? I never thought."

"No. And I'm afraid you should have, shouldn't you? When you were relying on her to look after these two."

"Has she been gone for long? I know I'm a few minutes later than usual . . ."

"Well, I've been here over an hour. And that's not really the point, is it? Little fingers get into everything, don't they? Even five minutes unsupervised can be disastrous."

"But Gloria's too small to get around much on her own yet."

"I'm not talking about Gloria."

"Johnnie's a sensible boy, very practical —"

Sheila interrupted. "So practical that he offered to plug in the electric fire; would have aired the baby's nappy in front of it, if I'd let him."

"There you are, then. He's really clever like that."

She'll never understand, thought Sheila. Whatever I say I'm wasting my breath. And if I stay here another minute I shall really lose my temper about such sheer negligence.

She made one last attempt. "Please don't leave them on their own again, Jane. Please," she said, and hurried towards the door.

I'm going to find out who I must contact in Kent about my concern for those children, she thought, as she strode out along the road. If anything should happen to them and I'd not reported what's been going on, I'd never forgive myself.

Todd was equally concerned when Sheila told him that evening. He had telephoned the inn where she was staying and they were sitting over sausages and mash in the bar there.

"I haven't been able to find out who to tell yet," Sheila added. "But I'm afraid I shall have to. I'm not going to have the accident that's bound to happen on my conscience. First thing tomorrow, I'm starting by contacting the local council. If nothing else, they should be able to tell me who is responsible for those kids' welfare."

Sheila took the bus into Maidstone and found the council offices, where a succession of busy clerks passed her from one to the other while she explained repeatedly what she was trying to do.

After waiting around for ages at another office, she finally got someone to take down details of the situation she had found in Jane's home. The elderly man heard her out, shaking his head, sighing occasionally. But when Sheila supposed that she had his sympathy and understanding, his response disappointed her.

"These are difficult times, dear me, they are! Anything but ideal. But you say that normally this landlady looks after the children whenever the mother is out at work?"

"Sometimes, yes. But she's quite old —"

"Many of us are," the man snapped. "And lots of you young ones are glad enough to find we still have our uses! It sounds to me as if the elderly lady does more real caring for those children than the mother!"

"Happen so, but she shouldn't have to. That's my point. Jane ought to be looking after them every minute that she's not at work. Or should make absolutely certain that somebody is in charge of them."

"Oh, I agree with you there. And we'll send someone round to check on the family circumstances." He continued taking down details. "And you are . . . A neighbour perhaps?"

"A friend of Jane's," Sheila told him, although her feelings towards the woman at that moment were anything but friendly.

"But you aren't able to superintend in the mother's absence?"

"Hardly. I'm from Yorkshire, actually. Have had to leave my own little girl with my mother so I could come down here."

"Ah — well, so *you* are fortunate. Maybe this person isn't lucky enough to have her mother so readily to hand."

He's making excuses for Jane, thought Sheila as she left the office. But she could only rely on the promise that Jane's home would be visited and, presumably, assessed. She couldn't think that would do much for her own relationship with Johnnie's mother, but that was just an unfortunate fact.

Strangely, when Sheila called at the house again, she found that Jane's attitude towards her had not been adversely affected.

"There's been a woman here to see how I'm coping," she confided. "They're doing a lot of checking up on mothers that's on their own. Anyhow, she said the room is nice and bright for somewhere that's so small. And Johnnie was ever so good, he passed her a biscuit to have with her tea. Held the bag out to her, I mean — he didn't just give one to her in his hand."

"And did she ask about arrangements for while you're at work?"

"Oh, yes. And Mrs Foster was in, so she got to know her as well. She said she seems nice."

"And you do understand now that it might be dangerous to leave Johnnie and the baby alone in the house?"

Jane gave her a scornful look. " 'Course. I said, didn't I, the other day? It was just that I — got held up, like."

Even though far from satisfied by Jane's account of the visit that she'd received, Sheila felt that for the present she had done all that she could. She had alerted the authorities to a potential danger. For a few more days she herself would watch what was happening. Todd wasn't on duty and they'd promised to sit with the children that evening. She would try to vet their wellbeing more thoroughly. She also would make a start on impressing on Johnnie what some of the dangers were. If there were going to be occasions when he was left without supervision, he must be given more idea of behaving sensibly.

Jane had asked that they should arrive by seven. Sheila expected that the boy would still be up, if in his pyjamas. He seemed so at ease with her these days that talking to him wouldn't be difficult.

Looking forward to an evening together, she and Todd were chatting animatedly when he parked the jeep outside the cottage in Frittenden.

Sheila was surprised that both Johnnie and Gloria were in bed already.

"I'm so grateful to you for sitting in, I didn't want you to have any bother," Jane exclaimed.

She was dressed for dancing, and waiting behind the door as though eager to be off.

"I thought your jeep was my date!" she continued. "But I think I can hear him now." She leaned out around the door frame to check. "Yes, here he is."

"And have you left something ready in case Gloria takes up?" Sheila enquired. "And what about Johnnie — has he had his supper?"

"Oh, they'll be all right," Jane called over her shoulder.

Sheila felt her concern increasing, and her indignation. Hadn't she brought Johnnie here because he needed to eat more, because he wanted good meals to build him up?

"That was rather nonchalant," Todd remarked, watching through the window as Jane got into the jeep. "I know that guy — he was based at Biggin Hill for a time."

"The reason Jane was asked to leave there?" Sheila speculated.

Todd shrugged. "Could be. Whether he was or no, it sounded as though he was just one of a whole string of them while Jane was working there, didn't it?"

"I wonder if he was the fellow who dropped her off here the other day when she was so late arriving home. I never thought to look."

"No matter really. All we need to know is that the kids aren't at risk whenever she is out of the house."

"Or when she's in, I suppose," added Sheila wryly, as she hastened towards the bed and cot to take a closer look at them.

Gloria was sleeping contentedly, but Johnnie was wide awake and tossing about. His grin when Sheila leaned over the bed delighted her, but then she wondered if he would have been just as glad to see anyone. He appeared thankful for a diversion, perhaps because of being put to bed long before he was ready to sleep.

About to ask if he wasn't in the least tired, Sheila checked herself. She must not imply criticism of his mother to him, it was up to Jane to decide the boy's bedtime.

"Are you too hot or something, Johnnie love?" she enquired instead.

He shook his head, and pulled the covers up more tightly around his neck.

"It's all right," he told her valiantly. "I'm just not very comfy."

"Let me look — I think perhaps you do have too many covers," Sheila persisted, a hand outstretched to draw them back.

"Mummy said we haven't got to move. We mustn't get out of bed," he protested. "We've got to stay like this."

Sheila noticed then that he had evidence of jam around his mouth, and also a grubby mark on the side of his face which continued beyond his hairline as a layer of mud. He hasn't been washed tonight, she realised, and turned to look more carefully at his young sister.

Gloria's face also was dirty, streaked where she clearly had cried until tears made a track through the grime. Together with the boy's insistence that they must remain in bed, and having the covers tight against their necks in summer, this made Sheila more suspicious.

So gently that she wouldn't disturb Gloria, she uncovered her. The baby was fully dressed in a little print frock that, from its grubby state, had unmistakably been worn throughout the day. From the smell arising from her, she should have been changed hours ago. And that nappy wasn't merely wet.

"Have you got all your clothes on as well?" she asked Johnnie.

He bit his lip, torn between loyalty and discomfort. "It's all right," he asserted again.

"Eh, love, let's have a look at you . . ."

He was wearing a shirt and pair of short trousers that he'd all but outgrown. Both were clinging to the sheets, twisting around his slender body so badly that Sheila cringed, thinking how uncomfortable they must be. Below the shorts Johnnie's knees were filthy, and one had bled following a fall.

Before she decided how to persuade the boy to cooperate, Sheila heard Todd approaching from behind her.

"Is something wrong?" he enquired. His voice

was so gentle that she sensed as never before what a compassionate man he was.

"I'll say! Look how she's just popped them into their beds."

Chapter Eight

Sheila was extremely upset. She was afraid she'd be compelled to see the authorities a second time. Someone ought to be told what was happening to these children. But she loathed reporting anyone; before resorting to that she would have one more try at convincing Jane that she wasn't looking after them properly.

By the time Jane arrived back in the early hours of the following morning, Todd had had to return to Headcorn airfield, but Sheila didn't let his absence deter her from tackling the woman about her attitude. "You're beginning to seem like a feckless mother, Jane. How could you put those kids to bed without washing or even undressing them?"

Jane shrugged. "Oh, you know how it is when you're going out — there's never enough time, is there? I had to get them to bed before you came, and —"

"I'd rather have put them to bed myself than have the poor little beggars expected to sleep fully dressed. Any road, Todd and I have cleaned them up a bit. I had to bath Gloria, her nappy was filthy."

Once over her initial dismay, Sheila had quite enjoyed bathing the baby and slipping her into the nightdress she had managed to find — which was infinitely cleaner than that dress. Gloria was so lovable. Todd had helped Johnnie while he undressed and had a thorough wash, talking easily with him, reminding Sheila of how he had always encouraged the lad to be more forthcoming.

Once the children were back in their remade beds, she and Todd had paused for a while, gazing down at them.

"You're a lovely mother," he had told her, husky voiced, and she had understood that she was not alone in longing to share more than the care of someone else's children. In a different time and place, in different circumstances, they might have been happy together. But that was only a fantasy, no doubt generated by his consideration.

Todd was certainly marvellous with kids. Like many of his fellow-countrymen, he was generous with supplies of fruit and the sweets that they all called 'candies'; rarely arriving at Jane's without one or more of the things that had become luxuries to English children.

One evening when he and Sheila were baby-sitting he announced a further way in which the local kids were to be given a treat.

"The guys on the base are planning a party — next Saturday afternoon. I'm gonna persuade Jane to let young Johnnie come along."

No persuasion was needed. As Sheila expected, Jane vas only too eager to agree. What surprised Sheila more was Todd's insistence that she herself must be there.

"I won't take no for an answer," he declared. "And you'll be doing us guys a favour. We've got to have a few females around for any kids that get sick or start hollering — that sort of thing."

The Yanks had hired a hall in Egerton, a village just up the hill from the airfield. Sheila called for Johnnie on her way there and they walked along to wait beside the church in Frittenden where other village children were assembling.

They were picked up in a USAAF truck, piling into the back of it with a lot of laughter, and grimaces from the two other adults accompanying the kids.

I don't know what I'm doing here, Sheila thought. I'm in anything but a party mood. The days since arriving back in Kent had done nothing to diminish the unhappiness about her marriage. Every time she had a moment for thinking, memories of what she'd discovered surged in until she felt humiliated again, as well as betrayed.

But there was to be no time for reflecting on her own emotions today. Present difficulties soon jolted her back to where she was, and the reason that she was sitting on the floor of this truck. One of the boys already installed there when they clambered aboard was eyeing Johnnie curiously.

"Are you a Yankie kid then?" the lad enquired.

"I don't know," Johnnie whispered nervously to Sheila. "What does he mean?"

"He wants to know if you're American, like Todd, love."

"Yes, I am," Johnnie said assertively. " 'Cos my Uncle Todd is one of them."

"Is he the same colour you are then?" another boy demanded.

Johnnie shook his head. "No. But that doesn't mean he can't be my uncle."

One of the other women turned to Sheila. "Is your husband working at the airfield?"

"No. And Johnnie's not actually my son. I'm just looking after him. You might know his mother, she lives —"

The woman sniffed. "Think I know the one you mean. I see her around with him. And with a baby, a fair-haired toddler."

Sheila began to wish the journey was over. Bouncing along the narrow lanes like this while they endured what promised to be quite an inquisition, was not her idea of fun. She wished that Todd was here, or that she possessed his ability to make Johnnie, and other folk with him, feel easier about the shade of his skin.

But Johnnie himself surprised her. Looking directly across at the two lads who had questioned him, he drew in breath that Sheila could feel as his chest expanded while he sat beside her.

"Say," he began in a tiny voice, cleared his throat, and started again: "Say, have you seen the Mustangs, like my Uncle Todd flies? They go real fast, and they can fly as far as Germany."

"Have you been in one?"

Johnnie shook his head. "Not yet, but I will soon. And I've seen lots of them on the ground, lots and lots."

The airman who was driving heard, and glanced briefly over his shoulder. "If you guys wanna see planes, just keep your eyes open wide. We pass close by Lashenden any minute. Then a mite further on you should look over on your right and you'll see our air base."

Looking out for aeroplanes diverted attention from Johnnie and, together with interest each time they stopped to take on more passengers, kept everyone entertained until they halted in Egerton.

The hall seemed quite full already, with men in the now-familiar USAAF uniforms and a mass of surging, shouting youngsters. Despite the throng, Johnnie spotted Todd immediately and raced across the wooden floor to fling himself at him.

"He's white then," the woman beside Sheila murmured, and became embarrassed. "What am I saying? You'll have to forgive me, I didn't really think —"

"Or thought aloud?" said Sheila and smiled. "Don't worry. Todd's just a friend of ours, a great friend."

"Well, that young man there certainly thinks so!"

"Oh, Johnnie's taken to him from the word go and he doesn't take to everybody."

"You say he's not your kid, though?" another woman asked. She sounded interested, rather than challenging now. Sheila's wariness began to wane.

From across the room Todd sought her eyes, raised a hand to greet her, and smiled. He had Johnnie by the hand now and suddenly placed his uniform hat on the lad's head. Astonished, Johnnie looked up at him from beneath its peak and, with his free hand, touched one of the ears which were all that prevented its slipping down over his face.

"We're gonna start with some of your British games," one of the other lieutenants announced as the uniformed private at the piano began playing 'The Grand Old Duke of York'. "We need two of you to lead this," the lieutenant added.

Todd bent to question Johnnie, then urged him forward. "This young fellow has played it at school, we'll lead off."

From where she was standing Sheila saw the lad hesitate, frowning. For one awful moment she thought he was going to retreat into the corner he was eyeing. But Todd would have none of that. Sliding his hand to Johnnie's shoulder he encouraged him into the centre of the floor where some of the adults were forming children into two lines.

Todd nodded to Johnnie as the singing began,

they joined hands and, after a faltering start, soon were side-stepping briskly between the two rows. Sheila smiled to herself as she saw Johnnie explaining to Todd that they must now separate, march behind their lines to the end.

Keeping so many kids in something resembling order took quite some time. When the music ended, some who had just got the hang of the game were clamouring for more. This time, when the pianist started up Todd detached himself from Johnnie, leaving him to partner another boy.

The people who had been marshalling the children were watching now, clapping with the beat. Surprising Sheila, Johnnie was relishing his role, his step jaunty, white teeth gleaming in his thin brown face and whenever he'd a hand free he saluted against the uniform hat.

The men loved it, pointing and laughing, exclaiming, "Say, did you see that?" "Sure is one bright youngster!" "So long as folks produce kids like that there's hope for us all."

The only time when Johnnie seemed about to be embarrassed was when the tune finished and the little girl immediately behind him took his hand. Sheila watched as he tried to free himself from her clutches, but the girl still clung on. She was a sturdy child with light brown hair, from the rear reminding Sheila of her own daughter. And Barbara could be equally tenacious if the mood took her.

To everyone's delight, Johnnie eventually capitulated. Shrugging, he let the girl lead him off towards her mother.

"Sure is right, son, let her take you to meet mom!" someone called.

Johnnie grinned and pushed back the hat, in what was meant to be a nonchalant gesture. It fell off and he giggled, turned, and bent to retrieve it, and in the process hurled the little girl around with him. In his haste, she almost lost her balance and toppled.

Briefly, she appeared bemused. But Johnnie, fully in command, continued in the direction they had been heading. The girl's mother went down on one knee to speak to them both and seemed enchanted when Johnnie gravely offered his hand to be shaken.

Where on earth has he picked that up, I wonder? Sheila thought. Life on Hardaker Farm wasn't exactly full of introductions. Everything there was very relaxed; especially with the Land girls there. Lots of comings and goings and never time for much formality. And yet his learning such graces from Jane seemed even more unlikely.

Todd was making his way across the room, and smiled after greeting her. "Did you see that? I'm going to have to be real careful, if the boy's taking to copying everything I do. He was with me only the other day when I met up with an old buddy from back home. I guess we shook hands that time."

After only a few minutes to cool off and regain

their breath, the children were ushered on to the floor again. This time, for 'The Farmer's in His Den'. When the other children appeared reluctant, Johnnie was urged to take the major role again, and seemed to relish ensuring that the rest understood what they were doing.

Musical chairs came next and proved less of a success for him, he was among the first children to be out. Sheila smiled to herself as that same little girl, equally unfortunate, seized his hand again.

More games followed, some of American origin which involved everyone in demonstrations and quite a bit of hilarious confusion ensuing. Throughout them all, Johnnie appeared to enjoy himself unreservedly, so much so that when tea was served he became the centre of attention.

Hurrying across to see if he wanted any help from her, Sheila found him surrounded by other kids eager to say hello, and US airmen only too willing to ensure that he shouldn't miss out on anything.

"What happened?" she asked Todd. "What have you done to him — where's the little lad who wouldn't speak above a whisper, if at all?"

Todd laughed. "Don't ask me, ma'am! Not my doing."

But I know differently, thought Sheila. Today is merely the blossoming of something that has developed during this relatively short time that Johnnie and I have known you.

Tea was followed by a demonstration of jitterbugging by one of the lieutenants and a woman who evidently frequented dances organised by the base. The lively music soon got the kids on their feet and joining in.

By this time the airmen were encouraging some of the parents to give the dance a try. Sheila felt a hand on her shoulder and turned to smile into Todd's grey eyes.

"But I've never done this," she protested.

"Are you questioning my ability as a tutor?"

The dance was too swift for her to become happy about her own performance, but trying to learn the steps was fun. And being held by Todd — even when there was hardly time to appreciate it — was so exciting that she felt quite dizzy.

Eventually, they paused for a moment to watch Johnnie who was still shedding inhibitions, and in the process winning himself a string of diminutive partners.

"Sure wish this wasn't just for kids," Todd murmured to Sheila as they finally went off the floor. "I'd be requesting a smoochy number."

She laughed, but she was belying her own emotions. And she silently condemned her private longing. Was she determined to be an irresponsible fool? She'd no business letting herself even think like this. She had seen, only a matter of days ago, where attraction could lead! Hadn't everything recently made her utterly determined that she would not allow herself to be vulnerable ever again?

The fun of this occasion was too powerful to

dismiss though, and as she was preparing to take Johnnie back to his mother, Sheila realised that he wasn't the only person who had changed during the course of that afternoon. She had discovered that she could still enjoy herself so much that she forgot the black side of life. If she could stay here for a bit she might become strong enough to survive.

In the truck dispatching them to their villages, the children chattered readily, laughing and shrieking over remembered incidents. Johnnie was as talkative as the rest, seeming at last to have become oblivious to any differences between himself and the other kids. And he'd developed quite a liking for that little brown-haired girl who now had set off home in another direction.

"Will I see her again?" he asked Sheila as they walked down the hill in Frittenden. "I like her. She reminds me of Barbara."

"Me too," she agreed.

That reminder renewed the longing for her own daughter, making her wish she could have brought the child down here with her. This shuttling back and forth between Yorkshire and Kent wasn't doing them any good. And right now Barbara needed her mother, needed more security to enable her to adjust to the radical changes in her life.

Although she felt that this growing unease about Barbara was irrational, Sheila telephoned Hardaker Farm next day.

As soon as she heard Enid's voice she knew that something was wrong. "What is it, Mum? What's happened?" Her heart thudded in alarm while she wished to goodness she could see her expression.

"Nobody's poorly or anything, don't go thinking that," Enid said swiftly. "But I think you'd better come home as soon as you can." Sheila heard the deep sigh at the other end of the line, and her mother's steadying breath. "You didn't let on who it was that our Pauline had taken up with, did you? Well, we know now, all right. And him and her have been trying to get Barbara to live over there . . ."

"At Pauline's?" Sheila was horrified. "You haven't let them have her?"

"What do you take me for? Of course I haven't, love. Just the opposite, I've told Edward he can't see her. Oh, I know I can't stop him, not legally; your dad's explained that. But I shall keep him away from Barbara for as long as I can."

"Thank goodness for that. Oh, Mum — I'm sorry you've had to be involved. It's not right —"

"None of this is right, is it? I shall tell our Pauline just what I think of her as soon as I see her."

"She wasn't the one who wanted to take Barbara then?"

"No — Edward had the brass neck to try that on. Came here as nice as pie, making up to us while he was talking Barbara into going with him. Then she let slip about seeing him at Pauline's, like. Well, he seemed to lose his tongue at first, then he evidently assumed we knew what were going on. I put two and two together, of course, realised why it was that you'd been so upset about our Pauline carrying on."

"What a mess! I'll get home as fast as I can. And I'll go and see Edward. At the army camp if I have to."

Jane's children would have to wait. How could she possibly remain in Kent, sorting out their problems, when she risked having her own little girl taken away from home?

At the other end of the line Enid felt tears rushing to her eyes. She could see Edward Calvert now, smarming round them, making such a fuss of the child. And then there'd been that sickening shock when the truth came out. She'd been cutting bread, had had to chuck the knife in the sink because she didn't trust herself not to harm him. Even with their Barbara standing there, still smiling up at her dad.

Sheila left a message for Todd at the airfield. He was in the air when she rang so there was no possibility of speaking with him. She only hoped that the message would be passed on.

As the train bore her along the track towards London, she stared out of the carriage window, wondering if she would ever be able to return. She hated leaving anything unfinished, and knew already that her anxiety about Johnnie and his sister would always haunt her. But she would feel the absence from Todd equally keenly, especially when she had been obliged to depart without saying anything to him.

She so admired that American for the unstinting use of his rare free time in helping those children. Few single men would show that degree of real caring. And there had been his concern for *her*. But for him, she would still have been containing every bit of the anguish induced by what her husband and sister had done.

As the train began running into London, Sheila was appalled by how much devastation there was in the suburbs. It seemed as if her own distress made the ranks of ruined houses more upsetting. She had thought the situation was bad enough in Kent, which had suffered repeatedly in recent days. The centre of Pluckley had been damaged, and a poultry farm at Smarden had been destroyed, killing six people. On the day she went into Maidstone Sheila had seen a photographer from the *Kent Messenger* recording the departure of evacuees for somewhere safer. Nearer to the centre of the capital now, though, she could tell how many V1s had reached their principal target.

The news on the wireless had mentioned the havoc caused by this new kind of bombing, but nothing had prepared her for seeing how much had been wrecked in addition to the damage caused earlier in the war.

Leaving the train at Charing Cross, Sheila wished that she was bringing Johnnie and his sister away with her. Hundreds of children were on the move. When she crossed London to find her train for Yorkshire, she discovered masses of young folk again, all heading for homes in the north.

And I thought I had problems, she reflected. Yet my own family's lives aren't threatened. Even if I do feel so angry I could kill those two who have ruined everything for everybody!

As well as evacuees, the train carried innumerable servicemen, most of whom were injured and en route to hospitals. Many wore airforce blue, providing a reminder she could have done without. Along with every man who took to the skies, Todd was in danger each time he flew. And not only then, she thought grimly, reflecting again on the quantity of flying bombs that came crashing down every day.

Midway between Kent and her home, she felt an almost physical pain, tearing her apart in her love for these two important regions in her life. Whatever can I do? she wondered. I can't look after everyone.

It was almost dark when she reached Halifax; a summer storm had blackened the sky before nightfall, rain was splashing down in drops as big as half-crowns and thunder groaned beyond the surrounding hills.

As she sat in the bus taking her along the Calder Valley, lightning flickered ahead, illuminating mills and stone-built houses, making the slopes to either side of them appear menacing. And then they were climbing one of those hills, the effort required by the engine of the bus drowning out the repeated growls of thunder.

The rain had ceased temporarily when she got off the bus at Midgley, a paler sky shone beneath heavy clouds, now purple-tinged with a fine gold line where they concealed the dying sun. Staring to the west, Sheila watched misty rays descending in bands to the earth as another deluge drenched the distant horizon.

Like this, her home territory appeared unfamiliar, disquieting, strangely attuned with her own personal unease.

She ran the rest of the way to the farmhouse, nearly fell over the step in her relief when the door opened as she turned the handle.

Her father was sitting at the kitchen table, reading the *Halifax Courier*, drawing on the pipe which he always relished when work for the day was completed.

"Eh, Sheila love, come on in . . ."

Nat had risen swiftly on seeing her, was rushing with unaccustomed haste to embrace her with equally rare emotion. "Eh, lass," he sighed. "It's that good to have you home! We didn't know, you know — never suspected a thing. Hadn't any idea what them two were up to —"

"I know, Dad. I didn't mean any of you to find out."

"There was no need for you to keep it to yoursen."

She smiled, however ruefully. "I dare say. Happen I was being daft, but I could see how upset everybody would be."

"Your mother's taken it badly, I won't pretend otherwise."

"But — she's not poorly or anything, is she?" Sheila glanced around the kitchen, puzzled by Enid's absence.

He shook his head, pulled out a chair from the table. "Sit down, love, you must be worn out," he said, patting her shoulder before he turned from her to go back to his own seat. "Young Billy and Louise went off to their own homes at last, yesterday."

"Oh? But I've just seen lots of evacuees heading north."

"Aye, well. I think their mothers said they're not getting any of them doodlebugs in Hampshire. Any road, they wanted 'em home." Nat smiled. "Your mum's made up one of the beds for you. She doesn't like to think of you sleeping over in the cottage tonight."

"And Barbara — she'll be in bed by now, I suppose?"

"Aye. She went up like a good 'un at the usual time. We told her you'd be here later on, but Enid said she'd gone to sleep when she checked a while since."

"I'll look in on her in a minute. How's she reacted, Dad? Does she understand what's been going on?"

"Only that her father wanted her with him. But we explained to her he's still in the Army, of course, that most of t'time he's at camp."

"And she's desperate to live with her Auntie Pauline." It wasn't a question, she had tried for weeks to accept the fact that Barbara idolised her aunt. And knowing that was breaking her heart!

Nat sighed again, shaking his head. "You're aware of that then. I was afraid you might be. Barbara has given us a bit of a time, I'll admit. Your mum had to get quite cross with her, telling her she'd got to stop here."

"I'm glad you've both tried to impress that on her. How I'm going to make her happier about the arrangement I cannot tell."

"No — well, it's early days yet. Happen if you and your mother have a bit of a talk you'll work something out."

"We will that!" a voice exclaimed behind him as his wife came down the stairs and into the room. "No, don't get up," she told Sheila and hurried across to hug her.

"Thanks for all you've done," Sheila said, kissing her. "I'm only sorry that you've had to be involved in this wretched business."

"And how would we not be involved?" Enid demanded, her hazel eyes glossy with unshed tears. "Anything that upsets you affects us an' all. You need folk on your side now."

Despite being grateful for their support, Sheila couldn't avoid wondering if they didn't have some amount of sympathy for Pauline.

Her mother answered her unspoken question. "Me and your dad are finished as far as Pauline's concerned, you know. Don't want owt to do with her, not now. And as for Edward . . . Well, he knows he's muckied his ticket. We might have got on once, that's all over."

"Do you — do you happen to know if he has taken his things out of the cottage?"

"If he hadn't, there'd have been none of his stuff there now," Enid asserted, cheeks which reddened suddenly seeming more lined. "When he dared to try and take our Barbara away, I told him straight. I gave him till the next morning to pack it all up and get it carted away."

"And your mum made sure Barbara didn't see what were happening, like," Nat added. "She took her off for a few hours, till it was her bedtime. You can rest assured, though, that he has cleared everything out. I made certain of that after he'd gone."

"When you're ready, Sheila love, you'll be able to settle in there again without being surrounded by — well, you know . . ." When Enid's voice trailed off she managed a smile. "But we want you to sleep here tonight at least."

Sheila smiled back at her. "Dad told me, and I'll be glad to. Only for the one night, though. I'm not letting myself turn soft."

Seeing Barbara sleeping quietly made her feel better, and content to be under the same roof, with her parents to hand. Tomorrow would be soon enough for facing the cottage. And for beginning to edit out so many of her dreams of the life that she had visualised there.

"How is young Johnnie?" her father asked

while Enid was making supper.

"Physically, he seems a bit better, not quite so thin. And he's becoming more talkative, much more like a kid of five." She would tell them later all about the party that had changed Johnnie so greatly.

"That'll be his mother's doing, I dare say," Nat observed.

"To some degree, perhaps. But I'm afraid Jane's still not looking after them right, not him or the baby." She told them how the children were not only left alone at times, but were being put to bed unwashed and fully clothed.

"Well, I don't know!" Enid exclaimed. "I've never heard of such a thing. I think that's disgusting."

Sheila nodded. "If this hadn't come up, I'd have seen the authorities again. I've told them once about her leaving them on their own while she went off gallivanting. Trouble is, Jane doesn't seem to take notice of anybody." And she herself must not be lulled into thinking everything was all right, simply because Johnnie had discovered the ability to enjoy himself for a few hours.

"What about their father, isn't he around?" Nat enquired.

"There's no sign of him — that's if there isn't more than one man involved."

Nat sniffed. "Like that, is it? Time somebody brought that Jane to her senses then, reminded her about her responsibilities."

"Sounds to me as if she has no idea," said

Enid. "Lasses like that didn't ought to go in for children. Is there somebody keeping an eye on things now you've come away?"

"Not all the time. Jane has a landlady who helps a bit, but she's getting on, and she has her own life. Then there's — there's that American pilot we met, the one that let me know how bad things were again. He helped when Johnnie and I were looking for his mother, helped us a lot. Jane was working at an airfield — did I tell you?"

Just mentioning Todd made her ache for his company, to talk things over with him. Coming back to the West Riding was ramming home to her how different life would be now that she had to manage on her own. She and Edward had been together for so long that he had dominated her life. Ever since getting to know him she'd grown apart from most of her old friends. And Todd had taught her how to value friendship.

Remembering that day when Barbara had pestered to be taken to visit Pauline, Sheila had been afraid that there would be tantrums about the refusal to let her go there now. She was agreeably surprised next morning when her daughter seemed so pleased to see her that she was tending to cling in a way that she never had in the past.

It began as soon as she went into Barbara's room to see if she was awake and was greeted with an excited yell of "Mummy!" Barbara leapt from the covers and came trampling across the bed towards her.

Young, sturdy arms were thrust around her

neck and after a succession of moist kisses, she felt Barbara's warm cheek held affectionately against her own.

Happen I needn't have worried as much as I have done about this, Sheila thought, and thankfulness threatened to overwhelm her. She would have to talk to her daughter though, about their future, about not having Edward around any longer.

Along with being obliged to speak with him, this chat with Barbara loomed ahead of her, driving away her immediate delight and generating as much disturbance as the storm she had witnessed last night.

During the morning Sheila discussed with Enid her intention of going to the Army camp to see Edward. "I was wondering if you'd mind looking after Barbara yet again. I can't think this encounter's going to be one at I want her to witness." If only things had come to a head during term time, arranging everything might have been easier.

Sheila telephoned to make certain that her husband was at camp, and that he would be available to have this discussion. Just going there would only be achieved by exerting her will power to the utmost; she didn't mean to go through all that only to find he was busy elsewhere.

Edward looked well when he strode into the office they'd been allocated for their talk. He also seemed less daunted than she herself was feeling.

Listening to his familiar footsteps approaching along the corridor, she'd felt that the clatter of his boots was threatening to crush the whole of her life as she had known it. But wasn't that crushed already?

"Hello," he said, coming in, and "You're looking tired," as he crossed to take the chair behind the desk.

I've been proper daft, thought Sheila, I should have occupied that chair. Now he's going to appear as if he's in charge here. As though to confirm that, Edward sat and gestured towards the chair on her side of the desk, the one nearer to the door. Sheila ignored it.

His back was to the light, giving him another advantage because it tended to conceal his expression. Standing, she could look down on him. She needed to avoid any position where she might shrink.

Taking a few steps nearer to the desk, she inhaled deeply, swallowed. "Thank you for taking all your stuff away from the cottage, I'm glad that's one thing sorted."

Edward seemed about to say something. Sheila did not give him the opportunity. "There'll be a lot to organise, but now we've made a start I want it all over and done with as quick as possible. When I leave here today I shall see a solicitor about the divorce."

At last he appeared disconcerted, although his steady voice told her that he was holding his emotions under control.

"You don't mean that, Sheila. Think what you'd be discarding —"

"*Me?* I've never done anything to undermine our marriage. But I'm not here to apportion blame. As I say, I only want to make sure we get this over and done with."

"Isn't that rather hasty? Surely we ought to talk this through first, discuss what's best . . ."

"I want a divorce. You've made your choice plain enough, now I'm having my way."

"But think of the effect on Barbara —"

"You've a bloody cheek telling me to do that! You never thought of her. How do you suppose she felt, seeing you naked with my sister? Nay, Edward, where's your common sense? You can't expect me to believe you've considered our daughter at all."

"Actually, I have. Both Pauline and I have. She's extremely fond of her."

He sounded very cool again, as though he had got his mind onto this track where it was firmly fixed; but even without seeing his expression clearly Sheila sensed that Edward was becoming aware that he'd have a battle on his hands.

"I dare say there's some truth in that, about Pauline," she acknowledged. "But I don't give a damn now what either you or that sister of mine want. I'm going to make sure first what my rights are. And then that I get them."

"You realise, of course, that I have rights as well, specially regarding Barbara . . ."

"You'll not be denied access, I know I

shouldn't do that. But I shall do my damnedest to stop her staying with you two —"

Edward interrupted with a smile in his voice. "I think you will discover that you'll be unable to prevent such visits."

"Well, we'll see. So long as Barbara doesn't suffer, even that could be worth it. If it's the only arrangement to ensure that I don't have to spend any time with either you or Pauline."

He sighed, shaking his head. "Sheila, Sheila . . . I wish you'd calm down and discuss this rationally. There's no need for everything to end in divorce, and there's certainly no need for any acrimony."

"I didn't set out to be acrimonious," she reminded him. "And nor did *I* set out to destroy our marriage. You might remember that, before you start advising me about my attitude. Whatever is said or done from now on, I shan't be able to forget how badly you've let me down. There's got to be some compensation for that. And you'd better believe that I'm going to find it!"

Sheila hadn't said one half of what she had intended, had failed to satisfy herself on several points which she had meant to thrash out today. But suddenly she'd had enough. Much more of this, and the tears now pricking at her throat and behind her eyes would come. This man was still recognisably the one she had loved, the one with whom she had created a home and started a family. And in whose company she had expected to spend the rest of her life.

She hated him for reducing her to this emotional wreck. She certainly wouldn't permit him to see her weep for everything that he had ruined.

"My solicitor will be in touch with yours," she announced, and was thankful that her own voice sounded devoid of emotion.

"That's as may be," Edward remarked tersely. "But you haven't been listening to what I've said. I'm not really sure about a divorce."

"It only needs one of us to be sure now," she told him quietly. "You've already provided me with the grounds."

Chapter Nine

Being tough had taken it out of her. Sheila was compelled to stop and find a café where she sat with a pot of tea and prayed no one she knew would come in. She had to compose her emotions sufficiently for the appointment with the solicitor her father had recommended.

Nat Hardaker had offered to accompany her, just as he had volunteered to be present during the meeting with Edward. Sheila had been touched as well as grateful, but had explained that she needed to do all this on her own. She had met Edward while she was so young, what she must do now was practise standing on her own two feet. She would begin that today.

Laurence Crowther was an elderly solicitor, and not inclined to make trivial conversation, which suited Sheila. Resolved on what action she must take, she could do without any frills, they would only have distracted her. In a few short sentences, she explained the situation, then sat back to listen while he outlined legal procedures.

By the time she left his offices she was rather awed by the lengthy nature of the course ahead, but she was already beginning to count her blessings. If the divorce took a long time that would allow her to adjust to the new life that stretched before her. When the day finally came and she was free, she would be ready for whatever lay in store.

Answering her parents' concerned questions about those two meetings was almost as draining as living through them. Even though she knew that they deserved to be kept in the picture, Sheila couldn't help wishing that somehow she could have prevented everyone from learning what was going on. Having a divorce in the family was upsetting her mum and dad. And each time she herself thought about it she felt as though she was weeping deep inside her. Discussing the matter threatened to make her tears break through to the surface.

Barbara alone helped her to retain some composure, delighting her with sudden hugs and eager chatter which provided assurance that all the time when she was away in Kent she had been missed.

Barbara also produced the first fragile hint that their future might work out more happily than Sheila had feared. It was two days later, and explaining to the little girl could be delayed no longer.

They were living in the cottage again now, and as they sorted out some of Barbara's toys and her clothes which they had carried across from the farm, Sheila began talking.

"I'm glad we've had lots of hugs again since I

came home, love. And I'm pleased that you've talked to me about what you've been doing. You see, most of the time now we're going to be on our own here. But with your Grandma and Grandad just across the yard there, of course."

Barbara was nodding seriously. "Only Daddy won't live here, will he? Not all the time . . ."

"Not at all, I'm afraid. I'm sorry about that, for your sake, love. But grownups don't always live together for ever and ever, you know. And he still loves you just as much as he has always done."

"He said. When he came to talk to Gran and Grandad. He's going to be at Auntie Pauline's house a lot. But . . ." Her voice trailed off.

"But what, Barbara love?"

"It's not the same there any more. He's not always like my Daddy. He didn't have any clothes on —" The child looked alarmed now, still bewildered by that glimpse of her naked father which evidently continued to perturb her.

Sheila hoped that there had been only the one occasion, that Edward hadn't ever had sex with her sister while Barbara was around.

"I thought it might be somebody else 'cos he didn't even smile at me that day we went there; he turned his back on me," Barbara added. "And Auntie Pauline didn't like me then, did she?"

"It wasn't you they didn't like," Sheila heard herself saying. "I think they were a bit embarrassed." She was surprised by the alacrity with which she was explaining on behalf of those two.

But she was only thinking of Barbara's feelings, of not wishing her to be hurt.

From what her daughter said, Sheila began to wonder if Edward could have hoped to share his time between the cottage here and Pauline's house. If that were so, she had put him right with her insistence on a divorce. She was thankful that she had clarified the future situation. Nothing would have made her able to endure any frequent comings and goings. A clean break would, if nothing more, leave her knowing where she stood. And with fewer painful reminders.

Todd had telephoned the farm that morning to inquire how she was, and what she had found on returning home. She was glad to be able to report that she had started proceedings against Edward, and that she felt better already for being able to begin looking ahead.

"Have you seen Johnnie and the baby at all?" she asked. "How are things there?"

"Sorry, honey, I haven't made it over to Jane's since you left. We've been on stand-by most days, and also taking off at night."

He sounded perturbed; Sheila longed to reassure him. "Don't let it worry you, Todd. You've done a lot already, especially for Johnnie. And it's not your problem, after all." Nor mine really she thought, but couldn't believe she would ever leave it at that.

"No, but . . . Well, I'll try and keep you posted." The truth was he was exhausted, and depressed. Several buddies had failed to return to base. One of their aircraft had been seen coming down over the Channel. And there was more — he himself had made it back, but the landing-gear was jammed, he'd crash-landed, damaging the Mustang and putting himself out of action with a mass of injuries, including a fractured arm. Hearing Sheila's voice was a real tonic, only it did make him wish they were together, that he could *see* that she was OK. Being grounded provided too much time for worrying. For missing her.

Todd's promise to contact her again materialised in late July, sooner than Sheila had dared hope, but his news was anything but encouraging.

"I need to know who you spoke with regarding Jane's neglect of those kids," he explained, sounding overwrought. "I know you were reluctant to report her again, but I went over there last evening. They were on their own yet again. No sign of Mrs Foster. Of course, I couldn't get into the house. I waited and waited, Jane eventually came on the scene at two A.M. Decidedly worse for wear . . ."

"You mean — ?"

"Drunk. And dishevelled, her clothing all over the place."

"But was Mrs Foster out till that time as well?"

"When I got some sense out of Jane, I gathered the old lady'd been left in charge. From what was said, Mrs Foster wasn't all that well. She had complained of a pain, not that *that* stopped Jane from going on her date. It turns out the old lady was whisked off to hospital — suspected heart attack."

"But whoever arranged all that should have made certain the kids weren't left on their own . . ."

"Ah. That's easily said. Seems it wasn't that simple. Mrs Foster staggered as far as the telephone kiosk to ring for help herself. She collapsed mid-call and didn't regain consciousness until she'd been hospitalised. No one else but Jane knew that those kids were alone."

When Sheila came off the telephone she was terribly anxious. She had no confidence in Jane's staying in to look after Johnnie and his sister, or even in her organising someone else to care for them. In any case, if she came home drunk, Jane herself wasn't a fit person to look after those children. Although she'd given Todd details of where she reported what was happening, he hadn't been able to guarantee that he could update the authorities. Until she heard from him again she would continue to feel extremely uneasy.

When it came, his further call did nothing to relieve her anxiety. "They have got someone to keep an eye on Johnnie and Gloria *pro tem,*" he told her. "Trouble is, they need to take action to prevent Jane from neglecting them in the future, and for that they require more than my word. The idiots have lost their notes of your original report. I know this is going to be difficult, but they ought to have you here to witness to what has been occurring — how long it's gone on, and that."

"I'll do my best," Sheila promised. "I'll talk to my mum, see if it'll be all right to leave Barbara with her again."

It wasn't entirely for the sake of those children that she would try to return to Kent, though. Todd had sounded strange — evasive. And that wasn't like him. He'd given her a new number where she could telephone him, but he hadn't answered when she'd asked if he had been transferred to another air base. She wondered if his squadron had moved right away from Kent, but if that was so why hadn't he said? She wouldn't have an easy minute until she learned what was happening.

For once, Enid agreed only reluctantly to enable Sheila to get away. She had recognised how anxious her daughter was to see Todd Albany. "I hope you're not letting yourself in for even more trouble! It's easy for these Yanks to impress, with their posh uniforms, the brass they've got to throw around, and their free and easy ways."

Even before she reached Kent on the first Monday in August, Sheila heard enough about the damage there to appal her, and to have her cease worrying about where Todd might be, and to pray instead that he was still alive, and Jane's children as well. Praying had become a means of getting through the succession of problems, although she felt in her heart that she might be undeserving of help. So constantly since this war began had church-going been crowded out by being busy.

She became upset while waiting for her train in London, people all around her were talking about the tragedies.

"It was last Thursday," one woman was telling another. "And it was three doodlebugs, not two."

"All in the centre of Maidstone, were they?"

"No — one was out at Allington. But the one that hit the goods yard did the most damage."

"I suppose it put the station out of action."

"A lot more than that! Several people were killed, and a great many injured. And then there were the homes it wrecked. Over a thousand, they say."

"What — with all three of them V1s?"

"No, just one. They reckon there was close on five hundred houses destroyed by the first that came down there that day."

Further along the platform two elderly men were discussing an incident in Tunbridge Wells. Sheila was saddened by their grave faces.

"I've known him all my life, we went to school together," one man said, his voice trembling as he sighed.

"And you say he bought it just sitting on the Common here?"

His friend nodded. "Well, he died soon after in hospital. Yesterday. Came crashing down it did, near the Spa Hotel. George was in that thatched summer house — you know . . ."

"And he'd no time to take cover then?"

"Evidently not. I gather there was a battle going on overhead. Knowing George, he'd be watching. Well, this blighter brought the doodle-bug down and it exploded."

It was only because she was so concerned about the people she knew in Kent that Sheila had resisted the temptation to remain at home. She hadn't wanted to leave her own daughter yet again, but she couldn't let those children down. At least, today, she felt better about one aspect of coming here — almost glad that Barbara and the rest of her family *were* so far away. She could at least feel thankful that they should be safe where they were in Yorkshire.

She didn't know when she would see Todd, or where. But when she'd rung the new number he'd given her, he confirmed that Jane did indeed have permanent help with the children: a retired schoolteacher, who was coming daily to the house.

Unable to wait one minute longer than she had to before seeing Johnnie and his sister, Sheila got out of the train at Staplehurst. When there seemed no sign of a bus going in the right direction, she set off to walk the few miles to Frittenden. She still had the map that she'd used when first trying to locate Jane, and she'd brought only a small suitcase light enough to carry.

The weather was better than it had been in July and as she walked up the incline from the station, Staplehurst looked bright and clean, very appealing. I wouldn't mind staying here, Sheila thought, and decided immediately to enquire about accommodation.

The first likely place was the sub Post Office, but even from across the road she could see it was crowded with customers, and she couldn't waste time waiting around to speak to the owner.

It took her only a few minutes to reach the heart of the village where the smell of new bread drew her to the open door of a bakery.

"Excuse me," she called to the man who was handling a batch of fresh loaves. "You won't know me, but my name's Sheila Calvert. I need somewhere to stay, I wonder if you could recommend a place?"

He introduced himself as William Hodges, then grinned. "I dare say that won't be too difficult." He came to the doorway to point towards several wooden houses. "There's lots of people are willing to take someone in now," he assured her. "We get men from the forces, and their families. Try the house just this side of the main Post Office there, and if she can't put you up she'll tell you somebody who can."

After thanking Mr Hodges Sheila walked up the road, looking to either side at the range of homes and shops, thinking how picturesque they were. The house that he had pointed out was to her left.

The lady who came to the door apologised at once and explained that all her rooms were taken. "But if you go over the road to that row of cottages, my friend will put you up, I'm sure."

Fifteen minutes later Sheila had approved her room, agreed a price per night, and was glad to leave her case, which by now was feeling less lightweight than she had thought it was.

With only her handbag to carry, the day felt even pleasanter and relishing the country air she continued heading south. Passing the church, she descended a slope where the road ran on in a straight line into the distance. Fields, with hedges and the occasional farm, stretched towards low hills on the far horizon, a scene that seemed more spacious than many in her native West Riding. She was used to the steeper hills there which often enclosed their valleys so effectively that only their summits provided breathtaking panoramas.

Just at present there was no sound of aircraft overhead. This rural landscape appeared so peaceful that Sheila felt revitalised. For the moment, she might believe no further signs of war would ever materialise. After glimpsing the huge rectory between trees over to her left she crossed the road, ready to take the next turning.

Frittenden Road was narrower than the village High Street and, had it been lined with stone walls rather than hedges, would have reminded her of many a lane near her own home. Still enjoying her walk, Sheila glanced again at her map, and tried to calculate how soon she would be with Jane and the children.

She kept noticing how different many of the houses were from those in Yorkshire. Constructed mainly in wood, most of them were painted entirely in white. And the few that were brick-built seemed to have tiled facings, especially on their upper storeys.

When she reached Frittenden and began heading towards the house where Jane was staying, Sheila ceased to enjoy the day. Determined though she was to do something for Johnnie and his sister, she hadn't fooled herself about the encounter with their mother. She knew how she would feel if someone implied that she couldn't manage to look after Barbara. She was well aware that Jane would be on her guard.

Sheila knocked on the now-familiar door and waited, trying to form in her head a few words which might deflect any animosity. The door was opened by a stranger whose austere hairstyle increased the severity of a face where a tracery of lines in no way weakened its forcefulness.

"Thank goodness!" the woman exclaimed. "You must be my replacement. For once, they've sent somebody immediately."

"No," Sheila contradicted gently, rather bemused. "Actually, I've only called to see how the children are."

The woman groaned. "You're the one from up

north, are you? The one Johnnie calls 'Auntie Sheila'?"

"That's right. You say you were expecting someone else?"

"You'd better come in. The children are out in the back garden, it'll give me a chance to explain. I'm afraid I had to put Baby in her pram, if only to get my breath back."

"You *are* the lady who's been . . . Well — appointed to help look after them though?"

" 'Help' was the operative word, or so I was led to believe." The woman sighed, indicating the only chair not strewn with belongings. "Oh, please sit down. I'm afraid I'm so distracted that I hardly know what I'm doing." She waited until Sheila was seated, sighed, and then continued. "It's not the children, you understand. I've coped with worse, and with forty at a time in my day. No, it's the mother . . ."

Oh, dear, thought Sheila, but delayed commenting until the older woman had had her say. In a matter of seconds she was hearing the latest reaction to Jane's behaviour.

"I was told my duties would entail just a few hours of a morning while Mrs Richards was at work, with perhaps the occasional evening to enable her to go out. That seemed quite reasonable to me. The true situation, unfortunately, is already proving altogether different."

"Jane's not coming home to time?" Sheila suggested.

"Almost not at all, if yesterday was anything

to judge by! She arrived here at five o'clock in the afternoon, if you please — and here was I waiting to go and attend the rest of my responsibilities. I have a brother lives with me, you see. He was invalided out of the last war, can't make himself a meal or anything."

"Oh, I am sorry. I was hoping that Jane would have realised that she'd got to pull her socks up."

"Coming in from work at that time of day was bad enough, but she'd also stayed out till all hours the one night I obliged by letting her have an evening off."

"Eh, dear. I don't know what we can do for the best."

"You're not related to her, are you, Mrs . . . ?"

"Calvert. Sheila Calvert. No, I'm not. It was just that Johnnie was evacuated to our farm. In a way, I feel as if this is my fault. I only brought him back to his mother because he wasn't thriving at all with us. He might have put on a bit of weight since Jane took him back, but I'm afraid she's not looking after him at all properly."

"You can say that again! Well, Mrs Calvert, I've reported back that things are bad here, in addition to stating that I've had enough of this. Maybe something will be done, but our services are severely stretched. With most young women in the forces or doing factory work there are barely enough of us to go round when it comes to helping families to cope."

"I just wish I could make Jane see sense. If she doesn't watch out those kids are going to be taken away from her."

The woman sniffed. "From what I've seen, I wouldn't be surprised to learn she'd find that a relief."

"Oh, surely not —"

"I speak as I find, always have done. Normally, that means I stand by those who I feel are being misjudged. Sadly, in this instance, the situation is quite the reverse." With another sigh, the woman glanced at the clock on the mantelpiece, checked it against her watch. "She did explain that she would be out all afternoon today, but she was supposed to be here half an hour ago. And she has no idea of catering for their needs. I've changed that baby three times, but I can't do so again, there isn't one clean napkin in the place."

"Don't worry, you've done your best. And I'll stop with the children 'til Jane arrives, you can get off home if you like."

"If you're certain it's not inconvenient?"

"I've got to see Jane anyway."

After the woman left, Sheila went to the back door and called to Johnnie.

The boy turned from the corner where he'd been digging with a stick in the clay soil and looked towards her. His little brown face seemed to glow as his eyes shone and then his mouth opened wide until he appeared to be all gleaming white teeth. "Auntie Sheila!"

He ran to hug her. "Is Todd here?" he asked, trying to see past her into the house.

"Not yet," she told him. "But I'm sure he will come again soon. Now — how's Gloria, is she asleep?"

Johnnie hung back when Sheila began walking towards the pram.

"Don't know," he muttered. "I don't think I like her, she smells."

"Babies do, some of the time. They can't help it."

"I know. But she doesn't talk either, not properly."

And you used not to, only a short while ago, thought Sheila, and *that* wasn't because you were too young. But she couldn't help feeling sorry for the lad, left to his own devices for so much of every day, and receiving little assistance in getting to know his small sister.

Gloria was asleep and she decided to leave her that way while she worked at the affinity developing between herself and Johnnie. The boy had been so touchingly pleased to see her again, and there could be no denying that he needed some stability in his world.

They were still outside the rear door when the unmistakable rattle and roar of a flying bomb startled them. Johnnie looked up at her, his dark eyes round with panic.

"We'd better get inside, I think," said Sheila. "You run along while I bring the pram." Hurrying indoors, she asked if there was somewhere where they could shelter.

The lad shook his head. "Mummy says that if

we're going to be dead, nothing will stop it happening." The fear in his eloquent brown features revealed how the statement had exacerbated his dread.

Sheila managed a smile. "Well, that one's gone past, any road. Happen we shouldn't be afraid, after all. Let's think about something much nicer. Has your mummy taken you to see the school you'll be going to after the holidays?"

He shook his head again, and a fresh concern darkened his expression, a mood which although less afraid seemed to be perplexed. "I will go to school, won't I? I can learn, and I don't want to be stupid."

"Of course you'll go to school. Nobody's said you won't be going, have they?".

"Don't know. I heard the lady that looks after us saying that I'll be backward if I don't go soon."

"I'm sure it'll be all right. I'll find out, if you like. I'm certain you needn't worry yet — it's still the holidays."

Sheila heard a key turning in the lock and glanced towards the front door as the boy's mother came in.

"What are you doing here?" Jane demanded instantly, frowning. "I got somebody looking after them two."

"I know, I met her. But she had to go off home, so I said I'd hang on here because —"

"Always has to go dashing off, she has," Jane snapped. "Nobody'd guess this was her job. She is paid to be here."

"I wanted to see you, any road," Sheila persisted. "To see you all, just to find out how you are getting on —"

"Find out, find out!" Jane interrupted. "That's all you've wanted ever since you first came down here. Checking on what I'm doing, *finding out* if I'm looking after the kids proper, that's all you've ever done. I suppose it makes you feel superior, watching me! Well, I've had it up to here with your poking and prying, you've caused me nothing but trouble, endless bother. And for what — just to satisfy your urge to stick your nose in."

"Jane, it hasn't been like that. It's only ever been my concern for Johnnie, and lately for his sister that's —"

Yet again, Jane did not allow her to finish her sentence. "You don't convince me, you know, not with all your high and mighty talk. And you can make yourself scarce now. I've got somebody coming here, and I don't mean to have you prying into my relationships as well."

"I can't get away from here fast enough," Sheila retorted. "I shall go right now, don't you fret!"

"And you needn't come back. None of us wants to see you again."

Hastening away from the house as the door slammed to behind her, Sheila decided to try and get through by telephone to Todd. If Jane had adopted such a hostile attitude to both of them, she would save him calling at the house.

Although sounding pleased to hear from her,

Todd seemed quite strained. "Can't talk for long, I'm afraid, honey. Got to go out . . ."

"That's OK. I won't keep you for more than a minute or two, but I wanted to warn you. I've just left Jane's . . ." She went on to explain what had been said. "I imagine I shan't take no for an answer, and I'll be back when I've calmed down, but I didn't want you annoyed by anything she might say."

"Have to admit I wasn't thinking of going over there, but thanks for letting me know."

He sounded utterly exhausted. Sheila ached just to hold him, to help him unwind. She could believe he'd been putting in too many flying hours. When he suggested they should try to meet on the following day she felt relieved that she soon would see for herself that Todd was all right.

"Are you staying in that hotel in Headcorn again?" he asked.

"No, at a house in Staplehurst. The village looked so nice I couldn't resist . . ."

"Give me their number and I'll ring you tomorrow."

"Sorry, love, I can't. I don't even know if they're on the phone. I'll have to contact you."

"Give me their name and I'll find out if they are."

"Oh . . ." For a moment Sheila was silent, thinking. "I've been such a fool, Todd. I've let that row with Jane drive the woman's name right out of my head."

Even without a firm arrangement to meet Todd, Sheila felt infinitely better for their brief chat. Despite his evident exhaustion, his voice had had its usual reassuring effect upon her. No matter how awful the encounter with Jane, she was already beginning to feel that she and Todd would find some means of improving things for those two children.

Jane *has* annoyed me, though, thought Sheila striding out along the road back to Staplehurst. Can't the woman realise that I've only become involved in all this because I've felt somehow *driven* to do what I can for Johnnie? She wished with all her heart that she had more than her own intuition to guide her on what she ought to do next.

The evening was growing cool when Sheila eventually passed the village church and walked down the hill. Feeling idiotic again, she wondered if she'd even recognise the cottage in which she was staying.

She was relieved when the woman who opened the door looked familiar, but forgetting her name was embarrassing. And Sheila couldn't think how to put that right; she didn't want to have to ask her. It was anything but flattering to tell someone that you'd so readily failed to remember what they were called!

"Come in, dear, you look quite tired. Have you been far?"

Sheila told her about walking over to Frittenden, but nothing of the confrontation with Jane.

That wretched business was the concern only of those who might be called upon to help sort out the problems.

"I didn't ask if you would be eating out, or what," her hostess continued as soon as they were indoors. "We're having hotpot tonight, there's plenty if you'd like to have some with us . . ."

"That would be nice, thank you. I'm afraid I hadn't got round to making any definite plans. But I have got my ration book with me, you're welcome to some coupons while I'm staying here."

A couple of teenagers came down from their rooms and were introduced as Derek and Diane. They talked unceasingly throughout the meal which helped Sheila to feel at home there, although their chatter prevented her from coming up with a way of asking their mother's name again without sounding totally foolish, or even quite rude. Each time she thought about it she became more hung up. Nobody would like to be made to feel that they weren't particularly memorable.

"I'm afraid I'm only fit for bed now, it's been a long day," Sheila admitted afterwards. "I hope you weren't expecting a bit of company?"

"That's all right, dear," she was told. "These two have their homework to finish. They were given essays to complete during the long summer holiday, and I've had to get tough and insist that they settle down to work before it's too late. As for me, I've got plenty to do. It's make-do-and-mend, I'm afraid, with their school uniforms. We're just praying that there'll be some decent stuff in the shops before the winter sets in. They've both outgrown last year's."

The room Sheila had been given was small, and felt rather airless, despite the window's being open beyond the blackout curtaining. Overlooking the main road as it did, the sound of traffic and of people talking as they walked up or down the High Street threatened to disturb her. Even as she was noticing these unfamiliar noises, however, tiredness overcame her and she fell deeply asleep.

Sheila seemed to have been sleeping soundly for hours when she was jolted awake. Listening, trying to identify whatever might have roused her, she could hear nothing. The silence, in fact, felt quite eerie.

The crash was the loudest she'd ever heard, hurting her ears, while the house shook as the noise reverberated all around her. After the initial impact further sounds of shattering glass and crumpling masonry continued on and on until she was afraid that the whole of the village was being destroyed.

Chapter Ten

Eventually the noises diminished to a steady scattering of breaking glass and what sounded like bricks falling. Sheila took a deep breath and tried to steady her agitated heart-rate. She was unhurt and the house around her seemed relatively intact. There was a strong smell though — soot mingled with dust — which was beginning to make her cough.

The night was so black she couldn't be certain whether some of the shattering glass had been the window of her room. As a precaution, before moving away from the bed to investigate she thrust her feet into the shoes she had left beside it. She smiled grimly. Still possessing a bit of forethought surprised her.

Despite the effort to calm down, her legs felt weak, ready to give way beneath her as she stumbled through glass shards towards the window and drew aside the blackout material.

It was still dark outdoors. Through missing panes dust came swirling into the room like fog. Running figures became visible with wan beams from their torches as they sped towards the far side of the road. Sheila was trying to make out more when there was a tremendous knocking on the door of her bedroom.

The woman who had seemed so cheerful last night was looking years older now in the light from the candle she held. Putting it down on a table, she struggled with shaking hands to knot the cord of her well-worn dressing-gown.

"You're all right, thank goodness," she exclaimed when she saw Sheila. "I was almost afraid to check, with you sleeping at the front of the house. It's one of them things, isn't it — a doodlebug?"

"I think so, yes. There's no light of course, and that much dust about I could hardly see."

"Let's have a look . . ." Sheila was followed through the room as they both went to stand at the window.

"Oh, my God! It's only just across the road — my friend's house has caught it. I'll have to see if she's all right."

"But you're not dressed," Sheila reminded her, but the distracted woman was tearing down the stairs already.

Sheila was wondering if she ought to throw on some clothes and go after her, when she heard Derek and Diane hurtling out of their rooms. She called to them, but they seemed too upset to notice. They had evidently thrust on trousers and sweaters over their nightwear, as they dashed downstairs after their mother and out into the street.

"I'll get dressed an' all, happen I'll be more

use then," Sheila thought, and realised she was asserting this aloud.

She dragged on her clothes with half her attention on the view through the window. The clouds formed by dust were settling a little, dim, hand-held lights revealed that several buildings across the road had been damaged severely. One, which had contained the Post Office, looked worse than all the others with huge timbers displaced among heaps of rubble.

The NFS and regular firemen were working already among the wreckage. Sheila marvelled at the speed with which they had reached the site. And then she recalled seeing a fire station near to where she was staying. She thanked heaven that they had been so close at hand when the missile landed.

As soon as she was dressed Sheila ran downstairs and out through the door the two youngsters had left open. I'd better not shut that either, she thought, or they might all be locked out. There had certainly not been time for anyone to think of picking up a key.

Outdoors, the air seemed heavy with dust. As she hurried it fell into her eyes and felt gritty on her lips when she struggled to breathe. On her own side of the street the narrow pavement was covered in broken glass and other debris, but as soon as she stepped onto the road itself she was in the thick of it, shoe soles crunching on pieces of brick and glass, chunks of wood impeding her progress.

There was frequent shouting between people who were trapped and their rescuers. The shifting of wood and plaster, stone and brickwork made sudden alarming noises. And above all these sounds a motorcar horn was blaring.

Sheila reached the other side of the road as a man in NFS uniform stumbled out from the remains of a grocer's shop. She heard him shouting to a regular fireman: "Quick, behind Mr Harmer's — there's paraffin leaking all over the place. The van's electrics have gone, it's all sparking!"

Someone attempting to take charge of onlookers urged them to get well back. "If that van ignites the paraffin, there'll be another explosion."

Already aware that she wasn't doing much to help, Sheila was about to heed their warning when a lady emerged from the ruins of a house. It was the person who had been unable to accommodate her, and she was being led out by the owner of the place where Sheila was staying. Oh, Lord, I could have been asleep in that! The thought made her sway as already-fragile legs threatened to let her down completely.

Breathing deeply to steady herself, she willed shock under control. She had got to pick her way through all this rubble towards her landlady.

"We're taking them across home," Sheila was told. "The youngsters are giving a hand with the others. The rest of them were sleeping at the front, their rooms didn't catch it quite so badly."

Once they arrived indoors Sheila went to find things for making a pot of tea. Everyone else seemed too shattered. All they could do was keep asking their friends in turn if they were all right and help each other apply first aid to their many cuts and bruises.

More neighbours came streaming in, directed by Diane and Derek who were helping those people who weren't in need of medical attention.

"They're getting the Misses Clinch out now," they reported at last. The sisters kept the Post Office and had been trapped when it was damaged. "And William Hodges has to go to hospital. He's lost a lot of blood since the bakery collapsed, but he's insisted on helping to get his family out first."

"I heard he made a point of informing the food office, so's the village won't run short of bread," their mother put in. "That's just the sort of thing he would think of, injured or not."

"Mr Hodges, you say?" Sheila checked, recalling the man who had assisted so readily when she was seeking somewhere to sleep.

Her landlady was recovering now; reassured by seeing that her friend from over the road was regaining a little colour, she was turning to practical matters. "I've a few rashers of bacon in," she announced. "And I can reconstitute some dried egg, scramble it. It's going to be a long day, I'm afraid, we'll cope better with something inside us. Even if we don't feel much like eating."

Sheila was glad to be able to help, and relieved

that the people rescued from the wreckage were beginning to respond to being somewhere rather more safe. They were now discussing their experiences.

"That'll help them all," someone said. "They'll get it off their chests like this, and realise that they're lucky to have survived." She paused, gave Sheila a rueful smile. "Of course, it's easy for me to talk, I know. *My* house hasn't been entirely flattened."

Sheila continued to assist where she could as daylight came and people went in and out of the cottage, relating more details of the damage sustained. She could share their relief that no one in the neighbourhood had been killed and only one person in addition to Mr Hodges had been taken to hospital.

The devastation to property, though, was appalling. Sheila was reminded of the house at Benenden that had been destroyed, and of the damage to Halifax much earlier in the war, when the bomb that had fallen near Hanson Lane wrecked such a large number of houses. Rare as that incident was in her part of the world, it had brought home to her how serious such loss could be.

Here, however, she suddenly felt out of place, as though she might be in the way now that there seemed nothing practical that she could do. Someone had come in from the street to say that the WVS were setting up a centre for those who had become homeless.

"If it's all right with you, I'm just going out for a while," she announced and left them to it.

The flying bomb had fallen somewhere behind the Post Office, but the area damaged was quite widespread. So many people were outside now, that Sheila suspected the entire population of the village had gathered to help, or perhaps to enquire concernedly after friends.

Passing a group of women she heard someone say that the church had also suffered. "There are tiles off the roof and lots of the windows have been blown out."

And I haven't even seen that church properly, thought Sheila. All at once, going there seemed imperative. Continuing to pick her way through the accumulated rubble, she carried on uphill, until the church was visible to her left beyond a row of houses. Dust was stirring here as well, its inability to settle seeming to emphasise a general unease. Part way along one of the side walls of the church she could see a group of people gazing down at heaps of tiles, and shards of glass that had scattered. As she watched they leaned back to stare up at the roof then sprang away hastily as a few more tiles came clattering down to shatter.

There was no one to prevent her entering, and somehow she felt compelled to walk into the cool interior. Seeing any building damaged distressed her; when that building was a church the destruction seemed symbolic of the evil generated by war. Or, thought Sheila ruefully, the evil which generated wars.

Seeing one of the stout pillars that had lasted for centuries only to stand now with its base deep in dirt and debris, she felt strangely bereft. If folk continued to ruin everything that represented good, where would people turn for comfort? For solutions? People like those in the village here who just an hour or two ago had been bombed out of their homes?

Perhaps because the area around her own home had seen so little war-damage and she'd been protected from its savagery, this bombing now hit her all the harder. She'd never felt more defenceless. Is there soon to be nowhere left? she wondered. Nowhere which might breed answers to the carnage? Nowhere to bring reassurance as people face up to loss? Where shall we find guidance as we try to pick up the pieces after all the years of this terrible fighting?

Suddenly exhausted again, Sheila went into one of the back pews intending to sit. Impelled to kneel, she closed her eyes for a moment, but the words would not come. She was unable to pray, unable to form coherent sentences of any kind. The failure seemed akin to yesterday's inability to remember people's names, only far, far worse.

One of the heavy doors creaked, and she heard men talking as they came back into the church and began walking down the aisle, their feet crunching on broken glass and bits of rubble.

And then one of them laughed — actually *laughed.*

How could he? This was their church. *She* was upset by what happened here, how could they be other than destroyed by what had been done to it?

Out of nowhere the words came, words from a foundation stone laid thirty-odd years ago, in St Paul's church at King Cross, not far from her home. She could see them cut in stone: **YE ARE GOD'S BUILDING.**

All these miles away here, in a life that seemed distanced in more than the physical sense from everything familiar, that eloquent reminder made more sense than ever in the past. Perhaps we shouldn't be afraid, she thought — not even if everything that made us feel we belonged were taken away. Perhaps the truth might be that whatever was really essential would still remain.

I ought to learn to cling to that idea.

Sheila stood up, turned to walk away. But already she grew afraid that when life was busy convincing her everything was lost her mind would not have room for such an understanding.

They were cordoning off several areas that had suffered the most severe damage. People were sweeping part of the road, trying to clear a route through the debris. She would offer to help where she could, but first she must go back to that house.

There was no real reason for her to remain in Staplehurst, and with so many homes damaged or destroyed accommodation would be scarce. By moving out, she would leave her landlady space that would be more useful for her local friends. Staying as near as possible to their own homes, folk would more readily rescue whatever possessions they could; begin to organise their immediate future.

Sheila was surprised how hurt she felt on behalf of these people whose lives had been disrupted in those few minutes by that V1. She had been shaken, of course, at the time of the impact, but the pain had grown worse while witnessing these villagers as they coped with the destruction.

Walking down the hill, she noticed her landlady plus son and daughter struggling across to their house with armfuls of their friend's belongings. And then the now-homeless woman herself, turning at the pavement edge to gaze back dismally at her ruined house.

"Thank God you're OK!"

The voice immediately behind her startled Sheila. She swung round and there was Todd, the shadow of anxiety only now disappearing from his grey eyes.

So pleased to see him that she ached to give him a hug, Sheila stopped immediately she noticed his left arm was in plaster.

"Oh, Todd, you're hurt! What happened?"

His grin was meant to be reassuring, but he could feel the stitches pulling beside his right ear where a gash acquired during that crash had been repaired.

"Your RAF boys would call it a prang. It wasn't that serious, really. At least, I got her back to base."

"You mean your plane crash-landed?" Sheila felt weak with shock. "And it isn't just your arm, is it," she added when he turned his head and she saw the dressing on his face.

Suddenly, though, Todd was hugging her, fiercely, making up with the one sound arm for any immobility of the other. He smiled approvingly as, growing less careful of hurting him, she was drawn more closely against him.

"You see," he said, "We're neither of us all that fragile." And kissed her, fervently on the mouth.

"You might not be — I'm not so sure about me!" Sheila exclaimed ruefully, gazing up at him.

"I heard what happened here, Sheila, I had to come."

"You haven't walked all the way from — from wherever you're based now?"

He shook his head. "Left the jeep the other side of the hill there. Didn't want to add to the chaos in the village. And it looks as though there's barely room for vehicles to get through."

Sheila smiled back at him. "Am I glad to see you! I've felt so confused — relieved that so few were injured, but shattered seeing what has been done to these people I was just getting to know. The baker's had to go to hospital. He was the first person in Staplehurst that I spoke to." She still found his being injured upsetting.

"You're staying some way further down the hill, I take it?"

She shook her head, and pointed. "No, not far away at all. In that house there. As you can see, the ones on the opposite side of the road caught the brunt of it. The thing fell behind the Post Office."

Todd frowned. "You were right on the edge of the damage then. It must have come down with a terrible crack!"

"It certainly did, shook everything. We were just very lucky."

He was watching the rescue operation, all the people salvaging what they could from houses and shops that weren't too dangerous to enter. "Where will they all go?"

"That's what I was wondering, Todd. Or rather — won't it be best if I give them a bit more space tonight. Those who still have homes intact seem to be taking in friends or family."

"If you mean you want to move on, we'll find you somewhere else to stay. How about picking up your things now?"

"Sure. That's if — if you've got time to give a hand?"

"That's why I'm here. Or to be assured you're OK."

Her landlady couldn't disguise her relief to have another room available. "You are certain it's not terribly inconvenient for you to find another place?" she asked as Sheila settled with her for the one night's stay.

"I've got someone to help me look, and Todd knows the area better than I do."

He was waiting outside. There were still so many people taking refuge in the house that the downstairs rooms were crammed with possessions ranging from clothes to rations that had been salvaged.

"I'll never forget this place," said Sheila quietly, as Todd insisted on taking her case.

They began walking up the hill and he tried to disguise the limp, which wasn't easy with strained tendons and bruising of both legs.

Sheila noticed of course. "I shouldn't have let you carry that case. You're limping, aren't you?"

"It's nothing serious, honey. The arm's the only bit that's broken." He didn't mention the suspected concussion that had kept him under observation for several days. And about which, even now, the doctors were not entirely happy.

They reached the spot where the jeep was parked and still the air about them felt heavy with dust. Sheila blinked eyes that seemed so gritty they'd never be really clear again.

"We'll find you a bed for the night," Todd announced after helping her into the jeep. "And then I guess we'd better discuss what we're gonna do about those kids. That's if you're up to that . . . ?"

"Sure. I'm fine really, Todd. I didn't even get one scratch."

"I wasn't talking about physical damage, honey. I know what shock can do to you."

She grinned. "Don't know which was the worst really, the V1 or learning yesterday that Jane's behaved so badly to the babysitter the woman's on the point of giving up."

"That Jane's real stupid, you know," Todd remarked, starting up the jeep and turning it around to face south. "She doesn't seem to realise it makes a whole lot of sense to co-operate when that would produce all the help she needs."

"We shall have to report her again, shan't we? Press the authorities to ensure that Johnnie and his sister don't come to any real harm. I'm getting scared now that something dreadful will happen before Jane comes to her senses."

Todd nodded gravely. "Me too. I was hoping to arrange to see someone today, but I think it'll have to be tomorrow."

"Fine. That'll give you time to refresh my memory on what they said to you before. What they need from me, and so on . . ."

"I will eventually, sure. First, though, it's more urgent we check on those kids. From what you said, it's anybody's guess who'll be looking after them."

Sheila was hoping that someone new might have been assigned to caring for Johnnie and Gloria. She had sympathised with the lady she'd met there yesterday, but felt that she disapproved too vehemently to be able to show Jane's kids any degree of patience.

As soon as the door was opened to them Sheila wished that the elderly lady could have been in charge today. Instead of her, it was Jane herself who confronted them.

During the first second Jane's smile faded. "Oh, it's you," she said, and Sheila wondered who she'd been expecting.

Jane's deflation emerged in a sigh and then she spoke again, sounding far angrier than they had ever known her. "I can't think how you dare show your face here!" she shrieked at Sheila. "You've ruined everything for me. That woman won't come here again, and now I shall lose my job. There's dozens of other girls wanting work at the airfields, they'll not keep it for me now I haven't turned up today."

"You could phone through, surely," said Todd swiftly. "Explain that you couldn't leave the children on their own."

"I did that already. Got a mouthful from her in charge. Any more big ideas?" Not waiting for an answer, Jane looked at her watch.

"We're only trying to help, Jane," Todd began steadily, though Sheila could see that he was exasperated.

"I've told *her* I can do without help from you two. Just keep away, the pair of you. I'm up to here with you telling me what I ought to be doing. You want to try it sometime, you'll soon find it's different when you're struggling to earn enough to keep them fed."

Beyond Jane's raging the house sounded strangely quiet. Sheila began to wonder uneasily where the children were. Since their mother was making such a fuss about having stayed here to look after them, they might have been expected to be visible.

"Where are the kids now?" asked Todd, becoming equally concerned.

"Playing out. Can't keep them indoors all the time, you should know that's not good for them."

"In the back garden, are they?" Sheila enquired, hurrying through the room to look.

"I suppose so," snapped Jane. "You find them, you're the one that's creating all the fuss."

Neither Johnnie nor his sister was in the rear garden.

"They're not there, Jane," Sheila announced. "Where are they?"

"Playing out, I told you. I had to get on, couldn't do with them round my feet. You don't know what it's like now there's two of them going on at me all the time. Can't get nothing done . . ."

Todd had walked across to the front door and opened it, was staring now towards the centre of Frittenden where the road climbed up to the church. "Christ!" he exclaimed and set off at a limping run.

Following, Sheila was in time to see him scoop up Gloria and order Johnnie to quit walking in the middle of the road and come with him.

"They were just strolling along, they'd have bought it if anyone had driven over the brow of the hill there," Todd told her, appalled.

"You should know better than wandering

about in the middle of the road like that, Johnnie," Sheila reproached the lad. "You ought to look after your little sister."

"Don't go on at him, honey," said Todd softly. "We don't know what provoked all this."

"Mummy kept saying to go and find my daddy," Johnnie said firmly. "He's got to look after us now."

It wasn't until they were in the house a second time that Sheila noticed the suitcase beneath the window. Todd was speaking to Jane, his quiet, distressed tone more affecting than if he'd been shouting.

"They were right in the centre of that road, near the top of the hill where any car heading this way would have mown them down. The baby can scarcely toddle, how on earth could you permit them to go off like that?"

"I didn't know, did I?" said Jane. "You can't watch them every minute." She turned on Johnnie. "What were you doing, out on the road? You know you shouldn't have taken your sister —"

"— You told me," Johnnie interrupted, fiercely. "You did, you said to find my daddy, that he'd —"

"Nonsense!" Jane contradicted. "That's a wicked lie . . ."

"It's not, it's not," the boy insisted. Gazing up at Todd, he pleaded with brown eyes awash with tears to be believed. "She did say it. 'Cos we can't stop here any more."

Her attention returning to the suitcase, Sheila challenged Johnnie's mother. "Where are you going, Jane?"

Todd took one look at Johnnie's bleak little face and ushered him out to the back garden then set down the baby beside him on the scuffed grass. "Just you stay here this time," he warned them before turning to come indoors.

"Mind your own business," Jane was telling Sheila. "You're still at it, aren't you — interfering. And you needn't think I've nowhere to go."

"I suppose I am interfering. Can you blame me? I brought Johnnie home to you, Jane, because I believed he'd be better here. But I can't think of one thing that's reassured me I was right. And now the kids are allowed to go wandering off, while you prepare to make yourself scarce."

"You were taking them with you, weren't you, Jane?" said Todd, his grave eyes willing her to assure him on that point.

"Oh, I don't know. I thought I'd maybe go to that office — see them that sit there behind a desk and keep telling me I'm doing everything wrong. They think they've got all the answers . . ."

"Jane!" Sheila could not believe what she was hearing. "You wouldn't let anybody take the children over, surely? Think what that could mean. You might never get them back."

Jane ran a hand through hair which these days

looked quite lank. She glanced at her watch again, sighed. “According to you, they might be better off than they are with me. It’s not my fault. I need a break, can’t you see? I’m at the end of my tether. I’m not going to pass up my one chance of getting away.”

“OK, OK. But don’t simply walk out, think what you want. Tell you what, I’ll try and give you more of a hand. I can’t promise how long it’ll be for, I’ve got my own little girl to consider. But just ’til you get yourself sorted out —”

“No, no! I won’t have you here. Hasn’t that got through to you? You’re all alike, you think you know everything. Well, you give it a go — you try looking after them if you’re so bloody clever!”

Jane charged across the room, seized her suitcase and made a dash for the door. Todd tried to reach it ahead of her and cursed when his limp slowed him down as Jane sent an armchair skidding across the worn lino to impede him.

“I’ll fetch her back, don’t worry,” he said as the door closed behind her.

“She’ll soon be back any road, I’m sure it’s just a gesture,” said Sheila. She could imagine Jane hiding out somewhere, then coming home at nightfall. “Happen if we let her calm down it’ll be for the best, give her time to realise what her priorities are.”

While she was speaking they heard a jeep’s engine.

“She’s not taking —” Todd strode across to

open the door. It wasn't his vehicle, but one that had sped around the corner and was parked beside the spot fifty yards away where Jane had halted.

"If only I could run, I might stop them," said Todd, but one leg had given way when he tried to prevent Jane leaving the house.

Sheila crossed swiftly to take his good arm. "Don't worry. Let her go, just for a few hours. You said you knew where he was based, you'll be able to contact them."

"I guess so." Todd sounded doubtful.

"At least it'll give her the break she needs, if only for a few hours. Away from them, she'll realise how much they mean to her."

"I sure hope so. Some folks don't seem to have any knowledge of what's right."

"But I *do,*" insisted a tiny voice behind them. Johnnie had come back into the room. "I'm sorry. I was naughty to be in the road."

"OK, son, OK." Moving awkwardly on account of his injured legs, Todd went down on one knee beside the boy. "Your mom's had to go out, but we're gonna take care of you. You don't have to worry, not at all."

Johnnie and his sister seemed strangely indifferent to their mother's departure. The boy began exploring the cupboards in search of something to eat, while Gloria brought her teddy bear in from the garden and was hauling it around the room by an ear as she tottered from one piece of furniture to the next.

"Well," Sheila began in a whisper, hoping Johnnie wasn't paying too much attention to what was being discussed. "I can stay here, I suppose, see they're all right. Even for a day or two if — if she doesn't . . . You know . . . But what do we do about reporting what she's done? If we tell anybody that she's gone off, the kids will definitely be taken away, won't they? Maybe even permanently."

"Well, they sure would if this happened in the States. Can't say for certain about your laws over here."

"Nor can I really, but I'm positive about one thing — they wouldn't be left here. Not even — I suspect — with me in charge."

Todd was looking pensive. When he spoke his voice was hushed. "What Johnnie said a while ago — about his father, have you any idea at all who he might be?"

Sheila shook her head. "Haven't a clue, I'm afraid. Don't even know if he and Jane were married. Nor, come to that, if the same chap's responsible for both kids."

"From appearances, we must assume that's unlikely."

"Quite. I wouldn't be surprised if the second chap was just somebody she dated for a time. Could be the one she's gone off with now."

"I think not. He won't have been around here more than a few months. They moved us into the area during the build-up towards D-Day." Todd sank onto one chair and indicated Sheila should take the other. His face looked grey with exhaustion, or pain.

"What time do you have to report back to base?" she enquired.

"I don't." He hesitated briefly, shrugged. "I'm grounded, didn't I say? Not much use to the airforce until this lot heals. But I do have a billet where I'm expected tonight." He was not going to explain that the house was conveniently close to the hospital where he was attending regularly for out-patient treatment. And to have the effects of that blow to the head monitored.

"But if I rustle up a meal you'll have time to eat that with us?"

"Why not?" Todd paused, thinking. He didn't want to leave Sheila to cope on her own. Didn't want to leave her, period. "Say — why don't I go along to the call-box, tell the good lady I shan't be there before morning?" So long as he kept tomorrow's hospital appointment nothing else over there mattered.

Johnnie's search had produced a paper bag containing a few fragments of biscuit which he laboriously shared out between himself and Gloria. The eagerness with which he devoured his portion reminded Sheila of the urgency of providing that proper meal.

The cupboards yielded nothing more than a pack of dried egg powder, half a stale loaf and roughly two ounces of margarine.

"Thank goodness I've got my ration book with me," Sheila exclaimed when Todd came in from telephoning. “Can you keep an eye on things now while I dash to the shops? Or shop.”

“Sure can. You go right ahead.”

Todd sounded quite cheerful now. Sheila hadn’t the heart to tell him what she’d discovered whilst checking for stocks of food.

The children’s clothes and other possessions were still around, but not one thing she could identify as belonging to their mother. Jane had removed every last item of her own — with the thoroughness someone uses when leaving a place for ever.

Chapter Eleven

Getting out of that house was a relief. Sheila took her time walking as far as the nearest shop. The children would be fine with Todd, and she needed to think. She just wished she didn't feel so utterly worn out, too much had happened since arriving in Kent, and all of it upsetting.

She would have to sort out a few priorities, give her failing attention to whatever she must do to hold things together until tomorrow. Once the meal was eaten and cleared away, there was washing to be done. She'd seen that pail of dirty nappies, and she'd never bring herself to sleep in Jane's bed until she had clean sheets and pillow-cases.

The tiny shop didn't provide much of a selection of food that late in the day, but she was able to purchase bread, some spam, corned beef, and plenty of potatoes. They also had cheese — it wasn't very nice, dry-looking and of the pungent variety that Barbara always called 'sweaty-feet', but it should cook all right.

Thinking about her daughter, Sheila became horrified by what she was contemplating. While agreeing to stay on here she hadn't allowed herself to consider the anguish that she could be causing in her own child. And in herself. Just thinking about Barbara made her ache to be back in Yorkshire. She couldn't forget how reluctant she had been to leave on this occasion, being well aware of Barbara's need for a stable home life. How long would it be now before she ceased being torn between these kids and her own little girl?

Sheila forced herself back to concentrating on immediate needs.

"Oh — and I'll have to have something for doing the washing," she told the woman behind the counter. "Have you got any Rinso?"

Todd had found a kettle, filled it, and put it on to heat. He had taken Johnnie into the bathroom and persuaded him to wash his hands.

"I'll clean the little one up in a while," said Sheila. "Best not just yet, though, or she might need another wash before we eat."

Todd grinned. "Could be!"

While Sheila unloaded her shopping he had been observing Gloria's attempts to push the teddy underneath the bed that looked as though Jane had vacated it in haste. The child's feat was rendered all but impossible by a conglomeration of broken toys and what seemed to be a massive collection of film magazines. To say nothing of weeks of accumulated dust.

"Should I give a hand with the food?" asked

Todd. "I'm not that domesticated, but I don't mind having a go."

She smiled. "Your one good hand, you mean? It's OK, love. Just keep an eye on the kids, will you? I'm going to make something simple like a corned beef hash. Not sure it'll be ideal for the baby, but I suspect it'll be as good as most things she's been eating."

The meal was popular enough with the youngsters, and Sheila noted thankfully that Johnnie did indeed seem to have recovered his appetite since returning to Kent. Gloria appeared to be the sort of child who would eat enthusiastically for a time, and then grow bored. But at least both children had something substantial. She herself hardly noticed how the food tasted.

During the few hours they'd been together again she had become increasingly aware of Todd. His arrival in Staplehurst had been enough of a surprise to make her acutely conscious of how good he was to have around. Then there had been the shock of learning that he'd been injured; that he could have been killed. But she'd been allowed no time for considering how deeply that would have affected her.

Now that they had been thrust together caring for Jane's children, memories of previous occasions came flooding back, intensified now by the stark truth of Jane's departure.

With Todd to share it all even this situation did not feel entirely alarming. There was still a strange satisfaction in coping here beside him.

Changing the baby and finding a nightgown for her, then slipping the sweet-smelling toddler into bed, Sheila experienced as she had on another occasion the wish that this family was *theirs.*

Across the room, Todd was showing Johnnie some photographs. Pictures of his Headcorn base, they depicted several aircraft, among them his Mustang. He was explaining details of the plane, pointing out the markings on the fuselage, each representing an enemy aircraft successfully destroyed.

Listening intently, Johnnie was nodding seriously. "You're very brave, aren't you, Todd? I'd like you to be my daddy. Will you be, please?"

"I'd like that too, son. But you have a dad already, somewhere. Maybe we ought to find him. Like your mom said. Does he dress the way I do — in a uniform?"

Johnnie giggled, uneasily. "I don't know. Can't remember."

"Have you seen him, Johnnie, since you came back to Kent?" asked Sheila, turning away from the cot where Gloria was almost asleep now.

The boy shook his head. "Don't think I've seen him ever. He's not the man that's got a jeep like yours. Mummy said not. 'Cos he's white, like the daddy Gloria's got."

"And where is Gloria's daddy? Do you know?" Todd asked gently.

Again, Johnnie shook his head. "Think he went away. When Mummy smacked Gloria, she said he should have taken her. I don't want Gloria to go away, not really. Only when she smells nasty."

Later, when she turned away from settling Johnnie to sleep, the misery of the kids' situation hit Sheila really hard. Working to make them a meal, attempting to discover more about their parentage, and afterwards tackling some washing, she had kept going without too much difficulty. All at once she had no urgent tasks demanding attention, and the freedom to think caught her out again.

"God, what a diabolical day!" She leaned back against the edge of the table. "I thought it couldn't get worse when I woke to that doodle-bug bringing down half of Staplehurst, but this . . ." Her voice trailed off and she sighed. "Oh, take no notice of me. I've got the hump, that's all."

"That isn't all . . ." Todd was walking towards her. "You're a sensitive woman, a caring mother who's had her day shattered by another woman's indifference to her kids."

"But I suddenly feel so *soft*, and it's not like me, Todd. It won't do either. I've got to find the right way of putting life together again for these two here. And I don't know where to begin."

"*You* haven't, honey. *We* have. We're the ones taking this on."

Facing her as she stood there, Todd grasped one of her shoulders, gazed into her eyes, his own almost luminous they appeared so intense. He kissed her then, firmly on the mouth, lingeringly. And then he was leaning into her, his body an exquisite pressure, trapping her against the table while his arm slid around her, gathering her close.

"We've both survived this far, we'll see this through together," he murmured. "Whatever happens, we'll work things out." And for ourselves also, please God, he added inwardly. But he must keep that a promise to himself. Learning how narrowly she had escaped being injured by that V1 had made him realise how much Sheila meant to him. But she needed space — time as well — to sort out her own life. She had a husband. He would not inflict on any man the pain that he had been caused. Only if (or when) she was free of that guy who had not deserved her, would he try to make up to Sheila for all the heartache.

"There must be masses of things I should be getting on with," she said with a sigh.

"In a moment," agreed Todd. "And if that was a reminder of where we are, and what could happen, I'm telling you it won't." And surely not tonight, he thought. When I make you mine, that won't be some place where we're haunted by anyone's disasters. It'll be somewhere where we can simply be us, and by ourselves.

As though promising himself that, he kissed her again, fervently, passionately, his tongue tracing her lips then pressing at her teeth until they parted for him.

By silent mutual consent they moved to chairs either side of the table, where they continued to discuss arrangements for caring for the children. 'Until Jane returns' was what Sheila said, but she was already dreadfully uneasy about the question of whether Jane would ever come home.

They sat through the night, half-hoping that every vehicle heard outside might be the jeep that had carried Jane away. When dawn lightened the sky beyond the blacked-out window, Todd set out to drive to his billet. He kissed Sheila before leaving, assured her that he'd come back as soon as he could.

Just do come back safely, she thought, as she listened while he drove off into the distance. Even his going off in the jeep seemed dangerous. Since she had learned that he'd come so close to being gravely injured, she could hardly bear to have him out of sight. She needed Todd Albany. Without him, she'd never be able to face anything.

Johnnie and his sister seemed happy that Sheila was there, and were still not unduly perturbed by their mother's absence. Caring for them on her own, though, became a strain from that very first morning, and mainly because the place was so ill-equipped with the things the children needed.

Sheila hadn't expected (or wanted) any labour-saving devices. Being reared on a farm had accustomed her to a life without too many refinements, but she soon discovered how few necessities Jane had provided. The worst shortage was of nappies for the baby. She had washed those which she'd found soaking in a pail, but although she had hung them on the line in the garden overnight a sharp shower had prevented them from drying. Searching Jane's part of the house revealed there were no clean ones anywhere; she was obliged to get both children dressed for going out and take them on an expedition to the few shops in Frittenden.

As Sheila feared, no one in the village had nappies in stock. She felt daunted by the task of finding somewhere where there could be a supply. Before so much of it was wrecked, she'd have considered Staplehurst a likely place. As things were, she suspected very few shops there would have been able to open for business.

Taking the map from her bag, she decided to try Headcorn. From her earlier stay, she recalled that there were several shops. Studying the map also reminded her of the branch railway which had a stop for Frittenden, even if it looked to be some way out of the village.

Getting the children ready and installing Gloria in her pram had taken longer than she'd anticipated. Now Johnnie was complaining of feeling hungry again. It was eleven-thirty. She'd never get them to Headcorn and back before they all were desperate for something to eat.

"All right, Johnnie," she promised. "We'll pop home and make some nice sandwiches before we go any further."

And if Todd hadn't arrived she must leave him

a note, or he would wonder where on earth they were.

The front door was unlocked, slightly ajar when Sheila went to place a key in the lock. Todd *is* here, she thought, and started to smile. But there was no sign of him in Jane's room, and none in the back garden either when she looked out.

Jane's come home then, after all, was her next thought. Maybe she's just gone into the bathroom. But the bathroom door stood open, no one was in sight.

"Hello?" she called up the dark staircase, feeling perturbed now yet also rather ridiculous.

"Is that you, Jane?"

The voice was tremulous, familiar, if not instantly recognisable. And then the slight, elderly figure appeared at the top of the stairs. Mrs Foster. Amid all the upheavals, Sheila had almost forgotten her.

"You're not Jane. Who are you?" Mrs Foster demanded anxiously.

Sheila began mounting the stairs towards her. "You don't remember me, do you? I'm Sheila Calvert — Jane's friend. I'm looking after the kids for a bit, just while she — well, takes time off."

"Have I met you?" the elderly woman asked, sounding suspicious.

"Before you were ill, yes. But how are you now? You'll be glad to be out of hospital."

Mrs Foster nodded. "Well, I shall be all right. When my daughter gets here. She's going to live here now. The doctors say I haven't to be on my own."

"I see."

"Just as well that Jane has left," Mrs Foster went on. "Saves me having to ask her to go. We need the room, see. My daughter's got three children. Their schooling's all arranged, and everything. The eldest will go to —"

"When are they arriving, did you say?" Sheila interrupted. She was too appalled to wait to learn the worst. How ever would she find somewhere for herself, Johnnie and Gloria at such short notice?

"They ought to have been here now. They were supposed to bring me home from hospital. But my daughter rang through to say they'd been held up. She was driving down from Macclesfield. Ever such a good driver, she is. But they had another puncture. She'd already had one, so she said. She hadn't found somewhere to get that repaired when the spare let them down. You know what it's like in wartime . . ."

"Does — does that mean you'll want us to move out soon?"

"Afraid so. Got to sleep somewhere tonight, haven't they? Especially having driven all that way. Jane didn't have much to pack up, did she?"

No, thought Sheila grimly, and she's taken her own stuff any road. But that was hardly the point.

"Look —" she began, thinking as swiftly as she could, "I'll get all the children's things together. Put them to one side somewhere, perhaps you've a cupboard where we could store them, just till I find another place to live?"

Mrs Foster sighed. "Only for a little while, mind. I suppose that'll have to do. But I don't know really how we're all going to fit in here, as it is."

"I'll do my best to get out quickly," said Sheila, silently reminding herself that Mrs Foster had been very ill, couldn't be expected to be accommodating. Most likely the stroke had given her a terrible fright. And now the poor dear was obliged to adjust to needing her daughter's care.

Johnnie was sitting on the bottom step, his arms clutched tightly around his chest, huge dark eyes turned agitatedly towards her.

"Where will we live, Auntie Sheila?"

"I don't know yet, love. But it's going to be a big adventure."

"Will Todd go with us?"

"We'll have to see. Depends where he's working." She didn't really know yet if they'd given him an office job or something until his injuries healed. Was he still based at Headcorn airfield?

She would leave a note here in case Todd arrived after they'd gone, and a second note for Jane. Although she sensed already that Jane would not be back in the near future.

She could contact Todd by telephone as well, she would try that number as soon as she had collected together the children's belongings and was free to go out. She wished with all her heart that she had such a ready means of getting in touch with Jane.

I'd go mad if I didn't know where Barbara was, thought Sheila, and imagined Jane's horror if she should decide to return and these two kids seemed to be missing.

One of the nappies she had washed was fairly dry, and if not aired as thoroughly as Sheila would have liked, she was at least able to change Gloria. Then she tackled emptying the cupboards and drawers in the room.

She had told Johnnie to keep an eye on his sister, but he was much more keen to help turn out cupboards, in the process of which he paused to play with each item of interest that was rediscovered.

"No, Johnnie love, not yet," Sheila reproved him, when he kept removing his treasures from the large cardboard box that she had found. "You can play when we get to your new home. If you insist on unpacking stuff as fast as I put it away, you might find things get left behind here."

She was glad to see that he still had the toys Billy and Louise had given him before he left Yorkshire, although he possessed such a pitifully small collection of belongings that hanging on to those he did have was hardly significant.

At least his owning very little made her task easier, and when it came to Gloria she had even fewer toys, mainly because several were broken. Some furry animals were missing eyes or limbs, looking to Sheila quite dangerous in that bits from them might be swallowed. But she couldn't abandon anything here. Instead, she packed everything that was damaged in one small box, which she sealed against inquisitive fingers. At some time in the future somebody might be able to repair these satisfactorily. For the present, Gloria had her teddy bear and one little doll that was relatively intact.

Sheila made a pile of those film magazines Jane had discarded beneath the bed and left them on the table. If Mrs Foster's daughter chose to put them out with other waste paper to be salvaged, that was just too bad. She secretly hoped they would disappear. She was appalled that Jane had spent money on those while the children went short of proper food and other necessities.

Her hope that she would finish clearing out the room in time to make that trip to the Headcorn shops proved to be fruitless. Even when she had collected up all the children's belongings Sheila felt obliged to clean the place. If someone told her Jane had never even picked up a duster since moving in, she would believe them. She simply could not leave the room in such a state for someone else to occupy.

Sorting out the bedlinen had been another headache. When asked, Mrs Foster claimed most of it was hers, only allowing that the more worn sheets and blankets were Jane's. Lacking all knowledge of who owned what, Sheila could only take the old lady's word, and thank heaven that this was summer. Had it been the middle of winter the children would have been destined to shiver through every night.

The only good thing throughout that afternoon was managing to contact Todd when she dashed out to the telephone.

He sounded tired again when he answered, but he was at least *there* and, although shaken to learn they were expected to vacate the room that Jane had rented, he came up with a suggestion.

"Leave this with me, Sheila. I think the lady I'm billeted with now could be willing to take the three of you. It's quite a large house at Hawkhurst — a farm really, only the land is let to a neighbour. Mrs Darnton is a widow, you see."

Todd arrived in the jeep an hour later, with the good news that she had agreed to take them. "In fact, I guess she'll be mighty pleased to have you around."

He didn't add that this was partly because his own future there was uncertain. He had been delighted that the hospital was satisfied the injury to his head had caused no lasting problems. His legs were healing well, and he reckoned that even though the arm must remain in plaster it shouldn't continue to keep him grounded for much longer. He had telephoned his commanding officer, and expected to hear any day now that he must join the rest of the squadron.

His elation was quashed as soon as he saw how worried Sheila looked. He did not mean to burden her with the prospect of further changes.

With luck, he'd have a few hours' notice before being called to move on. He hoped that by then Sheila and the kids would be settled with Mrs Darnton, and better able to accept his departure.

His own emotions were very mixed. Joining his buddies, returning to the job he'd come over to England to do, would be offset by saying goodbye to Sheila. The fondness he'd felt towards her all along had increased so suddenly since that near miss the other night. He wondered quite frequently now how he would ever adjust to not seeing her.

That might have been easier had she been single — free to receive suggestions about the future. As things stood, he was still determined that he'd never contribute to the break-up of her marriage. He had seen how good she was with these kids and couldn't do anything to deprive her own daughter of the stability of life with both parents.

Because Todd had arrived at the house Sheila need only write a note for Jane, and she kept that to a few lines which explained she and the children would be with Mrs Darnton at the address enclosed.

"You will make sure Jane gets this if she comes back, won't you, Mrs Foster?" she said, as with Todd's help she finished taking their belongings out to the jeep.

"Of course, dear, of course," Mrs Foster assured her. But she seemed so different since her illness, really quite vague, that Sheila wondered if she would remember. All she herself could do was write later to Jane care of this address, in the hope that a letter which came by post would definitely be kept for her.

The moment they arrived at Hawkhurst and Todd took them indoors to be introduced to Elizabeth Darnton, Sheila thought what a pleasant lady she was. And she was a lady. Everything about her — from her stately frame beneath the elegant white hair that enhanced strong features, to her beautifully-cut dress — emphasised that she was cultured. A farmer's wife, she might have been, but her late husband must surely have been a gentleman farmer.

This seemed to be confirmed half an hour later when they were invited to sit down to supper. The pre-war china was so fragile-looking that Sheila immediately felt alarmed that either of the children might have an accident.

Mrs Darnton, however, read the alarm in her eyes and met them with a smile of amusement in her own. Sheila noticed they were of a blue which seemed familiar — they reminded her of Barbara's.

"Forgive me, Mrs Calvert," their hostess exclaimed, and rose from her seat. "It's years since our children grew up, and I've become accustomed to only entertaining the Bridge Club, my fellow JPs and so on. And I suppose for long enough before that it was mostly Jeremy's fellow growers. Fruit was his speciality, you know."

Crossing towards the kitchen, she added over her shoulder, "But I do still have the Beatrix Potter dishes and mugs that my children used when they were small."

She also had child-sized cutlery which, although of silver, was in proportions that even a toddler might manage. Sheila was thankful that Gloria, partly by herself but mainly by others, had been taught to use a spoon and fork quite adequately. Johnnie, of course, had learned table manners at Hardaker Farm. She was glad to notice the appetite he'd regained in Kent had not been diminished by this latest upheaval on top of his mother's disappearance.

Despite feeling easier about the children Sheila herself was not entirely relaxed yet. Charming though Mrs Darnton was, her home was so large that it felt daunting as soon as they entered.

They had come through double doors into a hall tiled in marble that drew the eye beyond to an equally impressive staircase. Carpeted in red and with a wrought-iron balustrade, it looked as luxurious as any Sheila had seen in films. The rooms on this ground floor all seemed to be designed at great expense and with an overall impression of elegance.

Even where the furniture was old, and some of it appeared very old, its patina witnessed to years of meticulous tending. Curtains and carpets throughout demonstrated the taste and wherewithal to provide beautiful furnishings which would outlast any shortages induced by the war.

"Todd tells me your people are in farming also, my dear," Mrs Darnton began when everyone was served with homemade pie and assorted vegetables.

Sheila grinned across the table. "Well, yes. All my dad's family have always been farmers. But not quite on the scale that I believe your husband was. Ours is just general farming. A herd of cattle, a few sheep. Now, of course, we grow a lot of crops, have done right through the war."

Their hostess nodded, smiling. "The kind of farming that often seems to me more practical during a war. There are limits to the amount of fruit a nation can eat — however much people are lectured on taking in vitamins and so on."

She is so gracious, trying to put me at ease, thought Sheila, and began to believe that if she could grow accustomed to her surroundings, she might one day feel more comfortable here. Todd seemed totally relaxed, which made her wonder if his home in the United States could be similarly sophisticated.

When Sheila asked to be shown where she might prepare the children for their delayed bedtime, Mrs Darnton demonstrated that she was not nearly so unbending as strangers might imagine on first acquaintance.

"I've been hoping you might let me help bath the little one," she exclaimed, hastening ahead of them up the stairs and along a carpeted landing to open the bathroom door. "I've been disappointed so far that neither of my two have given me grandchildren. Unless you object, I shall enjoy pretending . . ."

Gloria was already so sleepy that she was stumbling over her own feet; Sheila had carried her upstairs. When handed over the toddler simply gazed from beneath heavy eyelids and smiled at Mrs Darnton.

"I'm going to apologise for the state she's in before you undress her," said Sheila hurriedly. "Her mother hadn't left her enough nappies, and although I changed her before we set off, I'm afraid her little petticoat had been wet and dried on her. She doesn't seem to have a spare . . ."

"Not your responsibility though," Mrs Darnton reminded her. "You mustn't feel embarrassed. Todd has given me a hint or two about the situation. And I believe you've coped remarkably today, being asked to leave at a moment's notice can't have been easy."

"No, well . . ." Sheila didn't want to say too much. Johnnie was standing in the bathroom doorway, and she had no wish to add to the misgivings he was bound to be feeling about his mother.

"If you want to economise with the water," she suggested, "Johnnie won't mind having a thorough wash rather than a bath."

Mrs Darnton laughed. "I suppose that's true of most boys. But we're not short of wood for heating our water yet. Many of the orchards were cut down in order to convert to arable land. In fact, if you go to the next door along you'll find the second bathroom. I think I put fresh towels out, you must tell me if I've overlooked them . . ."

"Wow, this is great!" Johnnie exclaimed when Sheila and he were alone there. "Can I turn the taps on, please?"

"You can. You can also bath yourself. I'm sure you don't need any help. But I shall expect you to take care you don't make a mess. This isn't the sort of place where you go splashing around for the fun of it."

"I know, I know," he said.

"And don't get carried away just because you've heard there's enough hot water here. Remember we're still restricted to five inches. It's all for the war effort."

They leaned together over the side of the bath, earnestly discussing just how deep five inches would be.

After their baths Mrs Darnton insisted on seeing the children installed in their beds. "I think there's nothing more appealing than little ones with their covers tucked up around shining faces."

On the way back downstairs to join Todd, she enquired if Sheila had children of her own. When she heard about Barbara she insisted that Sheila must telephone home to let her family know where she was staying.

"Well, if you're sure that'd be all right. I do like them to know where I've got to."

Mrs Darnton showed her where the telephone

was, and then explained that she would be out for the rest of the evening. "Bridge with the Rector and his wife. And if I'm late back, you must feel free to retire whenever you wish. You know where your room is, and you must be exhausted. Are you sure you have everything you need?"

Sheila smiled as she nodded. "I think so, thank you, Mrs Darnton. And thank you for being so good to us."

Enid Hardaker was pleased to hear from her daughter, and glad to write down her new address and telephone number. They'd talked for only a few moments, though, when Sheila sensed something was wrong.

"What's up, Mum? You sound upset."

"There's an important-looking envelope come in the post for you, love. Your dad thinks it might be from the solicitor."

"But that's good, Mum. It'll mean the divorce is starting to go through then . . ."

"I know. I dare say it's just me being silly, getting upset —"

"Why not open it? I don't mind. It's no secret, after all. You'll be able to stick the flap down somehow afterwards so's you can send it on to me."

"Are you sure that's what you want me to do? I don't believe in reading other folks' stuff, never have done."

"I know, I know. But I'm going to insist —

can't bear to wait now 'til it reaches me."

"Tell you what — I'll hang up for now. Your dad and me'll have a look at it, then I'll speak to you again, straight away."

Todd had been chatting to Mrs Darnton before she went out and now came back into the room. Seeing Sheila's smile, he raised one eyebrow questioningly. "Better news for a change, this time?"

"Sounds like it. Mum says there's been a letter for me, she thinks it's from the solicitor. Oh, Todd — I'll be so thankful if it is. I need something to make me believe I'll be shot of all this bother one day. I can't wait to put it all behind me."

"Could take some long while, you do realise that, honey?"

"Of course. I was told that. But just to have things set in motion means such a lot." It meant there could be no going back, no looking backwards either. Whatever Edward might say or do. She would be having her own life handed back to her once more, to shape it in whatever way she wished. With a goal like that ahead of her, she could wait for as long as it took.

When the telephone rang again her father was on the line.

"Oh, hello, Dad. What is it — did Mum think you'd explain everything better than she could? I don't need to know every detail, not yet. I can read that for myself when it comes. It is the start of the divorce, isn't it?" she checked, afraid suddenly that this was something entirely different, that there had been a delay.

"It's that all right. That's what I wanted to talk to you about, love. It doesn't look so straightforward, you see . . ." Nat paused, cleared his throat.

She could picture his dear, ordinary face, the eyes dark with concern. Her father was always so dependable.

"What is it, Dad? Is Edward turning awkward now, claiming he doesn't want it to go ahead?"

"No. I'm afraid it might be better if he were. He's suing you, if you please — for desertion. And he's claiming custody of Barbara!"

"But — he can't be . . . He knows I've only come here for a short while . . . He *can't*," she repeated. And already suspected that he could.

Chapter Twelve

Sheila honey, what in the world is wrong?"

Todd sprang out of his chair and hurried across the room. He was appalled by the change in her. A moment ago she'd been so confident, looking ahead. Now she appeared fragile, defeated by whatever news she'd received. And she was weeping.

Almost falling into the arms he extended towards her, Sheila clung to him as though she would collapse. And those sobs that tore at his heart were shaking both of them.

"Honey, don't . . . We'll work something out. You can count on me."

"I know," she said in a ravaged voice. "But you can't do anything. In fact, if you even tried it might only make everything worse."

Well, thank you, Todd thought. Her refusal of his help when he had yearned for so long to do something for her, felt like icy rain when it beat down on the cockpit of his Mustang. But he would say nothing. He'd recover; he knew that Sheila didn't normally react in this way, and surely not with him.

"You could tell me, at least," he began softly,

willing his own feelings into submission. He would provide whatever she needed — even if that were for him to withdraw from her life. "If it's this bad, you ought to talk it through." Use me for that, if there's no other way you need me.

He felt her shudder in his arms several times before she was able to continue. "As you'll have gathered, that was my father. When he opened that thing from the solicitor it — it wasn't quite what we expected. Edward's suing me for divorce instead. For desertion . . ."

"But he can't do that, surely? He's the one who walked out."

"I don't really understand, but it's all because I've come down here. He's claiming I've left the — the marital home."

"That's nonsense. Can't be right. You want to put them straight immediately. Tell them your version, the true one. How you're only here temporarily, just to see Johnnie and his sister settled. To make sure they aren't neglected. Let me tell —"

"No, Todd, no. Thank you, but no. Don't you see? If you intervene everybody'll want to know where you fit in. What's going on between us . . . Edward would seize on that, make something of it."

"OK, OK. Forget all that. But you need someone on your side, Sheila. I want that someone to be me. Behind the scenes, if necessary, right. But here for you. Always." He was still holding her, and she was trembling so violently that he could hardly bear the pain of not helping. "Come along now, and sit down."

She went with him towards the sofa, half-stumbling over the thick pile of the carpet, as though her feet were weighted, her legs turned to putty. She seemed no more in control of her limbs than little Gloria had been of hers that short while ago.

"Your parents are forwarding on this correspondence, I take it?"

"Tomorrow, yes. Should be here the day after. Not sure I want to see it, not in black and white."

"If you'd like that, I could go through it with you, scrutinise the details, try to ensure you're equipped to put this one right. Shouldn't be that difficult. From what you've said, there's plenty of folks can witness to what he's done."

"You haven't heard the worst of it yet. He's claiming Barbara, thinks he'll be awarded custody."

"Don't see how, sweetheart. That just wouldn't be right. No lawyer would hand her over to him, the girl needs her mom. And besides, he's been sleeping with your own sister. What kind of a home would those two provide?"

"A loving one, that's the trouble. Barbara adores her Auntie Pauline."

"That's as may be. But it shouldn't count for too much with the lawyers, not when those two are committing adultery. And have shown no shame about what they're doing."

"Do you think so, Todd? Do you really believe they don't stand a chance of getting away with it?"

"Sounds that way to me. We'll know more when those documents arrive."

"I might have to go back there yet again, if only to put my solicitor right on what's been going on. I thought he understood."

Todd nodded. "Be best, I guess, if you go and explain. You even saw them together, didn't you? That time at your sister's house."

"I thought I mentioned that when I went to the solicitor's office. Happen I didn't emphasise it enough. I was upset."

"And this time you'll explain more fully, make sure there are no more hiccups. That's all this is, I guess. You'll soon sort it."

"I'd better be ready to set off as soon as that envelope arrives. Enough time's been wasted already." Suddenly, Sheila thought of something. "You'll be here, won't you, to help with Jane's kids? I wonder if Mrs Darnton will mind giving a hand? She was lovely with Gloria at bathtime . . ."

"There'll be some way done," Todd assured her. "Don't you go worrying over that." This was not the time for admitting that within the next day or so he expected to be called forward to rejoin his squadron. And that would no longer be anywhere in Kent.

As though talking about Johnnie and his sister had refocused her mind, Sheila became aware of the persistent anti-aircraft shelling overhead. With this latest return to the south the sound of shells had grown so familiar she didn't always notice them.

"I'd better go up and see if those two are still asleep. In strange beds, they might be restless and feeling frightened."

"I'll come with you."

Todd got to his feet before her, extended a hand for hers. When they reached the stairs his hand went to her waist instead. He felt glad when Sheila leaned into him.

Both children were sleeping, unaware of the gunfire.

"Do you know, I think I'll turn in. I'm absolutely whacked," said Sheila.

"Why not?" he agreed, although the shadow of his departure from here made every second together seem more precious — to be treasured.

He drew her to him for a kiss that was meant to calm, to give her strength. Somehow, though, the factor of having one arm in plaster prevented him from managing a reassuring embrace. Awkwardly, and feeling ridiculously inept, he tried with the one good arm to hold her nearer to him, to instill more comfort. Afraid of being ineffectual, he was putting all he'd got into the kiss, all the pent-up need to be everything to her, all the weeks and weeks of longing.

Sheila was kissing him back, her fervour increasing as her arms went about him, holding him to her, holding her slender form to the ache that he'd supposed might be there everlastingly.

"Oh, honey," he murmured. And wondered how much longer he could endure this great need.

Beyond the noise of shelling the menacing rattle of a V1 surprised them, shaking the house and its windows as it screeched overhead.

Sheila shuddered, a tiny scream was stifled against his mouth. "Do we have to have that as well," she sighed. "Does it have to be tonight? My nerves are shredding, it's as if every bit of me will disintegrate with just one more thing . . ."

"Hey, now — that's not like you." He'd been more moved than he could ever express by her tears. He had never seen Sheila weep for her own anxieties before. And he would not bear it if he wasn't able to make her feel better.

"Just let go, sweetheart. It'll all come right. I'll take care of that." His kiss now was full of promise, fervent with the need to love her, as much as with this ever-present desire. "You've got me now," he said. "Don't you forget that."

"Don't let me go, Todd. Hold me."

He held her in the doorway of her room, and again when they paused beside the window to close the blackout curtains, and held her finally when they reached the narrow bed.

"I'm not leaving you tonight, not alone, not after what you've heard today." And, please God, I'll provide the one comfort I know how.

They drew apart only to undress, and met

again beneath sheets which felt cool on that summer night. Without the sling, his plastered arm was less of an encumbrance, though he soon wondered if he would even have noticed so small a problem. Lying close in the tiny bed, her hair was fragrant against his nostrils, her cheek velvet-soft as he brushed its firm contour with his lips. One leg lay against his own, she moved slightly and her thigh brushed against his hip. He almost believed she felt no strangeness with him, and prayed that such signs were more than his own wishful thinking.

Their next kiss continued on and on, inflaming a passion which would require every last atom of his will to resist.

She moved against him, pressing nearer as though she might be seeking to use their closeness to exclude all her fears. Just as he wished. His need to love her surged through every vein, through each nerve ending, surged until he groaned.

He could feel her heartbeat against his naked chest, and other pulses that rippled with equal intensity against his lower body.

She found his hand, guided it to her breast, and did not protest when his caress travelled down over her stomach. He stirred at her touch, kissed her again, and relished this ecstasy.

There could be no turning back. The situation wasn't ideal, was not as, only so recently, he had pictured their first lovemaking: but this world of theirs was far from ideal, these times generated needs too fierce for governing within normal boundaries.

"I need you, Todd."

Those whispered words were perfect. Tenderly at first, then encouraged into increasing fervour, he began to love her, uniting them as one against the worst the world might do to them.

The next day provided hardly any time for themselves. Only by interlinked glances were they able to communicate this new togetherness. Johnnie and Gloria, refreshed by sleep, were eager to explore unfamiliar surroundings. Sheila hadn't the heart to deny them anything. Aware of her own body, of the joy Todd awakened in her, she was recognising just how easily she might grow heedless of her chief reason for being in Kent.

And Todd was fully occupied. He explained over breakfast about the check-up he must undergo at the nearby hospital, though without adding that he expected this to be his final visit there. From there he should go to Headcorn airfield, for one last time. None of his fellow US airmen remained in Kent now, but he was trying to discover where Jane Richards had gone with that man of hers. He'd also been asked to attend to certain matters at the base before quitting the area.

And still he hadn't told Sheila, had not spoiled their new fulfilment with word that he was likely to leave. Tomorrow.

The children spent the morning playing in nearby fields. After the lunch Elizabeth Darnton provided, Sheila took them to see Fred and May in Benenden. This was what Johnnie wanted, but Gloria adored the farm as well, tottering about after her brother on sturdy legs, giggling while she watched the animals. Keeping an eye on them, Sheila sat with May in the sunny farmyard; bringing her up to date with all that had happened. May was glad to hear that Jane had been found, and then appalled to learn of the woman's departure.

"Are you looking for her again now?"

"I was hoping to, but I've got problems of my own." She related Edward's threat to take Barbara from her, but no details of the adultery accelerating the divorce. The facts were too cruel to bear mentioning.

Sheila explained she expected to have to return to Yorkshire, yet again before she'd done enough. "It's lucky Todd is around, or I don't know what I'd do about Johnnie and Gloria. You do remember Todd?"

May had not forgotten him. "But I heard all the Yanks had moved on now, isn't that right?"

Sheila told her of Todd's crash-landing, and his injuries. "Thank goodness he wasn't hurt more seriously."

Mrs Darnton had the evening meal almost ready when Sheila arrived back at the house with the children. Todd had come in minutes before and was waiting in the sitting-room to give her news of Jane after the children ran off to see what was cooking.

"She's no longer anywhere near here, I'm afraid. I don't have an address for her, but I gather she's with that guy we saw, posing as his wife. In East Anglia somewhere. I ought to be able to learn more when I move on."

"Move?" Sheila echoed, alarm drying her throat as she panicked.

"Afraid so. The hospital discharged me at last. Except for having this plaster cast removed — and that can be done elsewhere — no further treatment."

"Well, that's good, of course, but —" She swallowed, sighed. "But if you won't be here what can I do with . . ." Aware of Johnnie and his sister now standing hand-in-hand near the door, her voice fell to a whisper. "With these two?"

"I am so sorry, honey, I know this puts you in a spot. But there isn't a thing I can do. I can only suggest that you take them along with you."

Sheila sighed again. "It's to be hoped Johnnie likes Hardaker Farm better than he did before. If he starts going downhill again, this entire exercise will have been wasted." And she couldn't bear that, she had been back and forth between the crises — here and at home — so many times that she was losing count of the journeys.

Todd's grey gaze linked with hers, held on, questioning her.

Sheila smiled. "Except for last night, naturally."

They both had possessions to pack after their meal with Elizabeth Darnton, who offered to help by preparing the children for bed. Sheila accepted gratefully.

Since hearing Todd's news her head was thumping, feeling so restricted that she felt as if a metal band was confining her skull. In not permitting herself to think, she was willing her body not to feel. There was only tonight. She might not see him for weeks afterwards. How would she ever endure?

Sheila took a couple of Aspros to ease her headache. They failed to have that effect, but made her drowsy. She struggled to recall where the children's things had been put only so recently when she'd unpacked everything here. Gathering up their belongings, trying to pack any that would not be required before they set out in the morning, she noticed she was moving more and more slowly.

When she had packed everything that she could, she went to find Todd. He and Mrs Darnton were in the sitting-room, talking. Sheila felt she had to join them for this last evening — Elizabeth Darnton had been such a lovely hostess, taking in the four of them.

By ten o'clock Sheila was compelled to excuse herself or fall asleep in the chair. The other two were talking still. Mrs Darnton had just said how thankful she had been to have their company.

Todd went upstairs at a quarter to eleven, limped along to knock quietly on Sheila's door.

When there was no response he opened it softly. She was sleeping. Between the bed and the darkened window were suitcases and various boxes, packed with her belongings and the children's, all left open for the addition of further items in the morning.

She had looked exhausted at dinner tonight; would have an early start tomorrow. He himself would have an even earlier departure. He leaned over to kiss her forehead, but knew he shouldn't disturb her.

And he needed to get away to his own room. Seeing Sheila like this, surrounded by all the trappings of a journey that would take the three of them away from him, he felt totally bereft. So unmanned by even the thought of losing them that his heart screamed the loss could be forever. It was so terrible. If he lingered he surely would give way to all this emotion. He would never, ever steel himself to leave her.

Sheila was awake when he looked in at dawn. Awake but barely conscious, dazed by seeing him already in uniform.

"What time is it, Todd?"

"Early yet. But I do have to go, honey." He came to the bed, leaned over and kissed her, but on her cheek as he might kiss one of the children. "I'll phone you at your home number, find out how things are going. When I get leave I'll come see you — wherever. Up there in

Yorkshire, or if you've got things settled and are back in Kent."

"Take care, Todd." Words were so futile, so dreadfully inadequate.

"Sure will. And you, sweetheart." Another kiss, on the top of her head. "See you, Sheila."

She heard voices distantly, Todd's and Mrs Darnton's. And afterwards the outer door closing, the limp of his footsteps as he walked to the jeep, its engine starting up, Todd driving away. Out of her life?

Why did she feel that? Because of that other loss, of the destruction of her home life, the uncertainty regarding her future? She wanted to scream her desolation.

The postman, whistling, advanced up the path. The letterbox clattered, mail dropped to the marble floor. Her envelope would be there. Todd was no longer here to bear the difficulties with her.

But if that solicitor's letter had arrived, she must be preparing to be on her way. She also must reserve time to show their hostess the consideration such willing assistance had earned her. And she had to explain to Johnnie and the little one about their journey.

Life had to go on.

And if it seemed now to be less of a life in Todd's absence, she would learn to live for the future, however insubstantial that seemed. For the time when he would come to see them again. And even, please God, when this long-protracted war finally ended, a time when they might be free to consider building towards their own happiness.

She could not be happy without him. Edward had gone out of her life, lacerating her feelings so dreadfully that she might never have risked another relationship. But already there was Todd — Todd, who was preventing her emotional hibernation, proving to her he would fulfil needs she was only beginning to recognise.

When Sheila went downstairs and opened the solicitor's letter, though, she wondered if she could ever be happy, even with Todd. Despite being prepared for the letter's content, reading the bald words that Edward was attempting to take Barbara away from her hit really hard. Anguished, she steeled herself against crying out. What would she do if he won? How on earth would she survive if she no longer had her daughter? These recent trips to Kent had shown her how just a few days away from home made her yearn for Barbara.

She read more from the documents, resenting the idea that Edward imagined he could get away with suing her for desertion, but it felt nothing like the pain generated by the prospect of losing her child.

So close to tears she was having to breathe deeply to control her emotions, she became aware that someone was watching her.

Johnnie's little brown face was full of concern as he stood in the doorway. "Are you poorly,

Auntie Sheila? Me and Gloria's having our breakfast."

"No, no — I'm all right. I'm coming now."

Evidently sensing something was wrong, Elizabeth Darnton fussed over the children throughout breakfast, chatting cheerfully about the birds in the garden, the squirrels she'd seen, and the rabbits that came to savage her vegetables; anything to keep some kind of conversation going.

"Are you fit to travel, dear?" she asked Sheila anxiously, while Johnnie was in the bathroom.

"Yes yes, thanks. I'll be OK. I've got to get home or I'll never have this wretched business settled." But she was sick of these journeys, back and forth, back and forth, covering the same ground, and never getting anything to come right.

Gloria was enchanted by trains. Her enthusiasm began in the first one that they took all the way up to London. Packed, as usual, with men in uniform — some with evident wounds, all of them looking shattered — their compartment still delighted the child.

Despite Sheila's frequent intervention, Gloria couldn't resist toddling from one passenger to the next, saying 'Hello' and winning smiles for tired faces. Johnnie was amused by her excitement, saying little but turning repeatedly to Sheila, dark eyes shining, teeth gleaming in a grin as he watched. His expression seemed to say how satisfied he was to see Gloria happy, but also to relish his own, more mature, understanding that his sister was to be indulged.

"Her hair is pretty," he whispered to Sheila once. "People like little girls that look nice." And still he smiled, wholeheartedly, with no atom of resentment in his eyes.

You've come on a lot, Sheila thought. Returning to Kent hasn't been wasted for you. She only hoped to goodness that the next few weeks were not about to undo all that. As soon as her own immediate worries were sorted out, she would need to give careful thought to the future of these two children.

If Todd were perhaps staying somewhere near the spot where Jane's chap was based . . . Mid-thought, she stopped, horrified. Todd had not told her where his new posting was, she had no idea where he would be. Three parts asleep this morning, she hadn't had the wit to ask. Last night they didn't manage to have the long talk she'd intended. God, she hoped that he would ring her at Hardaker Farm, and soon. She could not bear more than a day or so of being isolated from him.

Although the children were very good all the way up to Yorkshire, Sheila couldn't have been more thankful when their last train finally pulled into Halifax station. She flung herself at Nat Hardaker who was waiting on the platform. He had telephoned Mrs Darnton that morning, hoping to catch Sheila before they set out, and had been told which train they intended to take from London.

Gloria was sleepy and dozed off on Sheila's lap as soon as they were in the car. Johnnie had gravely shaken Nat's hand when he said hello, and was now chatting about the places they were passing.

"I remember that," he said, pointing off to the right to the parish church. "And you go along there to the moor and the swings," he added a little while afterwards, amazing Sheila, who could recall only one occasion when he had been taken to Savile Park.

As her father took the road out towards the Calder valley, Johnnie spotted more landmarks, and his enthusiasm seemed to increase. Sheila caught Nat glancing sideways at the boy sitting beside him, looking rather bemused by the extent to which he had changed.

Thank goodness he seems to like the place now, thought Sheila, glad to have these signs that perhaps Johnnie would no longer be miserable here. She herself was feeling quite strange. In some ways relieved to be nearing home, but also aware that the visits to Kent had changed *her*, maybe even more than they had changed the lad. She could not deny that, these days, she did not feel she belonged here so completely as she had in the past.

Her mother was standing at the farmhouse door, and bent down with her arms extended for Johnnie. He ran from the car to be hugged. Sheila smiled, seeing Enid Hardaker's delight. Gloria was beginning to wake up, looked for a moment as if she might wail, but when she noticed her brother was being hugged, decided she wanted to join in.

"So you're Johnnie's little sister!" Enid exclaimed, holding out her free arm while the boy bounced around, still clinging to her hand.

Barbara came running out from the kitchen and launched herself at her mother. "I didn't know you'd only be away such a little while, I've been marking off the days on the calendar I made at school. 'Cos at first Gran said you might be in Kent a long time."

From kissing her mother, Barbara turned to look at Johnnie. "You've grown," she declared. "And you're not as skinny."

"I've got a sister now," he announced. But then he remembered something and frowned. "Where are they?"

"Where are who, Johnnie love?" Enid enquired.

"Them two, Billy and Louise."

"Oh, they went back to their mummies," Nat told him, after locking the car and striding into the house.

"Super!" Johnnie yelled, and ran along on Nat's heels. He gave the impression of being eager to become reacquainted with everything about the farm.

Were those other two evacuees the chief source of his earlier regression? Sheila wondered. Had their attitude to his colour been the start of all his problems? She hadn't forgotten Johnnie's mention of the stories they had plagued him with in the early mornings. They seemed to have enjoyed tormenting him simply because, to them, he looked different.

Sheila made an appointment the following morning to see her solicitor. She couldn't bear to wait any longer than she was obliged to before putting him right on who had left whom in the first instance, and also to explain that her visits to Kent had only ever been just that — *visits*.

"I see," said Laurence Crowther seriously, when she finished repeating what she had told him previously. He thumbed through the documents in front of him on the desk. "Well, I'll certainly bring this to the attention of my opposite number. I notice that your original version of events does, indeed, show your husband as the one whose conduct created those initial difficulties."

"Difficulties? He broke up our marriage — I thought I made that plain enough when I saw you before. And he's got no right to even try to obtain custody of Barbara. He's sleeping with my sister, after all — you can't tell me that's a suitable home for a little girl."

"Well, no — on the face of it, I'm bound to agree . . ."

Then why didn't you make certain that the facts could not be misinterpreted in Edward's favour? Sheila wondered. But she didn't ask the solicitor that. She felt rather in awe of him still, and she wasn't sure how he would react to being criticised.

"Will you do everything possible then to make sure Edward doesn't succeed in taking Barbara away from me? And that he doesn't end up suing me? This was quite bad enough as it stood, without him turning the tables on me."

She wished she was more certain of how to cope with the whole business of a divorce. No one in her family — in fact, nobody she knew — had gone through the experience. As well as having no one to consult, this increased the feeling that it was all too awful to be mentioned.

Not entirely happy she had achieved very much that day, Sheila returned to the farm determined to throw herself into some hard physical work. It had succeeded in the past when she'd been determined to endure simply by keeping busy.

She was glad to see the children were playing amicably together in one corner of the field nearest to the farmhouse. Barbara seemed to enjoy 'mothering' Gloria and was trying to teach her to make daisy-chains. Johnnie, who appeared to have rediscovered his tongue with a vengeance, was regaling them with details of the party he'd attended at Headcorn airfield.

"There was a girl nearly like you," he confided to Barbara. "Only prettier."

Whoops! thought Sheila, but her daughter sounded unperturbed. "I'm the prettiest girl there is, some of the time, my Dad says. But everybody has their off-days. My Gran told me."

That sounds like Enid Hardaker, thought Sheila, smiling to herself before she called to the children on her way to join the Land girls.

The time spent away from the farm meant that she'd grown unaccustomed to hard work. When she finished for the day, she was exhausted and aching in every bone. With the children around at mealtimes there had been no opportunity for really answering her mother's inquiry as to how the visit to the solicitor had gone. She had merely said, "All right, I think." By the time Barbara and the other two were in bed, Sheila didn't feel like talking about it. She also needed to tidy the cottage, and do some washing. Even though she'd been in Kent for only a few days, there had been no chance of catching up with laundry while they were staying with Mrs Darnton.

Yorkshire seemed very quiet, with few aircraft overhead and, thank goodness, none of those screeching doodlebugs. Although in some ways welcome, this quiet did make her feel rather detached from life. A feeling which increased the unreality of the future she faced alone at the cottage with her daughter.

Barbara had asked tonight if Johnnie and Gloria would always live at the farm now. Sheila told her no, it was just a temporary arrangement, until they went back to their mother. Or fathers, she reflected now, wondering how she would set about tracing the two men responsible, should Jane never turn up again.

A telephone call from Todd brought news of Jane Richards, but it was news which made Sheila's spirits sink. The airman she was with had been posted abroad, and Jane had gone with him.

"But I can't look after these two for ever!" Sheila exclaimed. "And in any case that wouldn't be right." She told Todd she felt obliged to locate Johnnie's father. "Trouble is I don't know where to begin." And then there was Gloria's father — who on earth was he?

"Don't worry about it, honey. I'm going to come see you, soon as I get leave. We'll talk things through, decide what's best. You're not on your own remember . . ."

The prospect of Todd's visit was the only brightness amid all the problems. Despite her interview with Laurence Crowther, the solicitor representing Edward was still insisting they had a case for proving that *she* had deserted him. And Pauline and Edward were making a great show of creating a stable family home, where Barbara would be adored. Even when her own solicitor assured her they would be unlikely to win, Sheila continued to feel weighed down by this massive anxiety.

When Todd telephoned again to check if it would be OK for him to stay at Hardaker Farm for the second weekend in September, Sheila clung to the thought of seeing him as the one thing that might help her to survive.

Counting the intervening days seemed to make them drag, but she couldn't stop herself from doing so. And then she began counting the hours, crossing off each batch of twenty-four as she went up to bed. During the week preceding his visit, she told the children that Uncle Todd was coming, and smiled more frequently when Johnnie repeatedly told Barbara all about him.

Todd was due to arrive on the Friday night. Wanting to cook him a special meal, Sheila had asked what time to expect him but he hadn't been able to say. In addition to being uncertain how long the journey would take by jeep, he could not be sure until the very last moment he could have use of the vehicle.

"But I shall get there, you may count on that. I'll take the train if the jeep is needed on the base here."

She had been saving her meat ration, eating only vegetables for days on end in order to have some good stewing beef for a casserole. Kept hot in the oven it would taste just as lovely even if Todd happened to be late arriving.

Thankful to see Sheila smiling at last, Enid Hardaker had told her to have an hour off from farm work in order to take time over preparing the meal. And Sheila had revelled in every minute of getting the dish ready for the oven. Todd is coming, her heart kept singing, Todd is coming today. Todd. The only good factor in her life during all these dreadful months.

Once the casserole was cooking, she went back to the fields. Some of the Land Army girls had the weekend off and one or two, who lived a distance away, set off early for their homes. Their happiness accelerated her own excitement, making her glad that in spite of the war there were these highlights to give them heart.

Sheila sat in the farm kitchen with the children while the family had high tea; she herself ate nothing, because she would wait for ever to enjoy her meal with Todd. Tomorrow, she would be sharing him with the children, letting him get to know her parents. Tonight, he was to be just hers.

Eight o'clock came and she felt at a loose end. She helped her mother get Johnnie and Gloria ready for bed, and said goodnight to them at the farm. Barbara had gone to bed also, persuaded by the promise that she could read for half-an-hour if her head was on the pillow by eight.

Too agitated to read or listen to the wireless, Sheila willed herself not to pace up and down the room, and try not to dash to the window every five minutes in order to see if a jeep was turning in at the farmyard.

By nine o'clock sick disappointment had descended, and with it an anxiety which would not surrender to her own repeated assertions that Todd had only been held up somewhere en route. She ran upstairs to check that Barbara was sleeping soundly, then sped across to the farm.

"Is he late, love?" Nat asked, his attention

mainly taken by the nine o'clock news on the wireless.

"Aye, I suppose the roads must be busy. Or happen he's had to resort to coming by train. That was on the cards."

"You don't think he's got lost, do you?" Enid enquired seriously.

"I did explain how to find us. And he's used to going all over the place in England by now."

Sheila couldn't remain across at the farm for more than a few minutes, Barbara shouldn't be left on her own at the cottage. She didn't really know what she was doing here, except that it was nearer to the telephone.

Back in her own kitchen, she turned off the oven. If Todd did arrive tonight, it would be too late to eat a heavy meal. The stew would do for tomorrow. With plenty of vegetables, there would be enough for the kids as well. But it wouldn't be the same. Nothing would be the same as she'd visualised it.

When the clock struck midnight, Sheila went up to bed. She didn't expect to sleep, and it was no surprise when she lay worrying throughout the night. Surely if something had come up to prevent him from setting out, Todd would have let her know? Had there been an accident? And if so, where? How on earth would she learn what had happened when she wasn't even sure which route he'd intended taking.

On the Saturday her own distress and feeling of anti-climax was worsened by the children.

Johnnie's little face seemed to shrink with disappointment when at breakfast time in the farmhouse he asked where his Uncle Todd was. Even Barbara, who'd never met Todd, became miserable when she understood the promised excitement seemed likely to be denied her.

Trying to distract them, Sheila willed herself to put the dreadful worry behind her; but how could she dismiss it?

When Sunday dawned and there was still no word, she wondered how she would even drag herself from the bed to face another day. Only Barbara's demands for something to eat got Sheila up and moving zombie-like about the kitchen.

She was there when Nat came across to call her to the telephone.

"Is it Todd?" she asked, running to the farmhouse with him.

"It was some woman spoke to me. Of course, it could have been the operator . . ."

"Hello?" said Sheila into the receiver. Her heart had begun thudding agitatedly, ringing in her ears until she was afraid she wouldn't be able to hear what was said.

"Mrs Calvert? Sheila? It's Elizabeth Darnton . . ."

Oh, Sheila thought, is that all? Have I left something behind at her place perhaps? They had departed in an awful hurry.

"Sheila, my dear — there's no easy way to tell you this, I'm afraid. Todd left my number, asked me to contact you if — if I heard anything. I'm terribly sorry to have to tell you that his plane came down. Just off the French coast, I believe. His commanding officer says they're afraid he's to be posted as 'missing'. There was no trace of him surviving."

Chapter Thirteen

He was just a friend, a very good friend to us — mainly to Johnnie."

It was what she had said to her father, and afterwards to her mother as well on that appalling Sunday morning when she could hardly force herself to explain. And just as it was all she could say when she recovered sufficiently to speak, later on it was what she told herself when emotion overwhelmed her.

That first day was bad enough, but Sheila felt numbed by the news, so numbed that she could not believe it was true. Though, God knows, Elizabeth Darnton had sounded so sad she would convince anyone of the reality behind those dreadful words.

Sheila had not told Johnnie, would not tell him. The lad had responded so well lately, just by knowing the American lieutenant. Since returning to Yorkshire she'd seen even more clearly how beneficial Todd's influence had been. The boy was far more communicative than ever before; and knowing how ineffectual Jane had seemed, she was in no doubt who was responsible for the change.

"I don't want Johnnie to find out about Todd," Sheila warned her parents on the Monday morning. She herself was devastated, but felt certain that Johnnie could be even worse. She at least had Barbara, and her own mother and father, whereas that poor little lad would have no one until he was reunited with Jane — or until they were able to trace his father. Sheila began to suspect she ought to be putting some effort into trying to find the man.

For the present she would have to remain in Yorkshire, certainly until her solicitor was able to confirm he had corrected Edward's assumption that he would be allowed to get away with claiming custody of Barbara. Perhaps when she had that assurance she might feel better about everything else.

Even the prospect of eventually solving the problems surrounding the divorce did nothing to motivate her to set out yet again to search for Johnnie's family. The thought of Kent without Todd was unbearable. Each time she remembered the place her mind reconstructed so many vivid scenes from their time together.

He *can't* be dead, she thought, and recognised the classic signs of a subconscious instinct protecting her from unacceptable fact. She could not grieve in front of other people, which made her wretchedness even more intense. As well as the need to prevent Johnnie from discovering what had happened, she had to preserve the illusion that Todd had been no more than a friend. No one must begin to suspect that their relationship had become intimate. If Edward were to hear even a hint that there might have been a personal element deeper than friendship, he would seize on it as ammunition.

Sheila could see how her husband would relish declaring that all the time she was away from home she had been committing adultery. With Todd no longer alive to confirm they had made love only the once, her word alone could bear witness to the true situation.

And she certainly wasn't going to deny what had happened between them — she could not deny their love. Those few hours when they had belonged together seemed so infinitely precious. Memories of that brief period were becoming so potent they seared right through her. At night, the only time when she was free from masking her sorrow, she yearned with every part of her being to be with him again.

The envelope came on the Tuesday morning. Todd's handwriting made her spirits soar, nourished her self-delusion that news of his death had been an error.

She tore it open, read greedily his opening: *'Sheila honey,'* and began to devour the words that followed. The letter was short, hardly more than a note, and none of it personal to her.

> *'I have news of Jane, from a buddy of the guy she went off with. Seems she confided she was never legally married to Johnnie's father, but*

that he was a doctor at a sanatorium in Kent. Hope this helps you begin tracing him immediately. Meanwhile, I'm trying to get a message to Jane that you are looking after the children.

'Will talk when I see you. Forgive the haste, just about to take off again.

Fondest love,

Todd'

He's still alive! she thought, radiant with hope as all the dreadful despair fell away from her.

And then she looked at the date at the top of the page. Thursday of last week. Reality swamped her again, compelling her to understand that delays in the post meant this had been written before Todd took to the air on that last fateful mission.

Just looking at his writing made her cry. And she hadn't meant to weep, had sensed since Elizabeth Darnton's call that if she permitted herself to let go she risked disintegrating completely. It felt no more than a week or two since the start of all the upset between herself and Edward had made her go to pieces. She hadn't forgotten how alarming it was to feel her emotions slipping out of control.

Whatever else occurred, she had to keep going. There were the children to consider; always the children. Her own little girl, who didn't deserve a mum who wallowed in self-pity. Johnnie and Gloria as well, those two kids who were already deserted — however temporarily — by their mother. The pair of them were beginning to settle quite well across at the farm, but they needed her in addition to Enid Hardaker. Now, it seemed, Johnnie needed her more than ever — for who else could find his father?

This first clue to the man's identity was too important to ignore. Todd had made time to let her know. She owed it to him to follow this up. She must will herself to avoid giving in to tears and, for his sake, put all she had into tracing that doctor.

She promised herself that as soon as she had better news about the divorce she would give this matter her attention. Here was the sign that she mustn't even contemplate not following up a lead.

It was something to occupy her. Making plans for another journey to Kent blocked out some of the memories of Todd, some small degree of the pain generated each time she remembered that his plane had been lost. It seemed to Sheila that in a strange way *he* was now providing her with a means of enduring.

Later that day, when she had helped as usual with getting Johnnie and Gloria ready for bed, and afterwards crossed to the cottage to hurry Barbara along to her bedroom, Sheila recalled something.

Surely the hospital where Jane had once worked had been a sanatorium? Wasn't it likely that the doctor with whom the woman had had this child was someone she met there?

Sheila thought of writing to Benenden Hospital to enquire, then realised how difficult the explanation would be. She did not know the man's name. The only thing she could assume was that he was dark-skinned. Deeply aware of all the repercussions Johnnie's colour had generated, she had become inhibited about people's potential reactions. She could not think of any tactful way to put her supposition about the boy's parentage down on paper.

Although daunted by the prospect, she began planning to set out for Kent yet again. This time, she intended going there alone. Her mother was willing to look after all three children for a day or two. Everyone but Sheila herself seemed in a good mood these days — renewed by optimism. On the Sunday when she heard about Todd's plane coming down, her parents and the farm workers had been celebrating the news that allied troops had captured Zeebrugge. Ten days later they had taken Boulogne and by the end of the month had added Calais to the list of conquests.

When the next communication from her solicitor confirmed the divorce was beginning to go through according to her own original instructions, Sheila took that as the sign she must not delay her journey south any longer.

As soon as she arrived in Kent, she realised she had been wise to leave the children at Hardaker Farm. She was in no condition for keeping up a cheerful front for anyone's sake. As her taxi took her from the station to the sanatorium, every lane reminded her of Todd. She seemed to hear his distinctive voice, and even the car's engine appeared to take on the sound of the jeep he'd driven.

When they stopped before the hospital and she paid the cabbie, Sheila willed her feelings into submission. You've got to do this, she silently commanded herself, you're the only person who is going to trace Johnnie's father — and when you've succeeded you can run back home to Yorkshire.

Sheila recognised the woman who was on duty as the person she had spoken with on the previous occasion. Maybe this is a good omen she thought, as she began explaining what she needed to know.

After the earlier enquiry she had noted the dates when Jane was first employed in the kitchens. This simplified her quest, but finding the right words concerning the doctor she was seeking was anything but easy.

"There's no way of skirting around the details," she admitted to the woman. "The son Jane had is brown-skinned, which seems to indicate that his father was of a similar colour, or darker."

"Quite so," was the response. "Since I wasn't here at the time I'm afraid I wouldn't know anything about that."

"I understand that," said Sheila. "But I wondered — well, this doctor would probably have a foreign name, wouldn't he. I thought perhaps your records —"

"Look, Mrs Calvert, this really is not my province. We're not permitted to give out personal details concerning anyone employed here, past or present. If you're so concerned about tracing the father, shouldn't you be asking this Jane Richards?"

"I would if only I could." Sheila swallowed, sighed. "It's all so complicated. Jane ran off you see, with an American airman. So far as I'm aware, she's still abroad with him."

"And this child then, is . . . ?"

"Staying with me. And it's child*ren*, there's a girl as well."

"You mean the mother dumped them on you?" astonishment removed some of the austerity in the woman's expression.

"More or less. Only we didn't realise at the time she truly wasn't coming back for the kids."

"You can't be saying this doctor you're trying to trace has two children he's showing no interest in?"

Sheila shook her head. "Only Johnnie is his. Gloria is white — I believe her father's another Yank."

"Hang on . . . That rings a bell. When you called here that other time it set some of the women talking. They remembered Jane Richards having the little girl, because they said there were rumours she'd had to find somewhere else to live. Well, people might tolerate one mistake and the boy being born, but having another kiddie and her still not married . . ."

"I can't look after them for ever. In any case, not knowing his father is harming Johnnie, especially now that his mother has walked out on him."

"What year did you say you think the boy was conceived?"

The woman had taken out a fat ledger. When told the approximate date, she began flicking through pages.

"I'm not telling you anything," she said to Sheila but turned the open pages towards her on the desk. "If you will just excuse me for a moment, I must attend to something in the office."

There was one name only that seemed at all foreign. Dr Nathaniel Isiolo. According to the information listed, he had been at Benenden for only a few months, in 1938. From there he had transferred to Guy's Hospital in London.

"Thank you so much," said Sheila when the woman returned.

"Not at all, I haven't done anything," she responded, smiled, and added: "Good luck."

Sheila was turning away from the hospital, already preoccupied with plans to go up to London, when someone called to her from the opposite side of the road.

"Sheila! It is, isn't it? I was only saying to Fred the other night that we hadn't heard anything about you for a while."

It was May. Looking younger somehow, no doubt fully recovered from her illness. Sheila crossed to greet her.

May's insistence that she must stay the night

with them meant it was the following day before Sheila finally arrived at Guy's Hospital. The elderly couple had been so kind though that she could not regret the delay, and she was thankful for a good night's sleep to prepare her.

The hospital almoner was the first person Sheila saw — she'd been directed there in error by someone who had only half listened to her request for information. As it happened, however, the woman understood the importance of Sheila's quest; better still, she could suggest a doctor who might possibly be the one involved.

"I can never remember his name properly, but he is from Africa somewhere. And I know he's been here since before the war, the period you mention. Trouble is, I can't put you in touch with him, not today. He's on extended leave, you see — gone home to — to Kenya or somewhere. Yes, Kenya, I think it is, to visit his sick father."

"So that's where he's from then?"

"Originally, yes. Africa, certainly — as I say, I seem to remember it's Kenya. He came to this country to train. Did I say that was before the war? I suppose somebody here could have a note of where he was prior to joining us. That's if the records survived the blitz; not all of them have."

Sheila left Guy's Hospital with the almoner's assurance that she would make enquiries as soon as possible. She could contact Sheila if the doctor's name was Nathaniel Isiolo, which would seem to confirm that he was working at Benenden before transferring to Guy's.

Afterwards, the rest — making that difficult approach to him — would be up to Sheila herself.

By the time she learned the doctor's surname was Isiolo and he had indeed been at Benenden hospital, Sheila had had more than enough time to work out what she must do. Weeks had gone by, weeks during which she had given up hope of hearing anything further. And yet she had turned her mind to composing a preliminary letter to him. Weighing what she might say had been infinitely preferable to dwelling on the gap that existed in her life now Todd had been lost. Feeling she couldn't talk to anyone about how much he had meant to her still made accepting his death terribly difficult.

Her letter to Dr Isiolo was short, and stated simply that she was a friend of Jane Richards and was enquiring if he could be the person who had known Jane during his stay in Kent. She decided to give no hint of Johnnie's existence. That piece of news — and she assumed it would be news to him — was hardly the sort of thing to impart by mail.

The wait for a reply was long, so many months passed that Sheila concluded he either did not know Jane, or was determined to avoid renewing an acquaintance with her. She also wondered if he'd decided to remain in his homeland. So much had changed. The war had finally ended; families everywhere were reassessing their future, making plans. She herself had felt hurt by the air of celebration. *Of course,* she was thankful that they at last had peace but, deserted by her husband and alienated from her sister, life promised little to look forward to. And continuing to feel she could only grieve in private for Todd, Sheila was becoming haunted by an obsession with what might have been. If only they had been granted a future together. Normally strong-willed, she had become unable to steel herself against reflecting on the life they could have had.

Although so many months had gone by, Sheila was elated when she recognised the Kenyan postmark. She tore open the envelope, and was agreeably surprised.

'Dear Mrs Calvert,

I hope that you will forgive my delay in answering your letter. My father was seriously ill and I took a temporary post out here in order to remain near at hand. Since he died I naturally became involved in attending to his affairs.

I do, nevertheless, recall Jane well — as one of the first people in your country to make me feel welcome there. You do not say whether or not you are trying to arrange a meeting between us. If that should be so I have nothing against seeing Jane once more, although I have to say that I can visualise no reconciliation after the elapse of all these years.

I shall be returning to England next week and have promised to visit one of my former colleagues in Kent before starting work again at Guy's. I will telephone you once I land in England, when we may see what arrangements we might make.

Yours sincerely,
Nathaniel Isiolo'

The winter's day was brightened by his promised telephone call. Nathaniel Isiolo had such a delightful voice, deep and well-modulated, Sheila could imagine his manner of dealing with patients would be absolutely charming. He enquired carefully if she might be able to meet him somewhere in the south. Travelling to Yorkshire would be difficult for him as he was due to start work again in a few days when he would be obliged to make up for his lengthy absence.

"I suppose I could come down to Kent; that's where you are, isn't it?" Just in time, she stopped before promising to bring Johnnie with her. The telephone was no better than writing as a means of conveying news of the boy's existence.

"I am staying with friends in Tenterden, do you know it at all?"

"Not really I'm afraid." All-too-vividly, she recalled Todd's similar question. God, how she still ached for him!

"Then I shall give you this address, my friends will be happy for you to call on me here. Will — will Jane be with you?"

"Oh, no. No — I'm not even sure where she's been since the war ended." Sheila suddenly became aware of how idiotic the whole wretched business must seem to someone who didn't know the entire story. "It's just — well, there's something you ought to hear, and it'll be best said in person."

"How mysterious," Dr Isiolo remarked lightly. His warm chuckle came down the line. "I must thank you then for going to all this trouble in order that we may meet."

What *am* I letting myself in for? Sheila wondered as she hung up the receiver. Taking Johnnie back to Kent again without giving him any explanation would be difficult enough, but nothing when compared to the explaining she must do to Dr Nathaniel Isiolo.

Planning the trip took precedence over all other worries, especially when Sheila realised that she would have to take Gloria along as well. She was hoping against hope they would be able to contact Jane in order to formalise arrangements for Johnnie's future. In which case, someone would have to convince the woman that she ought to take responsibility for her little girl.

There was also Barbara. They had become very close since Edward moved out, and now that a few peacetime treats were available, were enjoying them together. Although maturing fast, Barbara wasn't yet of an age when missing a few days' schooling would do any harm. There were other reasons too why Sheila did not wish to leave her daughter at the farm. Enid Hardaker seemed to have aged this winter. A severe bout of flu had left her easily tired and, however willing, less likely to cope very readily with an energetic six-year-old like Barbara.

Sheila had kept in touch with Elizabeth Darnton ever since that dreadful telephone call about Todd's plane. Ringing her now, she was pleased to learn that she and the children would be welcome to stay with her again.

"But can you manage one more this time?" Sheila asked, hoping this wouldn't be too much of an imposition.

There was a smile in Elizabeth Darnton's voice. "I shall love to meet her. Do you know — I've felt ever since you left that there was something missing, that the children were all that had prevented me from becoming stale and stodgy."

As soon as he heard that Barbara was going to Kent, Edward demanded to have a few hours with her before they set out. Seeing how perturbed Sheila was by the prospect, Enid offered to take her granddaughter to Pauline's home.

"No, Mum, it's all right, thank you. I've got to face this some time. I can hardly spend the rest of my life avoiding those two. I shall leave Barbara with them for a while, but I don't want her spending the night there."

Barbara was elated when they set out on the Saturday afternoon — dancing along beside her mother both before and after the short bus journey.

Seeing her own husband and her sister together felt just as dreadful as Sheila had anticipated, but she willed herself not to show what she was feeling. She would not stay for more than the few minutes needed to explain what time she expected Edward to bring their daughter back to Hardaker Farm.

He and Pauline objected immediately to being obliged to return Barbara that night. As Sheila might have expected, the girl herself added her own insistence that she ought to be allowed to sleep at her Aunt Pauline's.

"I'm sorry," Sheila told them firmly. "I can't agree to that. I don't want her growing up with your ideas about what's right and what's wrong, about — being faithful."

Her outspokenness made Pauline wince, but Edward appeared unmoved.

"I'm entitled to more than a few hours of my own daughter's company. You must understand that."

"We'll discuss this when Pauline's your wife. Until then I refuse to compromise. And if you try anything on I'll have to see my solicitor about whether or not the atmosphere here is having a bad influence —"

"You can be very cruel," Pauline began. "You ought to think what you're putting Teddy through by being intractable."

Sheila snorted. "That comes well from you, when the two of you have connived to ruin everything for me." Somehow, she managed a smile when she turned from them to Barbara. "See you tonight, love. Daddy'll make sure you're home before nine o'clock."

She left them then to trudge back to the farm

through the bitter north wind instead of waiting for the next bus. Anything was better than remaining in that house a moment longer.

Relieved to see Edward escorting their daughter home that evening, the tension generated by fearing that he would go against her wishes faded. As soon as she opened the cottage door to them however, she saw that Barbara was in a mutinous frame of mind.

"Daddy says I ought to be staying with them when you go all the way to Kent. He would take me out a lot while you were away."

Hard lines! thought Sheila, but said nothing. These days, Barbara was enjoying this new experience of playing one parent against the other. And Edward, for all his reckless promises, was still in the Army. He was unlikely to have all that much spare time for laying on outings.

"We're not going to be away for long," she reminded her daughter as soon as Edward turned and walked away. "When we come home we'll have some fun together again — and we'll see what we can arrange with your daddy as well."

Barbara was learning that her mother could be firm; also that neither sulking nor screaming cut much ice with her now. And arguments did not work, not when grown-ups could make you do what they wanted.

"All right, Mummy," she said grudgingly. "But I shan't like it in Kent, I know I shan't."

The journey south was better than she anticipated. Johnnie had developed into an intuitive small boy. Sheila was thankful that he sensed without being told that returning to Kent was somehow an expedition made on his behalf. He helped with their bits of light luggage, and insisted on taking hold of the reins to keep his young sister within range at all times.

Seeing how helpful Johnnie was, Barbara decided she was not to be left out, and fussed over Gloria too until Sheila was forced to smile. Those two older kids were like miniature parents pampering their offspring, much to the amusement of their fellow travellers.

Sheila couldn't have been more thankful to be staying with Elizabeth Darnton. That lady's warm welcome — literally with open arms — made the children respond by being quite gregarious. Gloria was becoming quite a chatterbox now, and vied with her brother as well as Barbara, who always reacted well when an adult showed interest in her.

It wasn't until the children were asleep that Mrs Darnton asked how Sheila was. "I couldn't help sensing that you and Todd had become close during that short space of time. You must be missing him?"

Sheila nodded, and tried to smile, though her eyes had misted. "You're the only person who knows. I couldn't say much to my mum and dad — things are in such a tangle anyway, with the divorce and all that . . . Did I tell you my husband moved in with my own sister?"

Strangely, she did not need to say very much

more about Todd. Having Elizabeth Darnton understand made such a difference that Sheila already began to feel less oppressed by his absence. And her hostess was very interested in her attempt to identify Johnnie's father.

"I'm glad you've brought the children to me," she assured Sheila. "I'll enjoy keeping them occupied while you go to meet this doctor."

The address in Tenterden which she had been given was a large house a few yards along the road which led eventually to Appledore. Surrounded by a covering of fresh snow, it looked picturesque and would have felt imposing, had Sheila not already grown accustomed to Mrs Darnton's splendid home.

The door was opened by an elderly man who smiled as he learned her name and was soon taking her coat and ushering her through to introduce Nathaniel Isiolo to her.

Rising as she entered the elegant room, the doctor revealed that he was taller than she had expected; six feet at least. The hand grasping hers was firm, and seemed to convey a quiet strength that must be reassuring to his patients.

"Thank you so much for coming all this way, Mrs Calvert," he began, waiting until she was seated before returning to his own chair. "I must confess to being intrigued, to put it mildly, by the possible reasons behind your determination to contact me. I do hope that you are not intending to keep me in suspense for very much longer?"

Sheila smiled, but felt suddenly inhibited. Nathaniel Isiolo was so very likeable; she didn't want to shatter him by announcing that he had a son.

"Are you pleased to be back in England?" she enquired, intending to work around gradually to more personal questions.

He smiled, displaying very white teeth, and making her realise how handsome he was: with high cheekbones and a nose hardly any broader than her own. His eyes were his best feature, though, dark and arresting, reminding her of Johnnie's.

"Even in winter-time?" He gave the chuckle that had delighted her over the phone. "I always feel this is my second home, so — yes, I *am* pleased to be here. And when I return to Guy's I shall know for sure that I am where I belong."

"And your wife, does she like living over here?" Is she English perhaps? Sheila wondered privately, but could not ask.

"I am not married. Unfortunately, my father had been unwell for many years. I have done what I could to provide for him and for my mother. A small debt, in recognition of the sacrifices he made to enable me to study."

Sheila smiled. "No doubt the satisfaction of your work helps to compensate for any shortcomings in — well, in your home life . . ."

"Perhaps. To be honest, yes, it more than compensates. Except — doesn't every man wish at some time that there were children — people somewhere to whom they might pass on something . . . The things you've learned from life, maybe, the bit of wisdom culled . . . Or even simply the joy to be found in having the right job."

I'll have to tell him now, she thought, and felt her tongue and throat drying out, threatening to choke her. She coughed, swallowed. "Did you ever hear from Jane after you — after — ?"

"— We parted so abruptly?" He shook his head. "Did she tell you what happened?"

"Not at all. Nothing."

"Then how did you learn enough about us to begin to trace me? Why did you even try?" He was looking quite anxious now; a face accustomed to coping in difficult situations tensing because this related to a personal matter. Again, he reminded her of Johnnie.

When Sheila hesitated Nathaniel spoke once more. His voice low, the words prefaced by a sigh.

"She went off, you know. With some local man. I suspected it was only for a fling. I'm afraid Jane was like that. Unfortunately, I never have been. Our differing backgrounds perhaps. The end result was that when, only a short while afterwards, she was on her own again, I refused to see her." He paused for a while, scrutinising Sheila's face. "Does this explain why I did not enthuse about the prospect of seeing Jane again? Why I can think of no good reason why I should welcome her back into my life? That *is* why you've got in touch with me, isn't it?"

"Not really. As I said, I'm not even certain where she is at present." But she could not continue for ever to talk around the subject, even though there was no easy way of telling him the truth. "This will come as rather a shock, I dare say, but I believe you've no need to *wish* you had children. There — there's a boy — Johnnie. Jane's son. He — he's . . ."

"Brown-skinned?" When Sheila nodded he sighed. "How old is this — Johnnie?"

"He was six last March." She watched the dark eyes veil and his deep forehead wrinkle while he made the calculation. "I recall no other black trainee doctor at the sanatorium at that time, and I do not believe there were too many of us living in Kent either." He drew in a long breath.

"It must be a bit of a shock," Sheila began.

"Do you always go in for understatements? I'm absolutely astonished. Being a medical man, I assumed I was fully conversant with avoiding such a — complication. But I do know, of course, that one can slip up." He paused, considering. "Where is he? Or don't you know that either; I suppose he's with his mother?"

"He's not with Jane — she —" Yet again, Sheila hesitated, reluctant to spell out that Nathaniel's son had been abandoned. "As a matter of fact, Johnnie's in Hawkhurst at present, I brought him there. I've been looking after him."

"I hope you're not about to tell me that Jane abandoned him." He sounded angry now, fiercely defensive of the boy who only moments ago had become known to him. When Sheila didn't reply, he went on more quietly: "She never was any good at recognising when someone cared enough to depend on her."

"I think she'd become worn out by looking after them, they got her down."

"Them?" The question emerged as a roar. Sheila realised that she would not like to be on the wrong side of Nathaniel Isiolo when he sensed an injustice. His voice lowered again. "There's more than one child? Not mine, this time."

"A little girl — Gloria. I understand her father's American."

"Ah — the one Jane went abroad with. You did mention . . ."

Something in Sheila's expression told him otherwise. "Seems she's just as feckless as ever," he observed.

She found she was smiling despite the gravity of the situation. "That was my word for her as well."

"You'd better tell me the whole story — or from where you came into their lives."

Nathaniel listened attentively while she related everything she could remember from the time Johnnie had been evacuated to Hardaker Farm. When she reached present day events, Sheila noticed how solemn he was looking and she tensed, steeling herself to accept that Dr Nathaniel Isiolo was about to declare that he wished to leave things as they stood.

"I want to see Johnnie. Before I go up to London, I've got to see him."

"When can I meet him, tomorrow? He sounds nice."

Johnnie was hopping from foot to foot, too excited to run into the dining room where Mrs Darnton had their meal waiting. Sheila had avoided mentioning that Nathaniel Isiolo could be his father, but the boy had nevertheless become enchanted by her description of him.

She was thankful Johnnie was so pleased by the prospect of the introduction. She herself felt sure there'd be a restless night for her while she contemplated the potential outcome of that meeting.

The event itself began more promisingly than she could have anticipated. It seemed to her that as soon as he saw the lad Nathaniel accepted his identity. Going down on one knee in a way that made his height appear far less awesome, he beckoned.

"Come here, Johnnie. Let's take a look at you."

Sheila felt her eyes filling as she watched the lad walking swiftly to him, then holding out his small hand in greeting. Copying Todd.

"Good to know you," Johnnie said as the large brown hand grasped his.

"And to know you, Johnnie," the doctor responded. "It's been a long time."

Before their hands drew apart Johnnie gazed

down at their fingers, comparing skin to skin. He looked fascinated by their colour, then he smiled up at Nathaniel, delighted.

The man grinned back at him. Sheila recognised their kinship, and read in Nathaniel's softening expression confirmation that she was not alone in acknowledging its existence.

They talked, Nathaniel Isiolo's eagerness to tell witnessing to his acceptance of the boy, while he answered a lifetime's questions. Johnnie's dark eyes widened as he learned who this man believed he was; then later something about his Kikuyu heritage.

"Are we going to live in Kenya?" Johnnie asked.

Nathaniel shook his head. "I shall take you there, on a visit, naturally. But England will be my home for a long time. Yours also, I hope." He explained how he had first come here to train, intending to return when qualified. "But I am uneasy about the life there now. And those war years have taught me that when people strive towards a common aim differences of race should not matter." Turning to Sheila, he smiled. "If I ever go home to Kenya, it will not be before I put back some of the good that has come to me through living here in your country."

And wherever you live, she thought, wherever you take Johnnie, I shall at last feel happy about him.

Chapter Fourteen

It was lovely to be so happy for other people that some of the disturbance regarding her own life had slipped to the back of her subconscious. From the moment Nathaniel Isiolo had met Johnnie he had taken command of events, determined to acquire custody of the boy and to provide him with a home. Sheila felt infinitely relieved. Intuition told her that even if the doctor's parentage of Johnnie were never proved, no scientific proof would be needed. And before that first meeting was concluded the little lad clearly adored the man he accepted so trustingly as his father.

Nathaniel took over full responsibility, confident of tracing Jane and certain that he would assert the right to have Johnnie live with him. He told Sheila of the plans he already had for bringing his own mother to England. "I was hoping to install her here in Kent, she'll be pleased to have the boy's company; her grandson's. Her grandson's." Savouring the word, he repeated it, smiling.

Sheila was content to have Johnnie live with her until that time came. With so much responsibility removed from her, she could look forward to those remaining weeks with this boy whom she had grown to love. She would relish the Johnnie who was now so jubilant that he often appeared quite irrepressible.

Elizabeth Darnton remarked on how ebullient he seemed on the day after that visit to Nathaniel, and quickly reassured Sheila when asked if Johnnie was perhaps a little too overwhelming. Gloria seemed to notice the change in her brother, and to take his lead, growing exuberant. Barbara was the only person who was less enthusiastic about her friend's manner.

"Johnnie's silly now, Mummy," she complained. "Always laughing and playing tricks on me. He's always teasing now."

Sheila noted that the three children played together just the same, romping in the garden, building snowmen, or making a slide when the afternoon sun fell beyond the hill and the air grew frosty. Inside the house they loved to huddle in a corner, engaging in conversation which seemed quite earnest.

Glad she wasn't obliged to keep intervening in what the children were doing, Sheila began helping Mrs Darnton in the kitchen. They had been preparing the evening meal together when she went into the living room, and found only Johnnie and his sister there.

"Is Barbara in the bathroom?" she enquired.

"Don't know," said Johnnie.

"Don't think so," Gloria responded, and giggled.

"Up in her bedroom then?" Even as she asked, Sheila wondered why she should feel so uneasy.

A quick dash upstairs told her that Barbara was not in her room, nor was she in any of the other bedrooms, and the bathrooms were empty. Feeling ridiculous as well as anxious, Sheila went to tell Elizabeth Darnton.

Together, they searched every room of the house, each cupboard, and then the garden, the fields beyond.

Gloria came up to them as they returned indoors, tugged at Sheila's skirt. "Bab'ra's not here. She went way."

The girl was too young to give them any lead. Only one person could help them now. Trying not to over-react, Sheila turned to Johnnie.

"Where was Barbara going, Johnnie ? Didn't she say anything?"

"Don't know, Auntie Sheila."

The boy was looking miserably conscious of his inability to help. His face was scrunched up with anxiety, dark eyes narrowing when he looked away from her, down at the shoe he was scuffing against a chair leg. Sorry though she was for him, Sheila was so alarmed she was forced to press for an answer.

"Please try to think, love — Barbara didn't just walk off, did she?"

He shook his head. She steeled herself to be patient with him. He wasn't yet seven, after all, she mustn't demand too much of him. If only she wasn't so desperate to find out *something*, just one thing that might give her a clue to where her daughter had gone.

"Tell me carefully, what were you doing when she ran off?"

"Talking." He was the old Johnnie again, hardly communicating, only this time he appeared guilty.

"What were you talking about?"

"Just — things. Like Gloria might get a new teddy . . ."

Hearing her own name, the toddler stopped playing with a doll Enid had made out of old stockings before they came away from Yorkshire. She beamed up at them.

"Yes, love, and then what?" Sheila persisted, but Gloria's tiny voice answered.

"When my daddy comes," she said, nodding to emphasise her eagerness. "New teddy, and a proper dolly."

"Not *your* daddy, stupid," Johnnie contradicted. "Mine. You haven't got a dad . . ."

"Johnnie," Sheila reproved him, "you shouldn't have said that. It was very unkind, and not true at all." Kids! she thought, making a mental note to talk to the boy about his father — and Gloria's. But that would have to wait. They'd got to find Barbara first, and swiftly; it would be dark within an hour. And the snow was inches deep. There could be another blizzard tonight — it often started again as daylight faded.

"And what did Barbara say?" Sheila persisted.

"Nothing." Johnnie seemed embarrassed, awkward about something. *Concealing something . . . ?*

"What had you said to her?" she demanded, sensing that the words he was keeping to himself hadn't been Barbara's at all.

"He said she hadn't got a daddy," announced Gloria, gazing triumphantly at her brother.

"You promised not to tell," he snapped, sounding as if he was about to cry. He turned to Sheila, and now an appeal for understanding emerged as tears that ran down his brown cheeks. "I've never had a dad before. I've never been the one that was better than other kids."

"Oh, Johnnie, Johnnie!" Sighing, Sheila looked down at him. She couldn't help pitying the lad for wanting to relish what he saw as a new acquisition. He'd always had so little. But this was all beside the point, time was too short to explain anything to him.

"Come on then, tell me — you're going to have to. This is serious, you know. Was it after you'd said that about her dad that Barbara went off?" Her daughter could have run as far as the next farm by now.

Dismally, he nodded.

"She said she had got a daddy, so there!" Gloria chimed in.

"And . . . ? Johnnie, you've got to tell me."

"She was going to fetch him," he muttered.

Fetch? All the way from Yorkshire! Oh, God . . . Sheila couldn't bear to begin to think what might happen to Barbara on the way.

"What time was this?"

"Don't know," Johnnie mumbled.

"Had you had your tea?"

"Squidgy cake, yummy!" said Gloria.

Mrs Darnton came into the living room from the hall where she'd been telephoning the police.

"I'm afraid no one's reported seeing a missing child," she began. "Sheila, I am so sorry . . ."

"It's not your fault, I was here as well, wasn't I? Nobody should have to watch them the whole time. They were only building a snowman, after all. Any road, we're a bit nearer the truth now." She was fastening her coat, putting on her snow-boots. Glancing up, she told Mrs Darnton what Jane's children had revealed. "Knowing our Barbara, she'll have done just that. Set out to fetch her father."

"All that way? How would she know where to start?"

"We passed the station only the other day. She remembered arriving there when we came down to Kent."

"Well, if you think so. But a child of six — wouldn't she be put off by the sheer distance involved?"

"Barbara slept during part of the journey, they all did. And they were playing together. It probably didn't feel all that far to her." She glanced at her watch, sighed. "Look — do you mind keeping an eye on these two for a while. I've got to get to the station."

"Of course I don't mind. But I was going to drive you there."

"I'd rather you kept the kids out of mischief."

"Then take the car. You'll be much quicker."

Grateful though she was for the offer, Sheila soon became unsure about the speed. She had travelled no more than a hundred yards before she became aware that the road was so icy she wouldn't dare to move much faster than walking pace anyway. But at least she was dry, and if she — *when* she found Barbara, having transport would be a boon.

Flakes of snow were falling from a sky turning to cobalt when she parked the car. The station was totally dark, not one lamp shining through a gloom that reminded her of the blackout.

She can't be here, thought Sheila dismally, her heartache worsening. Barbara hates the dark when she's anywhere strange. The doors leading to the booking hall were locked, but she rattled at them despite her gnawing realisation that the place was unmanned.

But if Barbara hadn't come here, where was she? Where would she go, in an attempt to reach her father? Had she merely set out, Sheila wondered, and failed to reach the station?

She had looked frenziedly to either side whilst driving there, but could she have missed seeing her in the deepening twilight? Had Barbara fallen perhaps, was she lying injured beside the road? In a ditch?

She was turning away to return to the car when

she thought she heard a faint sound. Could it be a muffled sob? Swinging round on her heel so rapidly that she slithered on the ice and nearly overbalanced, she ran back to the station buildings.

Trying to peer through the glass panel in one of the doors was hopeless. It still had the remains of a coating of blue paint which in wartime had prevented light from gleaming through. She couldn't make out anything beyond the pane. Exasperated with her own inability to do a thing, she rattled the doors again. Distantly, she heard another faint sob, and a tiny hiccup.

She's in there somewhere, thought Sheila, and I can't get to her. The sensible way seemed to be to fetch the police, but the prospect of leaving this spot tore into her. So long as Barbara was here (and now she was certain that she was), she had to stay.

Desperate to find a means of getting into the station, Sheila turned to her right and hurried as fast as she could over the snow and ice along the outside of the building. In places snow had drifted up against the wall and she floundered through, clutching at window sills or door frames to prevent herself from falling.

The gate she reached was at least six feet high, but constructed from wooden slats. Through one of its narrow gaps she could see on to the platform.

"Barbara!" she called at the top of her voice. "Barbara!"

There was no response, but she thought she could hear a distant sound. It might have been a child's footsteps on snow-covered ground.

"Barbara! It's me — *Mummy*. Come to the gate, love."

Through the darkness Sheila could just discern a pale blur which she was sure was her daughter's face peeping around the corner of the booking hall.

"Barbara — here by the gate, darling."

Slipping and slithering, her daughter stumbled towards her.

"Oh, thank goodness!" Sheila cried, close to weeping herself when Barbara was so near that she could make out the tears streaking her cheeks. "Don't worry now, love. We'll get you out of there somehow. How on earth did you manage to get on to the station? Was it still open when you arrived?"

"No — they'd all gone away, and there weren't any trains." Looking exhausted, Barbara leaned her head against the gate.

"But somebody must have let you through before they locked up."

"No. They didn't. I got in by myself."

Barbara suddenly appeared proud of the achievement, a mood which contrasted strangely with the sobs still shaking her sturdy body. Sheila yearned to hug her and go on hugging her until everything was all right. She urgently needed to touch the child. Slipping off her glove, she managed to reach one finger between the wooden slats. Her daughter's cheek felt so soft, but dreadfully cold.

The wood was coated with ice that seemed to burn the skin of her hand. Where a knot protruded it grazed her knuckles. And she was wasting time.

"I'll have to leave you for a minute, love, but it will be only a minute. Just long enough to fetch somebody who'll help us get you out."

"No, no! Take me with you, Mummy!"

Barbara flung herself onto the snowy ground. At first Sheila thought it was in sheer panic, but then she looked down and understood. The child was wriggling under the bottom of the gate.

Hauling her up and into her arms, she kissed the icy little face over and over again.

"Is that how you got in there? Is it? Is it, Barbara?" she asked at last.

Her daughter nodded. "I was going to fetch my daddy. Johnnie said —"

"I know what Johnnie said, and it was very naughty of him. But we know it isn't true, don't we?"

Sheila was hurrying to the car with her now, not daring to run lest she might fall in the snow, but desperate to take Barbara back to Mrs Darnton's house.

"You know you've got a daddy, don't you?" she said as soon as she had placed the child in the passenger seat. "He'll be longing to see you as soon as we get back home to Yorkshire. And that won't be long now, I promise."

"But he doesn't live in my house any more, you know he doesn't." Her tone was harsh with accusation.

Sheila willed herself not to become any more upset than she already was, or she wouldn't be fit to drive the car even that short distance to Elizabeth Darnton's home.

"You'll still see him. Just as you have ever since he went to live with Auntie Pauline."

"Can I take Johnnie with me, then he'll know it's true, won't he?"

"We'll have to see about that. We're not sure yet where Johnnie will be living. His daddy wants him to live in his house."

"Johnnie might come to visit me."

Barbara appeared satisfied by that possibility. She turned her attention to picking bits of frozen snow off the front of her coat.

"You're very wet, aren't you, poor love?" said Sheila sympathetically, thankful that the house was in sight now, and she'd soon have the child in a warm bath.

"No, I'm not wet," Barbara insisted indignantly. "I couldn't get into the lavatories, the door wouldn't open. But I did a wee at a tiny grate where the water comes down off the roof."

"Good girl." Bless her for being good, bless her, bless her for being *safe.*

Mrs Darnton couldn't have been more pleased if Barbara were one of her own grandchildren. She welcomed them at the door when she heard the car pulling up, ushered them inside and insisted that they must go straight up to her bathroom.

Afterwards, sitting with cups of cocoa in front of the living-room fire, the three of them talked over the details of Barbara's adventure. And now she was reunited with her mother, in the warm, and away from that lonely station, Barbara did believe it had been an adventure.

"I've never been out for a long time like that before in the snow, have I?" she remarked, sounding full of herself again. "And I didn't cry for ages and ages. Not until just before you came to get me. I thought the train would come and then I'd soon be at Auntie Pauline's with Daddy."

"You'll have to remember in future that it's a long way away," said Sheila, seriously. Now the immediate danger had passed, she was becoming only too conscious of all the potential hazards that would have been present if her daughter had attempted the journey into and across London, and then all the way by train to the West Riding.

"But it won't be far when we're at Hardaker Farm again. I know it won't 'cos it's easy going to Auntie Pauline's from there."

When Barbara insisted she would go there often Sheila hadn't the heart to protest that it might not be all that frequently. Having her daughter go missing and then be recovered had taught her that finding a compromise between her own wishes and other people's might not be so impossible.

Shortly after Barbara's adventure, Johnnie's father came to take him home. Sheila liked the smiling doctor even better on this third occasion, and was delighted to hear that he had been in touch with Jane.

"I traced her through the USAAF, you see," Nathaniel explained. "She telephoned me then at the hospital. This boyfriend she has now sounds very good. He will make her happy, I think."

"Whereabouts are they going to live, did she say?"

"In America, of course. She is to become one of these many GI brides. But before leaving they will visit Johnnie, naturally."

"And what about Gloria, didn't she mention her?"

"She is writing to you, I understand. But according to her this new man has agreed to take the girl."

Because she's white, thought Sheila, but wouldn't say that to Nathaniel.

"I know what you are thinking," he told her, and grinned. "Believe me, I am not offended, or only a little on the boy's behalf. I am only very thankful that she is permitting Johnnie to come to me."

"And he certainly seems unperturbed by the prospect of living permanently away from her. I suppose he will be able to visit her later on."

"Jane stipulates that must be a condition of his

residing with me. Though from what I'm learning about her, I doubt that we shall see my Johnnie making frequent trips across the Atlantic."

Saying goodbye to the boy was very painful, but Sheila silently reminded herself that everything throughout the past eighteen months had been geared towards this. And the smile on Johnnie's lips — and more importantly in those dark eyes — revealed how happy he was to belong with Nathaniel Isiolo.

Barbara was sad to see him go. Sheila was surprised when her daughter hugged the lad and kissed him on the mouth, as though they might have been close friends for years. Neither of the two seemed conscious now of the coldness which existed between them during the time they were all living in Yorkshire. If only Barbara had been nicer to Johnnie in those days, she thought. But maybe if she had things would have worked out less well for the boy.

Even if Jane had reclaimed him as soon as the war ended, there had been nothing to suggest that she would ever have been anything but inadequate as his mother. And he would never have met his father.

Both Sheila and Mrs Darnton had wondered how Johnnie and Gloria would react to being separated. When the time came, however, the little girl's age seemed to protect her from any distress.

"Bye-bye, Johnnie," she said cheerfully, after

submitting to a final cuddle from him.

"I'll come and see you one day," he promised. "My dad says so."

"Next week?" she asked.

Perplexed, Johnnie gazed up at his father.

"Not next week," Nathaniel explained. "And not the one after. But you will meet each other again. When you are living with your mummy."

"Soon. She is coming for me soon."

Only a few hours after Johnnie left Sheila realised how heart-rending losing him was. She hadn't appreciated quite how attached to the boy she had grown during those months of searching. Nor, she supposed wryly, had she noticed how talkative he'd become. Without his chattering the house felt strangely quiet. She wished they could go home to Yorkshire, but she had agreed to wait in Hawkhurst with Gloria until Jane arrived.

On the day Jane and her fiancé eventually came for Gloria, Sheila discovered she was now almost as fond of the girl as she was of Johnnie. The only good thing about the whole business was that Jane did appear to have changed. Perhaps influenced by this new man; she seemed to have more sense of parental responsibility.

No matter how relieved she was on behalf of both children, Sheila felt an awful gap widening in her life. A gap that she was afraid might never be fully healed even when they returned to Hardaker Farm.

For Barbara's sake, she made a game of packing their things for the homeward journey. Forcing herself to laugh and to chat about the life they would have together now they were free to settle into their cottage, she did her best to convince her daughter that everything would be fun.

From the contented way Barbara went up to bed on that last night, she felt she had succeeded. Only when she joined Mrs Darnton in the sitting-room did she discover that her own cheerfulness had been recognised as no more than a veil for her true emotions.

"You've sorted everything out for those children," Elizabeth Darnton began, glancing up from her needlework. "Even your own little one is looking forward to the future you've worked out for her. I'm sorry you seem less enthusiastic."

Sheila gave her a rueful smile. "I'm that transparent, am I? Oh, dear."

"Perhaps because I recognise the signs. Adjusting's not easy, is it, my dear?"

"I guess being away so much has prevented me from dwelling on the divorce and how it's going to be — afterwards. I might have managed on my own for a while, but . . ."

"You were happier while Todd Albany was around."

Startled, Sheila gave her a look, but did not speak. What was there to say?

Mrs Darnton sighed. "It seemed to me particularly cruel that he — well, had to go like that.

You were really only just getting to know each other, weren't you?"

Sheila nodded. "When Edward ditched me for my sister, I thought I'd never get over the humiliation. That I'd never risk caring about any man again."

"And then there was Todd."

"If I'd been aware of it happening, I'd have been even more cautious than I was. Because of Johnnie, though, I didn't really notice how intense my own feelings were becoming. Until it was too late. If falling in love again had happened only a few months after my husband left me, I'd have thought I was an all-time fool. But it was only weeks. And I did love Todd."

Talking about Todd hadn't been the best idea Sheila had ever had. After a restless night, she awoke headachy and so tired that she wondered how she would survive the journey back to the West Riding. There had been some relief after revealing what she felt to Mrs Darnton. Today, though, she was raw with pent-up emotion. Emotion for which there could be no release.

Barbara exclaimed and chattered during most of the journey, which meant that at least Sheila did not have to do much to keep her happy. By the time Nat Hardaker met them at Halifax station, both she and her daughter were just very glad to be home.

She would have too much to do to dwell on her emotions. Masses of tasks awaited her. The cottage had been neglected for too long, and the farm always provided a constant succession of jobs. She was afraid she wasn't pulling her weight there. Since the war ended her father had been planning to expand, but he wasn't up to doing that alone. Sheila wasn't yet sure if farmwork would always be sufficiently fulfilling for her, but Nat needed help, and it did provide an occupation. She wished she knew someone who would learn to love the place; help him with the administration which seemed to be increasing now, and with forward thinking.

Gazing around her beloved hills, Sheila recalled her art training and how she had longed to depict her home county on canvas. With no one to help her, even with rearing Barbara, she could see little prospect now of ever having much free time for painting. Although practical enough to recognise that her family needed her in so many ways, there were times when possessing an artist's vision and being prevented from exercising it hurt.

The farm and her own cottage looked particularly lovely surrounded by a covering of snow, and with blue-mauve shadows on the neighbouring hills. Todd never came here, she thought, and yearned to have shown him all this; to have shared with him this home territory of hers.

Her father surprised her that night after supper by asking what she intended to do with her life. He'd been talking again about his plans for the farm, admitting now to misgivings regarding his ability to cope with the paperwork, which was becoming heavier.

"But I shouldn't be going on like that about this place. It's you that wants a bit of help, isn't it, lass? You that needs to plan."

"Plan?" Sheila snorted. "I only wish I could, Dad! I often think it's like all those journeys down to Kent."

"Well, you're done with them now, love."

"Aye. But that's how my life feels, these days. With the divorce and everything. It just keeps on and on, back and forth, back and forth, most of it covering the same ground — and never quite getting everything to come right."

Nat Hardaker nodded sympathetically. "But trying, still trying — always trying. That's what you do. Happen that's what life is really — a bit of a journey, like."

His limp seemed better today, or troubled him less than before that long talk with Elizabeth Darnton. He was thankful that he'd decided to visit her. So much had gone wrong for him that he had needed someone to help restore his sense of proportion. Without that he would never have had the guts to set out on this journey.

Being told that he would not be permitted to follow the only career he wanted had been the final blow. Up to receiving that verdict he'd somehow remained sufficiently optimistic to believe that he would overcome any and every handicap. And there sure were enough of those.

The past few months had been devoted to beginning the reconstruction process. Released when the war in Europe ended, he'd been flown to England first; for reassessment of the injuries which had merely been patched up all those months ago at the time of his internment. The news had not been encouraging, the only good outcome being shipped home to the States for treatment which they hoped would reverse the shortcomings of that initial surgery. He blamed no one for the results of inadequate facilities at that original field hospital in occupied France. But the truth was that elsewhere he might have been restored to nearer his former fitness.

He had thought the worst had happened when, back home, his parents flinched on seeing him. Only when the presence of fragments of fuselage in his skull were explained, together with the limitations they enforced, had he realised that each stage of this so-called recovery was bringing fresh disappointments.

The shattered leg and the arm where that old injury had suffered further damage were painful still, and inconvenient, but he coped with them. The instability within his head was altogether different. Alarming initially — as anything unknown is alarming — the problem created strangely conflicting emotions. In those early days, on the look-out for each possible sign of potential trouble, he'd developed an apprehension which had never before been part of his character.

Even when weeks passed and nothing untoward occurred he just could not accept everyone else's assessment that he was fortunate. He almost resented feeling so well because he felt he was a fraud — a factor which made him less able to adjust to being refused permission to take responsibility for other people's lives. As a pilot.

A part of him, however much he ordered it to the contrary, would not accept that he would never do the job for which he had trained. In unguarded moments still, he caught himself picturing the life he might have had; experiencing hopes which he knew full well were no longer realistic.

Elizabeth Darnton's home in peacetime had been quite an eye-opener. The tranquillity of rural England, now that it lacked the constant disturbance of overhead aircraft, had appealed to him. The only place which had done so since he had needed to avoid his parents' (however understandable) compulsion to ensure him a secure future.

When he met the farmer who worked the Darnton land he'd been reminded of his grandfather, who used to raise cattle in Virginia. He was impressed by the acumen now obligatory to the successful running of any business. For the first time in months, he wondered if there might, after all, be satisfying work out there somewhere . . . It could become a challenge. He could enjoy working the soil, needing to prove himself afresh before letting his parents see how he was doing.

London, as the train advanced through its suburbs, tore at his heart. Now that some of the bomb damage was being cleared, the gaping wounds of vanished homes seemed all the more evident. The evil of war which he'd seen chiefly as lives ruined or ended, was present also in shattered buildings. Houses, businesses, shops destroyed — and every one of those causing anguish to the folks who belonged here.

Central London was as bad, if not worse, with massive areas barren-looking under the snow; dead willowherb wilting, waiting for a springtime no more substantial than a vague promise.

The countryside was more acceptable, he decided later in the train heading north. He needed reminders of the constant renewal process; that he might be renewed. More at ease with himself now, he dozed when daylight ended, let the time pass, ceased to plague his own mind by looking ahead. He was past turning back, and need only let circumstances guide him towards future decisions.

The town seemed as dark as the surrounding night, despite gas lamps and the faint light reflecting from snow-covered hills. It stood enclosed in its valley, a mass of soot-blackened stone buildings. Slush had been cleared from the platform and lay in dismal grey heaps against walls running with thaw-water.

His own uneven footsteps echoed up the steps and thudded dully along the moist wooden flooring all the way to the exit.

The taxi he found was a surprise; he took it as an omen, smiled while he told the driver his destination.

"You sure, sir?" the Yorkshireman asked. "It's a tidy way, and there's buses running already, just up th'hill yonder."

He was sure. And ready to give reassurance. "I can pay you OK."

Noting the accent, the driver grinned. "Aye, I reckon you can. There's nobbut you lot have any brass to throw around, these days."

The route out of the town was lined with buildings. Shops, of course, other commercial premises, the local newspaper offices, factories from which spewing light witnessed to the day's work beginning. And then there was a park to their right. Although it was still dark, he could see its distant terrace, a bandstand outlined against the snow, the lake gleaming with fragmented ice.

A road led off to the left, and another at an angle on the right. There were houses now, mostly in rows, but some large, detached and imposing, many showing light behind their curtains where mothers would be getting children up ready for school.

He would not see Johnnie. Elizabeth Darnton had told him about the success of the boy's reunion with the father he'd never known. Lord, but he would miss that boy. But perhaps only so long as he had no kids of his own. Who could say? That threat of his own mortality had induced a mistrust of the future which would take some erasing.

They left rows of shops behind, and passed a cemetery made somehow more emotive by its spire which lacked a church. He hoped it was merely a sign that a larger building had been constructed, perhaps in a happier location.

More houses still as they passed through the convergence of several routes, but he sensed an opening out of the landscape beyond. Rows of lamps alongside rural lanes allowed him glimpses of surrounding hills, woods emerging from the snow, and rocks that looked as dark as the native sandstone houses.

Chapels and churches, factories and further homes were clustered in a settlement which seemed to cling to the road and centre on the industry rooted here for the past century. Or maybe for longer.

The cab began climbing then, up narrow lanes with the ever-widening view increasing in splendour as the moon emerged from cloud. He wanted to walk, to turn his face to the freshness of the air, to feel its sting, to know he was *here.*

"Hardaker Farm — that was what you said, weren't it?"

"Yes. Thank you."

Outside the car he noticed how much more light there was; that the sky behind him was paling. Searching for coins, taking out a wad of notes, he stared hard at the buildings grouped about the farmyard like family members gathered for mutual support. He took his time sorting out the amount requested for his journey, not only because these English pounds and pence now felt unfamiliar. He needed time, time in which to muster the composure which was less obedient than he liked.

Scarcely aware of having moved, he found he was standing, overnight case in hand, staring bleakly ahead, immobilized by uncertainty.

His own awareness had been honed by these last months, sharpened until it was so acute that memory painted his face as plainly as any mirror set before him. These external scars, however much they might be overshadowed by the internal, were no less real.

God help me, but I'm scared! There was only one hope remaining — she had let Johnnie's appearance make no difference to her.

Borne on the cold wind, the smell was warm, enticing, of bacon cooking. For the first time in long enough, Todd felt real hungry.

The woman who could only be her mother came to the farmhouse door after hearing the car. Older, more comfortably built, eyes hazel rather than that unforgettable grey/blue, she was still unmistakable.

He smiled, but felt his face stiffen, dread rendering even the simplest action awkward.

"Hi," he said. "I wonder, please — does Sheila happen to be home? I'm an old fr—"

"Todd!" She was there, easing past her

mother, running swift as the wind towards him.

His voice, at least, had not altered. He prayed she might not find too many differences that would matter.

A pace away from him she paused, gazing and gazing as the wintry sun appeared over the hill to the east, silhouetting him against a sky glowing brighter above the craggy horizon.

"I can't believe it, I can't!" She was in his arms, hugging him, looking up. "Is that the same scar, or did you get injured again?" She was full of concern, but not in any way put off.

The relief was so intense he could have collapsed at her feet. But holding her was better, kissing better still.

"I think you two ought to come inside. You'll catch your death of cold, and that'd be such a shame. From where I'm standing, it's catching up you need, and plenty of it."

Sheila laughed. It felt to her as though it might have been her first laugh ever. "Mum, this is Todd — Todd Albany."

There were further introductions. Her father, Nat, was a man moderate in height and seemingly moderate in his ways, with a quiet greeting enhanced by a handshake powerful enough to convince Todd of an eager welcome. A man he liked already, someone with whom to discuss his own future perhaps? And then there was Barbara, hurtling through from somewhere to the rear of the house to meet him.

"Mummy thought you'd died, she was upset.

She didn't tell me but I knew. You're a real American, aren't you?"

"Sure am, honey. And mighty glad to meet you all."

"You know Johnnie's not here, don't you? He's got a daddy now."

"So I hear, that's great, isn't it?"

Sheila was still looking at him, marvelling that he had survived. Now she was puzzled. "How do you know about Johnnie's dad? Who said?"

"Elizabeth Darnton. I just came from her place."

They needed to talk, to fill in all that had occurred since that dreadful day when his Mustang went down on the far side of the Channel. But Todd was obliged to wait through breakfast, during which he sketched in his months in a German prison camp. He made light of his injuries, while remaining acutely aware that as soon as he and Sheila were alone he would be compelled to tell her as much as he himself knew about the metal embedded within his skull.

He'd come all this way from Virginia praying they might spend the rest of their lives together. But that would only be if Sheila was fully conscious of what she was taking on.

Barbara attached herself to him from the start, pleasing Todd, if making him wonder how he would ever manage time alone with her mother. And then suddenly Barbara went off to school, walking with her grandmother, who was going to Luddenden Foot to shop. Nat Hardaker was somewhere about the farm.

"I want to show you the cottage," Sheila said. And it was only the beginning; Todd must see everything about her life here.

He'd forgotten that she had her own place. Thought ruefully that perhaps that was as well. Picturing her living among her family in the farmhouse had prevented him from fantasising about their reunion. If emotions had run free, he might have failed to weigh the nature of what he had to offer.

"How've you been, honey?" he asked when they finally were alone with the door closed behind them.

"If you want the truth — just existing. Living for the kids, glad in a way that having to find Johnnie's father kept me busy."

"And the divorce, what's the situation?"

"It'll go through. Of course, it's taking time. But Edward's been prevented by my solicitor from suing me, which means there's hardly any chance he'll be awarded custody of Barbara."

"So, although there'll be some delay you'll be free one day." He could hesitate no longer. "I want you to marry me, Sheila. But there's a whole lot of things you need to know."

She was about to interrupt. Todd hoped that she would have said that she knew enough about him already, but he could not let her be so careless of the true circumstances.

"Please listen, darling," he went on. "I'm sure you can tell I was injured again. The worst is that I'm not allowed to fly — ever."

"Oh, Todd — I am so sorry. You'd set your heart on being a civilian pilot."

He nodded. "Must admit I'm still finding adjusting hard. Trouble is there are bits of fuselage lodged in my skull. The experts can't operate, and they're afraid they could mean potential problems. And that's what I've got to have you understand. I wouldn't have you commit yourself blindly to a guy who could be a liability."

"I'll listen," she said. "And that'll change nothing. Never for one moment did I dare to hope you'd survived. Now you're here, I'm not going to endure another parting. Ever."

We hope you have enjoyed this Large Print book. Other G.K. Hall & Co. or Chivers Press Large Print books are available at your library or directly from the publishers.

For more information about current and upcoming titles, please call or write, without obligation, to:

G.K. Hall & Co.
P.O. Box 159
Thorndike, Maine 04986 USA
Tel. (800) 223-2336

OR

Chivers Press Limited
Windsor Bridge Road
Bath BA2 3AX
England
Tel. (0225) 335336

All our Large Print titles are designed for easy reading, and all our books are made to last.

LT FICTION Ste
Stephens, Kay.
Dark before dawn /
S/01

$23.95 12/18/97 ACM-3896

DEC 28 2002
MAR 21 2003
MAY 10 2003

HQ
MID-YORK LIBRARY SYSTEM
1600 LINCOLN AVE.
UTICA, N.Y

A cooperative library system serving Oneida, Madison, Herkimer Counties through libraries and bookmobiles.

010100